CROSSING THE LINE

Crossing the Line

Published by The Conrad Press Ltd. in the United Kingdom 2023

Tel: +44(0)1227 472 874

www.theconradpress.com

info@theconradpress.com

ISBN 978-1-915494-51-1

Typesetting and Cover Design by: Charlotte Mouncey, www.bookstyle.co.uk

The Conrad Press logo was designed by Maria Priestley.

Printed and bound in Great Britain by Clays Ltd, Elcograf S.p.A.

CROSSING THE LINE

KEITH DOBSON

Dedicated to the closest and most influential people in my life who gave me inspiration and encouragement, you know who you are...

Crossing the line – to overstep a boundary, rule, limit, or go too far. Doing something that is outside the bounds of acceptable behaviour.

1

If thou gaze long into an abyss,
the abyss will gaze also into thee

Friedrich Nietzsche

The heaving prison truck swayed alarmingly and jolted abruptly, the partly worn tyres intermittently losing traction on the warm, dry tarmac.

The driver struggled to retain control of the almost three tonnes of lurching metal box as the vehicle tore around the tight corners of the streets of Cancún and into the hot, humid Mexican night. His ever-tightening grip on the uncompliant steering wheel caused his knuckles to stiffen and ache and momentarily lost control as he lifted a hand in protest and felt the tiny sting of a mosquito's hypopharynx push into the soft flesh of his salty and sweat-soaked neck.

The side-shifting momentum, swaying, and lurching of the vehicle was slightly increased by the weight of the human captives imprisoned and locked in darkness in the purpose-built cell attached behind the driver's cab.

The swaying motion convinced one of the prisoners to lie flat on his back on one of two hardwood benches positioned along the walls on each side of the cell and to prevent being thrown around as he tightly gripped the sides of the bench with each hand causing his wrists to ache as the muscles and tendons exerted and stretched to their extreme.

There were three others in the cell with him, but the only sounds came from the screeching tyres and the slight noise of groaning metal as the frame of the truck lurched objectionably against its own stiff and intended construction.

The others were silent and remained still in the moodiness and foreboding of darkness. He had no doubt they would be attempting to do the same as he was, bracing themselves against the tilt and momentum of the vehicle as if on some turbulent roller coaster ride.

As he lay on the bench, a surge of indignation overtook his thoughts taking his mind elsewhere and providing a brief respite to the ever-increasing pain and aching of his tiring wrists. His concentration turned to why he had been so unexpectantly and violently incarcerated with the other men; indignation intensified to fury as he thought of the events that had led to their inhuman confinement.

Of course, he knew precisely why he was here, it was all down to the stupid, irresponsible, and reckless behaviour of the burly and towering man from Wales who was sharing his imprisonment.

Jack's anxiety intensified the more he thought about it and continued to strain against the shift of the vehicle, fighting to retain its dignity on the dry, hot streets of Cancún City, Mexico.

He knew that if it hadn't been for the Welshman's bone-headed stupidity, which often verged on lunacy, he and the others wouldn't be lying in a urine-stinking mobile prison and being tossed around like rag dolls.

Occasionally, above the sound of the moaning engine and in the dark shadows of the cell, he heard the slight sounds of a shuffle and random mumble, sometimes followed by groans as those who also occupied the lockup tensed their sore and nagging bodies with every jolt and rocking motion of the groaning metal box.

From time to time, a tired and grouchy voice could be heard above the racket of the straining engine, as someone in the darkness cursed the driver for swerving sharply or pressing on the brake too quickly and caused those lying on the floor to roll around like eggs in an oversize tin box.

Jack remembered with anguish the earlier violence and pain he and the others had endured, so viciously inflicted by the two police officers in the front cab, the officers now taking them to their destiny. He recalled how they had viciously beaten him, and he seethed with rancour and loathing for the driver and his passenger.

Too many times, he feared that the sudden swaying and lurching of the vehicle would throw him from the bench to the floor. He was determined that that wouldn't happen, his nostrils stinging from the acidic stench of vomit and urine left by prisoners before him. Body fluids had more than likely been deposited by the numerous drunks, hoboes and prostitutes who would have been the frequent and regular residents of this dark and dismal hellhole.

Earlier, following the extreme violence of the evening, he had found himself on the wet floor for a short time, and it had not been pleasant, realising he had been sitting in what felt and smelled like human excrement.

He was conscious that time was passing and was becoming

extremely concerned. He sensed that he had been imprisoned in the vehicle's rear for maybe three or four hours; it was difficult to quantify in the complete darkness.

In any case, it partially explained why his back ached so much, mainly due to the time he had been lying on the hard and uncomfortable bench. His left leg and foot began jarring up with spasms of cramps due to motionlessness and inactivity.

The constant and sustained grip of the bench strained his tiring forearms and wrists, but it was all he could do to prevent rolling to the floor. Instead, he would put up with the aches and pain for as long as it would take, as he knew the other option was to be forced to lie on that stinking wet floor with the others, and that would be inconceivable.

Recalling the surreal events he had endured earlier, Jack recollected that over a single evening, at different times and locations, he and his three friends had been threatened, beaten, and manhandled by brutal and violent Mexican police officers only to be finally locked in the prison truck.

Now, the truck seemed to be continually driving around the city and had been for hours without reaching a destination. He assumed that in a large city like Cancún, with all the crime and disorder Mexico's second-largest city would surely encounter, there should have been a central jail or prison located in the city centre.

Again, his mind drifted to the thugs in the driver's cabin. If they intended to take them to the police cells, they were taking a damn long time or taking the longest route imaginable. He guessed the city would be beginning to quieten by now and it was probably the early morning hours, the roads would hardly be congested at such a quiet time. It would be ridiculous to

12

suggest that the police driver and his passenger were somehow confused and had forgotten how to navigate to the city jail.

Suspicion and doubt, heightened by inaction and impatience, began to course through his restless mind. He thought it possible they may be being kidnapped, then quickly dismissed the idea and recalled their uniforms, weapons, and the vehicle had all seemed genuine.

He recollected reading somewhere or perhaps had been told that the Mexican authorities had a reputation for being the most corrupt in the western hemisphere, second only to Guatemala.

On the surface, this charade could be a nefarious deception which may turn into something Jack and his friends would live to regret. He knew that only time would tell; just let it go a bit further, and if they still failed to reach a destination, he would have to work out how to escape this stinking wretchedness, either with or without his friends.

Then suddenly, the truck abruptly stopped for the first time during the long journey.

Hoping that they had reached their destination, he listened to the engine as it quietly ticked over. There was no movement in the driver's cab and realised they had probably stopped at a red traffic light or allowed another vehicle to pass.

In the silence, he could hear faint movement and regular breathing from the others occupying the dark space around him. With relief, he sighed, momentarily releasing his grip and readjusting his position on the bench. It was an opportunity to relax his aching limbs and provide much-needed rest for his muscles, and for the first time, he felt able to relax during the treacherous and unpredictable journey.

The heat and humidity in the cell were almost unbeara ble and very little air circulated in the box which accentuated the stench that emanated from the floor. He guessed that the temperature was probably thirty-five degrees at best.

He rubbed his wet face and neck with both hands and felt sweat trickle down his lower back and inner thighs then ineffectively licked his cracked lips with his rough, dry tongue.

He inhaled the cocktail stench of sweat and urine and suddenly felt a tightness in his gut as vomit refluxed into his oesophagus, rising from his stomach. He managed to swallow the acidity down, realising he desperately needed to drink something, his throat stinging from the caustic effect of the bile.

He knew that if he had to, he would drink his own urine if it came to it. He had done it before during jungle survival training, which he had completed in England in preparation for serving in Belize, he wasn't ready for that just yet, but that time might come later if he felt the need to survive.

After less than a minute, the engine accelerated slightly, and he gripped the sides of the bench as the vehicle lurched forward and continued its seemingly never-ending journey.

It was almost pitch black in the prison truck, making it difficult to see; the only light came from occasional flashes of streetlights and oncoming vehicle headlights, flickering across the ceiling above him like some broken monochrome kaleidoscope.

The dull pain of cramps surged through his calf muscles, causing him to sit up and place his foot on the floor. Maintaining his grip with one hand to steady himself, he rigorously rubbed the area of pain in his aching limb as the truck slowed down again.

Squinting his eyes and scanning the darkness, assisted by

the intermittent flashes of light, he made out the grey, murky shapes of the others sharing the dark space with him, two of them lying on the stinking floor and another lying on the bench running along the opposite side of the cell.

He looked for the source of the glancing lights, seeing they were coming through the square metal grill at the front of the prison chamber. Measuring about thirty centimetres squared, it was enough to allow some light to pierce the darkness of the cell and he could see the coloured lights of the dashboard in the driver's cabin and flashes of light filtering through the windscreen.

Then he noticed, caught in the rays of light, swirls of smoke and then the smell of burning tobacco. The introduction of this stench caused him to retch; it was the unique pungent smell of strong American cigarettes, the acidic smoke only added to the cocktail of odious smells already circulating in the cell.

Wincing, he recalled when the two feral police officers had so viciously beaten him, brutally pushed him through the rear doors of the cell and violently hit him with a police baton causing him to fall to the stinking floor.

Stan had followed, after being hit with a police baton across his shins, and unceremoniously collapsing into the cell and then, to his utter shock and confusion discovered his other friends, whom he had left earlier in the evening, were already incarcerated in the darkness of the transportable police cell.

Feeling that the unjust and inhuman ordeal presented the most serious predicament that he had ever experienced, and his previously unblighted career would surely be wrecked when this crisis was over. He thought there were two possible outcomes which would result from his desperate situation, either the Army would make official attempts to bail them out of a Mexican prison, or if the corrupt authorities failed to inform them, he and his friends would end up rotten in a stinking jail for however long it would take to make someone aware of their whereabouts.

His thoughts again turned towards Gareth, the Welshman, who was responsible for their ordeal due to his continual, irrational and idiotic behaviour; then he thought of the other two guys who were incarcerated with him and how worse it could have been if he had been alone in the cell with Gareth and felt a little cheered, knowing that the others were dependable enough if the time came to consider a plan to escape their suffering.

Again, the truck decelerated and slowed, giving him a reprieve to release his grip and allowing him to rub his sweating face then quietly muttered to himself, 'The stupid Welsh bastard,' while hoping the burly person the slur was aimed at couldn't hear him.

Lowering his hands, he squinted, attempting to focus his vision through the thick veil of darkness which shrouded the bodies that lay on the floor.

Shockingly, the truck lurched forward with a jolt, and he almost fell from the bench, only prevented by clenching the sides. Then the vehicle increased speed and continued its long journey through the quiet Mexican streets as dawn began to break.

Vibrant lights occasionally glinted through the metal grill, which separated them from the cab. Turning his head, he looked again at the dark shapes of the men lying on the floor and saw it had become easier to distinguish the larger of the two and responsible for their incarceration.

He looked up at the quivering lights dancing across the ceiling, and his thoughts drifted back to how events had begun when the police stopped them as they walked through the dark and empty streets of Cancún. What then followed shocked them both beyond belief.

Earlier, he and Stan had left a quiet bar after a few drinks and were feeling content and relaxed, mainly due to the copious amounts of strong Mexican tequila, they had consumed. They eventually found themselves walking along the main road and discussing how they may find a safe and comfortable place to sleep the night.

Then, to their utter bewilderment, the chaos and violence began.

They weren't even aware that the police had been searching for them when the law enforcement truck drove towards them in the street, tyres screeching, the vehicle coming to a shuddering stop, doors slamming, two irate cops yelling and running towards them.

Then, surprise and confusion, as one of the officers, who was shockingly overweight, drew a baton from his belt and began waving the menacing weapon above his head whilst incomprehensibly screaming and shouting towards them.

While trying to understand the distressing conduct of the lunatic in front of them, and to their further astonishment, a second policeman, who noticeably, wore a substantial black walrus moustache spreading across his lips and cheeks, failing to disguise his dreadfully pocked-marked face, was also holding a baton which he swirled above his head as if threatening to strike and screamed frenziedly and incoherently towards them.

The overweight officer nervously darted his gaze between Jack and Stan as if watching a tennis ball being thwacked forward and then back across a tennis court net.

Feeling warm spittle spray on his face as the indignant police officers continued their screaming rant, he wanted to raise a hand to wipe the foul-smelling sputum from his face but felt that if he made a move, it would send the two cops even more demented, and a baton could quite possibly strike him with pernicious consequences.

Both Jack and Stan were carrying backpacks containing their personal belongings and realising his bag was an additional burden, Jack shrugged the straps off his shoulders and dropped the bag to the floor, momentarily distracting the berserk police officers.

He was tempted to turn on his heels and run as fast as possible from the terrible anarchy and hostility unravelling before them but couldn't find it in him to leave his friend to the wrath of the two psychotic lunatics gyrating, yelling, and swinging their batons.

He felt it prudent to maintain eye contact with the moustached officer, who seemed to be about to swing his baton and strike either of them on the head.

Observing their fierce and erratic expressions, he thought that the whole situation made absolutely no sense and hoped that any second, the cops would realise that they had made a terrible misjudgement and had detained the wrong suspects; perhaps only then would they lower their batons, cease posturing, and apologise for the mistake and the inconvenience.

That did not happen, and their threatening display continued towards the two soldiers, then the overweight officer began shouting something that Jack half understood.

'*Detención penal, detención penal.*'

On hearing his police partner, the moustached officer stopped shouting and lowered his baton, swiftly forcing it into his belt. Then with both hands, reached forward, taking hold of Jack in an armlock and promptly twisted him around.

Jack complied and instantly felt immense pain spread across his shoulder, then, as the officer came closer, he felt warm breath on his nose and cheek. Panting heavily from the shock and trauma, he inhaled the acidic smell of cheap cigarettes.

The pain made it impossible for him to try and resist, as the cop swung him around and into the side of the truck; slight pressure was applied to the arm lock, which heightened the pain, forcing him to comply; otherwise, he knew his arm would be pulled from the socket.

A large hand pushed his face against the hard metal of the vehicle, causing a sharp pain to his cheek and jawbone. Suddenly, he felt a painful jolt in the small of his back as the officer's knee found more flesh to bruise and hurt.

Standing restrained against the truck, he heard a loud thud next to him, and the truck vibrated as Stan's head was also rammed into the side of the vehicle.

The hand holding Jack's face against the metal released, resulting in his head involuntarily falling backwards; then he winced as he was jolted sideways, still in an armlock and realised he was being pulled to the rear of the truck.

He stumbled as he was pushed towards the metal steps leading to the truck's rear doors and realised, before it was too late, it was time to attempt to reason with these lunatics before he was pushed into the dark abyss of the cell.

'Please stop; there must be a mistake, we haven't done

anything wrong,' he screamed above the chaos.

He felt the officer place his mouth close to his ear, and spoke in a hushed, calm voice, '*Detención penal.*'

Jack raised his foot and placed it on the bottom step then leaned slightly backwards as the officer continued to apply the arm lock pressure and pushed from behind.

Reluctantly, he acquiesced while shuffling up each step, supported from behind by the officer. After feeling the last step with his foot, he stepped towards the open doors as the officer released and pushed him forward. It was pitch black inside the truck, but he was more relieved that his shoulder and arm were not broken and knew there was no choice but to move cautiously towards the darkness.

The officer wasn't finished with him yet, which was evident as he felt the excruciating painfulness of a police baton swiping across his rear calves, causing him to collapse limply onto the truck's metal floor, the right side of his face cushioning his fall.

He screamed out in crushing pain then began to gag as he drew breath and inhaled the stench of something rancid and acidic, then lay choking on the hard, damp floor for what seemed minutes but was probably seconds.

His arm felt as if it had been pulled out of its socket by the armlock, both his calves ached from being struck with a baton, and his face felt swollen and bruised, amongst all the physical trauma he still did not understand why this was happening to him and his friend.

Using what little strength was left, he lifted his face from the metal floor to free himself of the acrid stench burning inside his nostrils, then began to shuffle further into the darkness as he heard the officers shouting outside the vehicle.

He guessed that the odds were Stan would be joining him very soon and didn't want to be in the same position when his friend was forcibly launched through the open doors.

Pushing himself to his knees and wincing with pain, he slowly clambered forward into the darkness until the top of his head gently touched the wall. Then slowly turning into a sitting position, he shuffled his bottom, feeling the cold and sticky dampness soaking into his trousers.

Seconds later, and as expected, he heard the sound of someone stumbling on the metal steps; the truck rocked gently as the silhouette of his friend appeared at the open doors. He knew what would happen next and waited for Stan to collapse into the space and could only watch as the officer appeared behind him, baton held as if about to strike.

2

Not today, Satan, not today

Bianca del Rio

The old and decrepit ex-British Army Land Rover spluttered and coughed as it was clumsily driven along the twisting and rocky Belizean jungle trail. The battered vehicle was curtained on either side by hanging green vines, ferns, and lush foliage. The murky brown waters of a ten-metre-wide slow-flowing river ebbed precariously close and just a few centimetres from the jaunting and bouncing rubber tyres.

The vehicle was one of the original models left by the British Armed Forces when they first extracted from Belize in the late 1970s, probably manufactured in the 1950s and due to its age, had more than likely experienced some military action due to its scars, displaying more wear and tear than it deserved. It was now being pushed to its limits and driven on the extremely rough and uneven jungle trail.

The prolonged Belizean humidity and extreme weather conditions had caused accelerated deterioration to its engine, not to mention the groaning dented chassis and severely bald tyres struggling to maintain the vehicle driving straight on the mud and rocks.

The driver fought to prevent the metal machine from sliding

uncontrollably into the deep river adjacent to the meandering trail and curiously felt the water beckoning him to steer into its depths of oblivion. Perhaps it was the high tensile steel wires poking out of the rubber tyres that provided much-needed grip to keep the vehicle on course and away from a watery peril.

The tired and weak diesel engine, belching a blue and greasy oil-smoked plume from the exhaust. It was obvious the machine was struggling to cope with the arduous journey, and the driver jerked and fought to retain the forward trajectory, forcing him to maintain a tight grip on the steering wheel, his hands uncomfortably shaking due to excessive wear and deterioration of the steering shaft. The vehicle had rarely seen any genuine care or maintenance for years but held its dignity and was trying to perform in the last of its days.

The man in the passenger seat was only too aware of the uncomfortable experience of travelling in the dilapidated vehicle but had little concern for such trivial matters. The position he commanded in his cruel world carried little sentiment for such issues, and his emotion and care for other human beings were even less.

He had known his driver, Mikel, for many years but held diminutive respect for him; he knew that if he failed to complete this critical journey, he would reduce him to dust as he had done to many weak people. Ordinary people possessed no value in his world; they either served him and were allowed to survive or if they failed him, would be hastily neutralised.

Mikel was very aware of his boss's, or *jefe's* contempt and utter disregard for human life. He had witnessed the malice and viciousness which occasionally led to the demise inflicted on people who had done nothing but disappoint him.

Refocusing on the challenging journey, he felt sweat trickle down his face as he tackled to control the old metal beast, but that wasn't the only matter that was uppermost in his mind; the main challenge was the need to get the malevolent and vile demon safely to his destination, the filthy shack owned by his low-life cousin, Baptiste.

Mikel had lived, mostly endured, life in Belize City for five of his twenty-two years and had worked for his monstrous passenger for most of his short adult life. The oldest of eight children, he had lived his preadolescent years in desperate poverty with four sisters and two brothers, loved but not all belonging to his natural parents.

He soon realised that his siblings' different colours and features did not match his parents. He had loved his father's generosity and devotion to all his bothers and sisters, and they never needed anything he couldn't afford.

His father's skills lay in carpentry, but all that changed when employment for indigenous people became complicated when the British government took control of his country for the second time in 1981. They shipped in their engineers, builders, and carpenters in a futile attempt to rebuild the industrial and economic infrastructure of their vulnerable and defenceless country.

At the same time, their military machine brought security and shored up his county's border to ward off the invading Guatemalan army who were intent on occupying his land. This led to businesses either shutting down or relying on the occupying British military system, from whom they were forced to buy cheap materials to rebuild their much-needed economy.

The British occupation had created a deep recession in a

county that already thrived on poverty and led to low-skilled workers losing jobs, livelihoods, and a future. Mikel's father became a British colonial statistic and resigned to carving rosewood ornamental figures destined for tourists, which he sold on the streets of Belize City.

His takings were barely enough to pay the enforced protection money to the Belizean mafia, the '*Sinaloa cartel*', along with taxes the corrupt government demanded, so his children were made to beg on the streets to feed their mouths and those of their parents.

Mikel was the oldest child but also the most awkward and inept. His father always said that he hated how skinny he was, and his unusual light brown skin made his father question whether he was his own child, but it wasn't surprising when he saw the variety of shades of colour of all his children.

Very quickly, he accepted that his hands did not possess the carpentry skills of his father and because he was unable to follow his trade, would be lured to the city to find any work which might provide him with a decent income and the possibility of a future.

Without any experience or money to support him, which added to his naivety, he was quickly recruited into the drugs and sex businesses, which were the primary underworld employment in Belize city at that time. He began working out in a gym to build his physique, quickly learning the street culture from the dealers and prostitutes and began creating a fearsome reputation amongst the higher criminal ranks.

It wasn't long before his reputation of being ruthless and violent assisted in quickly escalating him up the hierarchical rank structure. He was eventually accepted as a loyal lieutenant to the most formidable and sadistic drug trafficker in Belize and head of the Sinaloa cartel, Satan.

Today, his *jefe* would meet with his cousin, Baptiste, who was nothing but a petty criminal but critically important to Satan's cartel business and lived in a remote shack situated deep in the jungle north of Belize City. Baptiste was in the business of buying and selling stolen property, so his head was well below the attention of the Belize Drug Enforcement Agency. The shack was ideal for Satan to store his illicit and illegal drug consignments between transactions with the Mexican and Guatemalan cartels.

'Keep the vehicle on the track, Mikel,' his passenger said in a deep, gritty croaky voice, then turned and spat saliva through the open window to his left.

Mikel hated how Satan spoke to him and how he almost always spat afterwards. He wasn't alone in thinking like this; like most people who encountered Satan, his abhorrent behaviour almost always made them despise him. That was if they were fortunate enough to survive their first encounter with him.

The Land Rover jolted as one of the front wheels hit a mud patch making the whole vehicle slide slightly before gaining traction again. Satan braced himself and placed both hands on the dashboard while turning his head towards Mikel, grimacing. His driver returned a glance, smiled, and then refocused on the track ahead.

He had always tried to avoid looking at Satan whenever possible. Satan's face would instantly turn milk sour, perhaps due to his distressing gnarled permanent facial expression or maybe his dreadfully scarred face, but his repulsive, dark and empty eye socket made people fear him most, almost warning them of what would happen to them if they ever crossed him.

Many years earlier, Satan lost his left eye during a violent and murderous confrontation with one of his drug traffickers, which resulted in the usually terrifying and predictable consequences Satan almost always craved in most violent situations.

Invariably, whenever Satan visited his dealers, if they ever crossed the line or simply upset him, they would almost always become worse off. He was a large man with a naturally toned body and big arms and thighs and possessed astonishing strength for someone who had only visited gyms to deliver drugs.

Mikel had always feared his passenger, as did most men and women in Belize who knew him and his terrible and execrable reputation. Even the authorities and the police knew that if they ever tried to disrupt or challenge his business, any confrontation could lead to a fierce shootout, and they would probably come worse off.

There seemed to be an unspoken arrangement between the authorities and Satan; Mikel had seen money being exchanged, allowing Satan to continue his criminal business and the police to make their financial inducements.

Satan had led the most significant drug cartel in Belize for over fifteen years and was feared by all who were connected to him for the misery, death, and destruction he inflicted on the people affected by his drug empire and if not drugs, the protection money the Sinaloa cartel demanded.

Almost all the drug dealers across the country were in his service, and there was surprisingly little competition in his violent and perilous trade. His arrangement with the neighbouring Mexican cartel and the Belizean Government authorities helped him to continue his progressive and profitable business without threat or fear of disruption.

Like any other businessman whose only aim was to swell their fortunes to incredible levels, he would pay people to carry out his demands but only when it was of maximum profit to him. If he tired of their efforts or they became weak or simply inconvenient; he personally disposed them of service, that is if he could be bothered, otherwise, his loyal lieutenants were ordered to do it for him.

He liked to think that he held the lives of the people in the palms of his hands but otherwise held little respect for them, believing they had a choice in their pathetic and miserable lives but had taken the wrong choice at the crossroads of hope. If they had chosen to take the road towards Satan, he offered a hazardous and perilous short-lived future in narcotics.

He had absolute control over those he enticed to work for him, delivering drug consignments for a pittance, gradually reducing their reward, and forcing them to accept drugs instead of money until they became addicts. Then, he slowly increased the price for their fix until they owed so much, then had no choice but to work for nothing, and at that point, he would own them and everything they had in life.

Satan held an unshakable belief of privilege and infallibility, almost a god complex that would systematically consume and destroy those around him with hatred and violence over time. His wealth was envied but not the extreme nastiness, destructive treatment, and contempt he inflicted on everyone around him.

Today his purpose was to visit Baptiste and collect some of the drugs he purposefully stored at his shack. The drugs were for a transaction to raise cash to pay for a large consignment of heroin, which would eventually be smuggled across the Mexican border.

Satan never allowed Baptiste to see what he was hiding under the floorboards in his shack, and his cousin would ask no questions. He was ordered to wait outside his house while drugs were concealed or extracted. Even though he was family blood, Baptiste did what Satan told him to do because he feared him and was acutely aware of the consequences of defying his cousin.

The Land Rover suddenly burst into the clearing surrounding Baptist's shack; relieved, Mikel pushed on the thinning brake pads, and the vehicle eventually stopped in front of the ramshackle building.

They sat silently for perhaps a minute staring at the door; Mikel knew something wasn't right. Baptiste would usually greet them when they arrived, but not today; everything was silent and still.

Mikel glanced at Satan and saw an expression of suspicion growing across his grimaced face, confirmed when Satan took a small handgun from his shirt. Mikel had seen it before; it was his favourite and had been used resulting in devastating consequences. He spun the barrel, checking that every chamber was full, then twisted around in his seat, removed his machete from the back seat, and climbed out of the vehicle, pushing the handgun down the back of his trousers.

Mikel held his machete and followed.

Satan was well-armed and not afraid of anything, and Mikel was no saint either; he occasionally had to carry out his *jefe's* orders and inflicted pain and death on people when told to do so. He liked to think that he didn't have to carry out Satan's dirty work to the extremes of violence that Satan enjoyed, but he was also feared by many and kept his enemies close in the hope that he might live longer.

Together, their machetes raised, they slowly and carefully walked towards the porch.

As they stepped onto the wooden boards, Mikel noticed tiny water droplets of condensation on the inside of the glass window. Both men gripped their machetes tightly as Satan touched the door handle. He looked at Mikel and nodded, indicating that he was ready to pull the door open and rush into the shack. Mikel nodded in agreement, and a second later, they were standing inside the door frame, holding their machetes above their heads, frantically looking around the room.

Mikel noticed a shape lying on a mattress and concealed beneath a dirty blanket. Satan didn't have to check with his lieutenant; he carefully walked to the bed and quickly snatched the blanket from the mattress, at the same time raising his machete and revealed Baptiste's stiff and contorted body lying underneath, reddened blood-spattered froth surrounded his pale lips and chin.

Mikel walked to the sink and seeing a pan containing syringes and needles on the gas burner, placed his finger in the water; it was warm.

Hearing a noise, he quickly turned and watched Satan step over the dead body of his cousin lying on the mattress then stare at a hole in the floorboards, emitting a guttural groan. Mikel quickly joined him and saw that the place where the money and drugs had been concealed was empty.

'He will burn in hell for this,' he shouted in a throaty, grating voice, then spat at the body of Baptiste. Mikel watched in silence, afraid of what would happen next. Satan could be very volatile in the calmest situations; when he was enraged, it was not a safe place to be around him.

Satan swung the machete, lodging it into the wooden wall, then turned to Mikel, who saw something terrible and dark in Satan's deranged eye; it was evil and horrible. His eye became bloodshot, spittle ran down his chin, and he shook with fury.

He had seldom seen his *jefe* in such a state of uncontrolled anger before and knew he could never forget the pure malevolence he saw in his horrible single, staring eye.

Satan dropped down, sat on the mattress, and, realising he was sitting on Baptist's leg, roughly pushed the stiff limb away as if it were a piece of wood.

He then stood, and Mikel watched as he began to walk around the room as if searching for something. Satan examined the window, wiping the condensation from the glass with his finger. Then walked to the pan, touching the metal then dipped his fingers in the water. Next, he walked around inspecting the floor area. Finally, he looked behind the door, paused and appeared deep in thought for a few seconds then looked at Mikel and spoke.

'Baptiste was my cousin, but today has betrayed me and he will burn in hell because he no longer has what is mine. I swear I will find who did this and will avenge his death and inflict the most severe consequences on those who have stolen my *drogas*.'

Mikel was already becoming nervous as Satan dislodged the machete from the wooden wall. He continued to watch as he began to chop violently and repeatedly until the wood splintered, small pieces of wood dropping onto the mattress and the stiff body of his cousin.

Then Satan turned and pointed the machete threateningly at Mikel.

'I know who did this, and I will avenge my cousin and slice their throats slowly while they scream for their mothers and children. Then I will throw their limp bodies into the river for the crocodiles to devour.'

Mikel rarely asked a question of Satan; he never really thought it was a good idea to try to understand what was going on in his dark and hideous mind, but he was curious.

'You know these people who have taken everything?' he asked.

Satan looked at Mikel for a moment, replying.

'It is obvious, the British have done this; they have stolen what is mine.'

Mikel frowned and waited for Satan to continue.

'Baptiste was a low life, an insect; he didn't have the balls or the strength to join my affairs. He just did small transactions buying vehicle pieces from the British soldiers for meagre pesos, which I provided to him. He had no life and, without me, no future.

'I could have given him wealth, but he was weak and didn't have the courage or the respect to join me, and for this, he is dead like a cockroach squashed under my foot. He offered me no respect, and I only allowed him to live because he is family, and this was a safe place to store my property.'

Mikel quietly asked, 'Why do you think the British stole from you?'

'You dare to question me, Mikel, do you also want to die in this rat-infested place?' Satan retorted, spitting as he spoke.

Mikel, fearful, shook his head. 'No, Satan, I'm sorry, I believe you; I only need to understand how you know these things.'

'Nobody else but the imbecilic soldiers came here. I was here once and saw them visit to sell their junk to Baptiste. Did you not see the pieces next to that old vehicle outside? They are recent and untouched; the British have been here; they killed Baptiste and then stole my drugs.

'His body has been dragged from behind the door to the bed; the foam around his mouth suggests he has been poisoned.'

Mikel looked at the dead body.

'The blood is also there on the floor behind the door,' Satan added, pointing, 'he was dragged to the bed from the floor, and the blanket was thrown over him by those who were here; it does not seem he had the strength to do it himself, and the pan of hot water was turned off after he died, it is still warm and has caused steam to gather on the windows.'

'You think the reason they killed him was to steal the money and drugs?' Mikel asked.

'That I do not know; it does not matter now; they will tell me everything when they are painfully tortured, that I can promise.'

Mikel decided to gamble and cautiously asked;

'How will you be able to find the ones that killed him and have taken the drugs? There are many of them here in Belize, and they will have guns.'

Satan was becoming visibly agitated.

'Enough questions, Mikel,' he said, raising his voice, then continued; 'I have already told you I was here, and I remember one that visits. He is a very big man with black hair and hair on his lip. He spoke to Baptiste with a strange tongue. I can remember him. I believe he is the one who has taken what is mine, and I will ensure that he and his friends will die painfully remembering my name.

'They will come back here Mikel, they must return because many pieces of their equipment are here and surround a dead man; they will return to clean up their junk, and when they do, we will be waiting, then I will stick them like pigs.'

Mikel knew that Satan wasn't lying.

'Get rid of the pathetic body into the jungle. It will be eaten by morning; I need the bed, and you can sleep on the floor. You will light a fire and kill some hens for food; after we have eaten, hide our vehicle behind the shack so no one can see we are here.

'We will stay for as long as it takes until the British thieves return.'

There was no emotion or respect in Satan's voice for his dead cousin, and it did not surprise Mikel; the formidable *Capo* came from somewhere that lacked morality and compassion; he seemed to be from a place that ordinary people would find very dark and forbidden.

He began to roll Baptiste's body off the side of the mattress and into the stinking blanket.

3

Darkness is a prison from which only light escapes.

Matshona Dhliwayo

Stan stumbled up the metal steps and stood on a small platform outside the doors looking into the dark cell. The officer who had followed, poked him in the back with his baton, indicating he should continue into the darkness. He stepped forward then paused, and glancing over his shoulder, shouted, 'Fuck you, you demented whacko.'

The police officer, silhouetted in the open-door frame, swung the baton low and firmly thwacked the metal stick across Stan's calf muscles.

Jack, who was watching, winced, causing unexpected pain to his swollen jawbone and cheek. Then, trying to predict what would happen next, and before he could bend his legs to allow space for Stan to fall to the cell floor, a pair of large hands grabbed his shoulders, pulling and turning him into a sitting position on a wooden bench at the side of the cabin.

His eyes attempted to search the cell in the darkness, then heard the expected thud as Stan collapsed and occupied the space on the floor he had just left.

'Hello, boyo,' said the voice from his side.

He was shocked but curious to hear the distinctive Welsh

accent from the darkness near where he was sitting and knew that only Gareth Jones possessed the incredible strength to effortlessly lift him from the floor.

What paltry light there was in the cell came from the rear doors, which remained open as the officers hurled in the soldier's backpacks, both colliding with Stan as he lay on the stinking damp floor, moaning and gently holding his lower legs.

The two metal doors creaked, then slammed shut, plunging them into total darkness, engulfing the small room as muffled laughter was heard outside the cabin.

Then the cell gently rocked as the officers climbed into the front cab and sat in their seats, and following a short, indistinct conversation, the engine roared into life, and the vehicle jolted forward, driving into the evening streets of Cancún as the prisoners grabbed hold of what they could to steady themselves.

Jack looked again around the prison cell, but it was useless in the dark, even with squinted eyes. The Welsh accent had been the giveaway, and he knew, with certainty, it had to be Gareth sitting somewhere near to him.

'Oh man, there's human muck on the floor,' Stan said, his voice barely auditable above the noise of the diesel engine.

He could just make out Stan's shape moving in the shadows as his friend pushed himself up and precariously stumbled to his feet, bracing himself in the moving vehicle; he quickly sat down on a bench lining the opposite wall of the cell.

Jack held the bench he was sitting on and stretched his leg, his foot contacting what he thought was his backpack, and carefully pulled it towards him. Then using both feet, managed to shuffle the bag underneath the bench. He knew there was a fifty percent chance it was his and not Stan's and, more importantly, no longer lying on the wet floor. He gave the bag a heel kick to firmly lodge it under the bench and instantly heard a groan from somewhere in the cell.

Squinting his eyes, he searched the darkness and vaguely made out the outline of a person sitting on the bench opposite and next to Stan, as another familiar voice filled the space.

'Sorry it's come to this, mate; it's probably better than being alone out there and having nowhere to go.'

Jack responded by shouting above the loud groaning sound of the accelerating engine and grating of gears.

'Lewis! What the hell are you both doing here? I can't believe this, what have you and Gareth done to get us locked up? We only left you in a bar a couple of hours ago,' pausing for a moment, thinking, then said, 'oh, I know what you did; you went back to the hostel, didn't you? What have you two done to that reception boy? *(pause)* Answer me, for Christ's sake.'

Jack felt himself tremble as a mixture of uncertainty and anger erupted from deep inside. Lewis and Gareth seemed to be relentless and recurring nightmares, and on every occasion, he had tried to separate from them, they seemed to bounce back, always cloaked with trouble.

Then Stan's voice came from the darkness, feeling he needed to add to Jack's anger.

'You both did something stupid at that hostel after the cops told us not to return. I can't believe it; they almost locked us up when they caught you trying to kill that kid in the reception.'

Jack glanced between the dark outline of Lewis and then to the place he had last heard the Welshman, Gareth, impatiently waiting for one of them to explain what had happened and had resulted in them being arrested and locked in the cell.

The silence was unbearable.

'Look, I know it's better that we are back together again, a team, and we are all safe and well, but a short time earlier, we left both of you to find your separate way, and we were doing just fine.

'Whatever you have done has resulted in me and Stan having our heads rammed into the side of a vehicle and beaten with police batons. So, for once in your pathetic lives, have the decency to let us know what you did to get us banged up!'

Lewis asked, obviously feeling uncomfortable explaining himself. 'Do you want to tell them Gareth, or should I?'

The cabin rocked as Gareth stood from the bench next to Jack, then, using the cell walls as support and stepping cautiously, shuffled towards the bench opposite, stumbling as his foot struck a backpack on the floor which he crudely kicked toward the opposite bench, then sat down, forcing Lewis and Stan to squeeze together in the limited space.

Finding barely room for the three men, and feeling he was now on the wrong side, Stan quickly crossed over and sat on the bench next to Jack.

The consistent hum of the engine disturbed the cell's silence, then Gareth's voice was heard in the darkness. 'I'm sorry guys, I was just trying to save money; I didn't pay for the drinks in the bar before we split up.'

Stan quickly interrupted. 'Hold on, Gareth, you told us the drinks were on you; we saw you pick up the bill and then go into the bar to pay for them.'

Gareth replied: 'I just went to the toilet instead of paying, you see. When I had finished having a piss, I came out of the bar, and you two had gone, so I just left.'

Jack's turn.

'Is that all you did, you daft Welsh bastard? You've got us all banged up in a cell for a couple of quid because you didn't pay for drinks, and you expect me to believe these bruises on my face and body are because of that? Could it all be really that simple?'

Again, he felt himself trembling with anger and tightly gripped the bench with both hands, accepting that being annoyed wouldn't help the situation or assist in reducing the mayhem he had found himself.

Everything seemed to go south each time he put his trust in Gareth and Lewis.

He tried to focus on the shadows of his friends' opposite and knew with almost certainty that Lewis would have had a more significant part in the shenanigans that Gareth got himself involved with, as he always did.

Lewis was unfailingly the one who plotted and schemed; Gareth tended to act rashly and was ill-advised and Jack was convinced that Lewis, who could be pretentious and conceited, would have been complicit in Gareth's behaviour.

He shouted above the noise of the engine, 'Lewis, was it you that told him to leave without paying for the drinks?'

There was a short pause then Lewis's calm and barely auditable voice was heard in the darkness.

'No, I didn't, Jack; I had no idea he did one without paying; if I'd known he was going to do a runner, I would have told him to pay because it's not worth the trouble, is that the answer you want to hear from me?'

Lewis's smug reply did not surprise him, he responded angrily.

'Okay, Lewis, if that is all Gareth did, we can recover from this mess, can't we? Do me a favour please, ask the cops up front to take us back to the bar, and we'll pay what we owe.

That way, they are bound to release us, but the last time I checked the Mexican tourist information, nothing said that if you unintentionally leave a bar without paying for drinks, the cops will beat the fucking living daylights out of you and then throw you in prison for the rest of your natural life, did you?

'If that were the situation, almost every penniless student in Cancún would be rotten in jail by now. So, humour me, could it be that you did something else, something perhaps a little more serious? Come on, Lewis, let's hear the truth before this all gets out of hand.'

Jack was convinced there was more to explain, and both Gareth and Lewis were hiding something. He had been here before, not in a cell with them, but being told a watered-down version of the truth.

There was a crushing silence in the dark chamber, only interrupted by the engine's drone gently singing, as he waited patiently for those opposite to reply.

Lewis eventually disturbed the quiet. 'All right, asking the cops to take us back to the bar is probably not a good idea, Jack. It's a little more complicated than what Gareth told you, and before you ask, I swear I didn't know until after he had done it.'

Jack's heart sank, shaking his head, noticing the large frame of the Welshman shrinking into the corner of the cell.

Lewis continued: 'Gareth, just say what happened after we left the bar; we need to get this into the open before things get any worse.'

Jack interrupted before Gareth had a chance to reply.

'After you left the bar! Don't tell me you did something stupid after you left without paying; just what the hell did you two do that was so serious for us all to end up in a fucking cell?'

40

Realising his anger had been triggered again and he was shouting unnecessarily, and feeling the annoyance of a stressful pulse ticking in his temple, rubbed the throbbing vein with his finger, composed himself, and then spoke calmly.

'Gareth, would you please tell me what happened when you left the bar? It would be helpful to know so we can try to understand why we have all been arrested. On top of that, Stan and I have been almost beaten to death and we are not entirely sure why. Now go ahead, the floor is all yours.'

Gareth shifted around on the bench, nervously trying to compose himself, which only gave Jack more time to worry about their predicament and become increasingly concerned about what he was about to hear. The police obviously regarded them as a physical threat or potentially violent, evident by how they had dealt with them so far.

Not paying for drinks was not a reason to beat or lock them up, and he guessed that Gareth must have done something quite serious after he had left the bar.

It was hot in the cell, and the humidity increased mainly due to so many bodies in such a small space. He rubbed his sweating face and grimaced when touching his swollen cheekbone and jaw, recalling the earlier police brutality, then anxiously waited for Gareth to explain, expecting it would be something he didn't really want to hear.

'Well, you see,' Gareth began, then stopped and cleared his throat, allowing a bit more time to collect his thoughts, obviously finding it uncomfortable and preparing to explain something difficult.

The Welshman continued.

'Well, Lewis and me, we left the bar, see, and we had only

walked for a little while and were crossing a bridge over a river, like, not a big bridge really, well anyhow we heard a load of shouting from behind us.

'Well, so we stopped, and it turns out that it was the bloke who served us at the bar; anyhow, he caught up, you see. Now then, he started shouting in Mexican and he was like, really angry, and demanding that we pay for the drinks and if we didn't, threatened to call the police.

'Well anyway, he was making a real racket, and I'd heard enough from Mexicans at that point, mainly because that little bastard with the stupid hair in the hostel who nicked our money and passports, see, otherwise we wouldn't be in this situation if it wasn't for him. Well, I sort of lost my temper and just picked him up and threw him over the bridge into the river like.'

Only the swelling and soreness in Jack's jaw prevented his mouth from dropping open in utter disbelief and instead sat in silence and astonishment, desperately trying to make sense of the insaneness of what he had heard, which could have been laughable if it wasn't believable.

The temperature seemed to have increased considerably in the cell and intensified the feeling of his blood beginning to boil; anger swelled again, and he felt the need for some clarification.

'For god's sake Gareth! Are you absolutely deranged? You just threw him over the bridge into the river. Did you check on him, you daft bastard? Is he dead? I really can't believe I am hearing this.'

'Oh no, no, no,' Gareth quickly replied. 'The water was quite deep; I heard a splash, so I looked over and saw him swimming to the side like, then he climbed out and lay down on the riverbank, so I know he didn't drown you see, and that's when we ran away.

'A bit later, we saw police vehicles racing around the streets, so we thought that maybe they were looking for us. The cheeky bugger must have told them we left without paying and all that for a few pesos; you wouldn't fancy it, would you?

'He must have told them that all four of us were together at the bar, and guess that's why, after we were locked up, they continued to search for you and Stan.'

Jack thought the lunacy of his explanation was astonishing on many levels and attempted to focus on Gareth's face in the dark, knowing if he could see him, he would see an expression of childlike innocence. He had known Gareth for long enough to understand that throwing a guy off a bridge into a river wasn't that much of a deal to him, and probably would not have imagined the consequences could result in their incarceration.

He turned and looked at the dark silhouette of Lewis and wanted to know the part he had played in orchestrating the debacle. Then he asked:

'So then, Lewis, while Gareth is holding this poor bloke, who has lost some of his evenings takings and is about to be thrown over a bridge into a river, could you please allude to what noises you are making at this time in an attempt to bring some sense and order into the mayhem? For example, did you not think the idiot Welshman's actions could seriously hurt or even kill the server?'

Lewis replied with a raised voice; sounding upset and slightly wounded.

43

'For crying out loud, stop it, Jack; it was only at that point that I realised Gareth had done a runner without paying. We are where we are, and it's not worth getting all stressed out, Gareth has admitted what he did, and now we're locked up; that's the truth of it. I'm more concerned about what happens when we get to the actual prison because I'm not sure you have heard what I have, but the judicial system is a bit irregular in Mexico, no phone calls, no solicitor, and no food either, just a long time in a rat-infested cell.

'We have an awful lot more to worry about, so stop the "I'm holier than thou" crap because it won't change the situation. If you hadn't already worked it out for yourself, life's a bitch; let's move on and work on getting out of this mess instead.'

Stan, who had been silent during the heated exchange, decided to contribute, which later, and in hindsight, he wished he hadn't and was about to regret it. 'You stupid, stupid Welsh bastard....'

He had hardly finished the final consonant in the word bastard before the large clump of the Welshman's fist hit him squarely under the jaw, delivered with remarkable accuracy and surprisingly in the pitch dark.

Gareth was a large man; his reach was long and had hardly moved in his seat to execute the devastating manoeuvre. Stan immediately lost all consciousness and slumped forward with an awkward thud to the stinking wet floor.

There was a short pause then Jack, incensed, responded. 'Stop it! Just back off, Gareth; don't you realise you have done enough damage already?'

Dropping to his knees, he supported Stan's head and rolled his limp body over to a recovery position; a flash of light streaked through the cabin, probably from a vehicle's headlights, momentarily lighting up the space, allowing him to see a trickle of fresh blood around Stan's mouth.

He could see that the shattering impact of the punch had already caused bruising and swelling to his jaw, along with having his head rammed into the side of the truck earlier. He gently slapped Stan's face and pinched his nostrils until he half opened his eyes. Satisfied, he pulled his arm, bending at the elbow and lay his head on his hand.

Gareth and Lewis silently watched as the lights dimmed again, and the truck continued into the night on its momentous journey as if nothing had happened and no one cared.

Jack stood and cautiously walked, as if on a tightrope, to the front of the cell, then crouched down, putting his face close to the small metal grill which separated them from the driver's cabin.

It gave him a restricted view, but he could see the back of the officers' heads, who were talking and laughing excitedly, almost as if they knew what had happened in the cell; he tried to listen to their conversation, but it was no use as his grasp of Spanish was woeful, and their fast-paced dialogue made him realise he should have learned more when he had the chance.

Looking beyond their heads and through the vehicle windscreen, he saw that they were still driving through Cancún city centre and watched as they passed shops, bars and people, alone or in pairs, walking around the late-night city.

Then suddenly jolted forward, as the truck came to an immediate halt, causing his forehead to hit the grill, as the truck stopped at a red traffic light. He looked through the windscreen and saw a brightly lit shopping centre on the right side of the road, bearing ornate pink marble carvings around the entrance doors, the name 'Flamingo Plaza' embossed into a sign above pretentiously designed doors. Then, the truck lurched forward without warning as the traffic lights changed quickly to green.

He awkwardly made his way to the empty bench and was about to step over Stan's sleeping body but, instead, kicked something heavy on the floor. Bending down, he felt around, touching a backpack.

'That's odd,' he thought, as it hadn't been there before. He remembered pushing his bag under the bench earlier and had also seen Gareth kick Stan's bag under the opposite bench.

Gripping the shoulder strap, he pulled the bag as he stepped over Stan's prone body and then bending, waved his hand under the bench, nothing, confirming it was his bag and thought that it must have become dislodged because of the movement of the truck.

He pushed it under the bench, but this time it wouldn't go quite as far back, as if something else was under the bench and restricting it.

Leaving his bag slightly protruding, he began to mull over their desperate and insufferable situation, Gareth's reckless behaviour, and the consequence of the Welshman's stupidity.

Remembering the experience was supposed to be a holiday here in Mexico and they had spent weeks planning and looking forward to the three-day break to escape the monotony and tediousness of the British military base in Belize.

A few days in Mexico hadn't been that much to ask for, and nobody he was aware of, friends or family, had ever had the fortune or finance to travel to anywhere as exotic and captivating as this. Now, following all the chaos and mayhem that had been experienced from the moment they had arrived, he deeply regretted being there. Perhaps it would have been different if the two men sitting opposite had not caused the unsurprising bedlam.

Looking down, he saw Stan move into a foetal position and began snoring heavily, probably due to his sinuses being severely swollen. At least he would be unaware of the continuing situation and hopefully would sleep and rest for a while until they reached their destination, that's if ever they were to get to it.

The truck continued through the streets on its long journey.

He felt the cabin tilt and watched Gareth stand then bend over and search for something under the bench on his side of the cell. Removing a backpack, he lay down on the floor next to the person he had just punched into unconsciousness, and using the bag as a makeshift pillow, tried to sleep.

Jack rolled his eyes at the audacity of Gareth's behaviour but then remembering the revolting substances he was now lying in, felt a little less judgemental.

Movement on the bench opposite caught his attention, and he saw the silhouette of Lewis, who was trying to get comfortable and had laid down on the bench. It wasn't long before the sounds of grunting and snoring from his three friends joined the therapeutic hum of the engine as if a strange harmonious orchestral quartet.

Turning his wrist, he looked at his watch, the luminous blue hue of the hands barely readable in the dark; he saw that the time was just after 2 am and guessed that they had been in the truck driving around for at least two, perhaps, three hours. He was feeling tired and stressed and needed to get some much-needed sleep but felt the responsibility fell on him to remain awake and think of a way out of their predicament.

He thought of what might happen on arrival at the prison and how important it would be to alert Army chiefs back in Belize.

It had only been a day since they had left the Army base and they had all taken three days of leave, meaning it would be at least a further two days before they would be missed, if not more and it could be a while before anyone became aware of their absence.

Hopefully, if they failed to report back when their leave had ended, they would be reported *absent without official leave*, and enquiries should begin immediately to locate them.

Usually, the Military Police would try to establish if they were intentionally absent or had been involved in an accident or worse.

Would they go as far as checking Mexican prisons? Perhaps, after all, it wouldn't be the first-time squaddies had ended up in jail following a drunken fight or minor and occasionally more serious crime.

He hoped that on arrival at the city prison, and being British citizens, they would be allowed to contact the British Embassy.

Inevitably, the two police officers would have questions to answer for giving them such a gratuitous and violent beating.

The constant rhythmic movement of the truck, combined with the hum and heat of the engine, unruffled and calmed him, and his head began to fall slowly forward, his chin dropping to his chest.

Startled, he jerked and sat upright, rubbing his stinging and swollen face gently with his hands; he knew this was not a time to sleep; and it was clear, he had to consider options to find a possible solution that could end their consternation before it became worse.

His thoughts were interrupted by intermittent light flashes around the cell's walls. They were almost hypnotic, and he began to feel tired again; the stress caused by the anarchy, reducing his ability to think correctly, and he felt the need to have a power nap for just a few minutes which would energise his ability to think more logically.

Lifting his legs, he lay on his back on the bench, clasped the sides with both hands and closed his eyes. The truck was warm and quiet, and the movements were rhythmic and soothing.

He instantly succumbed to a deep but restless sleep.

4

If you do not change direction,
you may end up where you are heading.

Siddhãrtha Gautama

Only a few months earlier, he had boarded the aeroplane in England, having been posted to Belize for a six-month-long operational tour of duty.

The arduous flight lasted over fifteen hours from the military base in Brize Norton in Oxfordshire to Belize International Airport, with a short stop at Dulles International Airport, Washington. Even that had proved inconsequential as it was only to refuel the plane, and passengers were not allowed to leave the aircraft.

Thirty minutes strapped in their seats on the aeroplane while waiting on the tarmac had only added to the exhausting and herculean journey.

That was well behind him now. He was now over five thousand miles from home, sitting alone in an uncomfortably warm Nissen hut in a British Army base surrounded by an unforgiven and formidable primary jungle in Central America.

He looked around the office, which was only a third of the size of the entire hut and separated from the remainder of the building by a thin wall framing a single door. In the room, he saw an old wooden bureau desk with several drawers, a metal filing cabinet, and a waist-high, rusting Chubb safe.

A freestanding circulating fan on the desk made a low-pitched droning noise as it swept the room from side to side, the occasional breeze giving light relief from the sweltering humidity and heat. There was another chair beside the one he sat on, next to the bureau below a double casement window.

Through the window, the sky was cloudless, blue, and bright, the blinding sun shockingly hot, and there seemed to be a perpetual dampness in the air that clung to his skin and clothes. There was also a lingering and ghastly smell; he had noticed it when he had disembarked from the DC10 Royal Airforce aircraft; it was a musty, mouldy smell and had been ever-present since his arrival.

His attention was drawn to the window and movement outside. A green and black camouflaged Land Rover stopped outside the hut, the driver, climbing out of the vehicle and walking to the rear.

Jack was taken aback by the size of the tall man who had broad shoulders and a big chest. His jet-black hair, longer than normally acceptable for a soldier, was brushed back over his head and a thin moustache on his lip. He wore an olive drab military-issue tee shirt and shorts and, on his feet, jungle boots with green socks neatly turned over the top.

Then the passenger left the vehicle; he was smaller than the driver, more Jack's size and wore the same uniform as the tall man, he was clean-shaven and had very short crew-cut hair. Their shirts were soddened with sweat patches stretching across their chests, underarms and backs and helping him to understand that being indoors was a better place to be, away from the sun; the circulating fan was refreshing, making his damp shirt stick to his skin as the warm air circulated and fanned him.

He curiously watched the soldiers as they lifted equipment from the rear of the Land Rover, carrying the items past the window to the rear of the Nissen hut, then returned and continued to do the same with another load. He watched as they removed what appeared to be vehicle parts, batteries and tyres from the vehicle.

The internal door in the office, presumably leading to the rear section of the hut, opened, startling him; he stood up, pushing the chair backwards and watched as the shorter of the two men entered. The soldier, face dripping with sweat, smiled broadly, stepped towards Jack and began vigorously shaking his hand, introducing himself as, 'Lewis Williams.'

'Glad you made it, Corporal Wallace; it's Jack, isn't it; do you mind if I call you Jack? Corporal is a bit formal don't you think? We are a bit more relaxed here. How did you find the flight? It's a long bleeding time. The guy you're replacing, Jonah, flew back to the UK on Friday, so we were expecting you.

'Have they allocated you a room? Did you get breakfast this morning? It's bloody hot here, and the mosquitos are a real menace, but you will get used to them.'

Jack wasn't sure which question to answer and just nodded.

'Just a minute Jack,' Lewis said and stopped shaking his hand.

He walked over to the window and opened it. The other man was removing the canopy from the rear of the Land Rover.

'Are you all right to do the next delivery, Gareth? The new corporal is here, and I'm just about to brief him about what's going to Baptiste's, and then you can set off, is that okay?'

Jack watched as the man smiled, nodding to Lewis in agreement, then walked past the window, returning moments later, rolling a tyre to the Land Rover and then hauling it into the back of the vehicle.

'That's Gareth Jones; he's a big bugger, isn't he. It must be all that lamb they fed him in the Welsh valleys back home, don't you think?'

Jack had always avoided judging anyone in the first few minutes when meeting them. However, there was an obvious uneasiness about Lewis; he couldn't quite put his finger on it, sensing cockiness and arrogance leaking out in the way he spoke and in his body language.

Conscious it was just a first impression, and he was tired and weary from the long flight so could be wrong.

He felt he needed to adjust, allow more time to pass, and understand his new job and who did what in his new team. He had met enough soldiers whom he distrusted on the first encounter, only to become some of his closest friends later. Equally, he had met others who appeared honest but rapidly became untrustworthy and devious. He tried to guess where Lewis would fit.

Lewis slumped into the chair opposite and wiped his brow with the back of his hand then leaned towards Jack.

'You haven't been to Belize before, have you, Jack? I will give you a thorough brief tomorrow and take you around to meet everyone; I know that you will really enjoy your time here, but for now, we need to talk about something really important, and I feel it's crucial you know what we are doing from the outset.

'You see Gareth out there? He's loading the Land Rover with equipment; some Land Rover spare parts and tyres. It's because we are committed to making a delivery, and it is essential we get it to where it needs to be today, in fact, in the next hour, so I want to get straight to the point with you and explain so you fully understand what we are doing and the revenue for us, and because you are taking over, that includes you.

'Please don't be concerned until I have explained everything because the benefits are enormous for us all, and I promise you won't be disappointed.'

Jack remained silent and waited, curious to hear more.

'Could you excuse me for a second, Jack? I need to quickly speak to Gareth again.'

Jack watched Lewis walk to the window and gently tap on the glass with his knuckles, trying to attract Gareth's attention, then began to shout when he turned and looked at him.

'It's four tyres, Gareth; you've only loaded three; there must be another out the back. I'm sure Stan got it from the Parachute Regiment compound yesterday. Can you have another look for it please; you know that Baptiste prefers you to rock up at midday at his place, so you will have to get a move on; are you ok with that?'

Gareth replied, sweat dripping from his face 'Yes, I'll have another look around, but I will have to leave soon; otherwise, I'm going to be late.'

Lewis returned to the chair and, sitting down, said, 'Right then, let's get down to it, Jack, but firstly I have to ask you to promise not to say a thing to anyone outside our group; otherwise, we will be in more grief than you could imagine.'

Jack didn't say anything; he just sat silently, waiting for what Lewis seemed to be pushed for time to tell him.

'Belize is one of the best operational postings for a soldier and a fantastic experience; we are lucky to be here, right? A beer only costs a dollar, that's about twenty pence, and for forty-one dollars, you can buy an hour with a lovely girl in Raúl's Rose Garden, the local brothel, that's just eight British pounds. It's like being in heaven here, Jack; what more can anyone ask?'

Jack was aware the question was rhetorical and allowed Lewis to plough on.

'Well, as you already know, a soldier's salary isn't great, and there is more to Belize than beer and prostitutes. For instance, there are boat trips to the Caye resorts around Belize, St Georges, Caye Caulker and the incredible Ambergris Caye; that's the island where many married American ladies like to spend their annual holiday, without their husbands, if you get my drift.

'There is also the opportunity to visit Mexico City or Cancún; if you save up on your leave, you can also catch a short flight to Orlando and Miami for a holiday. Now, how many people do you know have the chance to do all that?'

He didn't wait for an answer and continued.

'The issue though is that it's not cheap, and transport and hotels can cost a considerable amount of money, much more than we can afford on our meagre wages. So, here's the bit I know you will like, we have an enterprise going on here which brings in a great deal of cash, giving us the fantastic opportunity to visit all those incredible places and enjoy the trappings, that normally only a wealthy tourist would be able to afford, without having to touch your salary.

'As you know already, we are only stationed in Belize for six months, and we all want to make it the experience of a lifetime. Critically though, as I mentioned earlier, you cannot let anyone know how we are getting additional funds to pay for paradise.'

Lewis stopped talking and looked at him, waiting for a response, as Jack sat in silence trying to take in what he thought was beginning to sound like a clever sales pitch, but he was curious.

'Why don't you get to the details, Lewis; you are aware that I have just arrived in Belize and don't know anyone here to talk to, never mind telling them what is going on here. I won't promise to be part of your enterprise, but if you explain what it involves, I can think about it.'

Jack couldn't deny it; presently, money was an issue, and he had intended to restrict himself to spending no more than twenty-five pounds a week while he was in Belize.

For the past five months, he had been eagerly saving everything he could for a second-hand Audi Cabriolet he had seen for sale back in England and was being kept for his return. It had seemed so long since he had been able to spend money, even moderately, on anything as a treat to himself, and he was really feeling the pinch.

He had planned to conserve and use his money wisely, and an hour of sex with a prostitute at the local brothel did not seem a good investment and certainly would not be top of the list of things he wanted to do whilst in Belize.

'As I said earlier Jack, just promise one thing, please; you must keep this to yourself; it can't be made public.'

Jack had already picked up on the continual emphasis on secrecy and had caused him to be suspicious.

Lewis stopped talking and stared at Jack as if waiting for some indication of trust before continuing.

Jack said nothing and waited.

'All right, so we are doing a little business, an enterprise we prefer to call it, on the side with the locals. It's been going on longer than I have been here in Belize; it's something I inherited when I arrived, and it's so important that we keep this under the radar; otherwise, not only those currently involved but guys who were here before us will be in an extremely difficult situation if the Army chiefs were to discover the operation.

'Don't be too concerned about agreeing to join us; it's been going on for ages, it's very straightforward, and there is no great risk.'

Jack continued to listen, being cautious not to show commitment until he knew more; aware that wherever he had served, he had heard of activities where soldiers had benefitted from the odd "enterprise" typically illegally selling something. Usually, something ordinarily assessed and deemed to be scrap, useless or otherwise unusable. "No longer in the public interest" was the phrase often used.

However, what he would not get involved in, and would expose if aware of, was trading operationally sensitive information, uniforms or weapons. Enterprises of that nature were criminal and resulted in those involved being, quite rightly he thought, court-marshalled and occasionally imprisoned. The Army hierarchy was aware of and proactive in exposing any internal illegal activity to prevent reputational damage to the UK Forces.

He reserved himself from commenting on what he had heard and decided to wait for more detail before responding.

'Look, Gareth needs to get off soon, so I will give you a swift potted history, and then you can decide for yourself; if you don't like it, you don't have to be involved; all I ask is that you keep what I say to yourself, that's all.'

Lewis looked out of the window and held up his hand as if to inform the other soldier to wait for a minute or two, then continued; 'I'll have to be quick because Gareth must leave in a few minutes.

'Twenty years ago, Belize was a British colony, but the UK decided to give back its independence and remove its military support. The logistical costs were massively expensive and involved returning a colossal stock of ageing thirty-year-old military equipment, generators, and vehicles to the UK. Most of which had become outdated and past their operational capability, so the Army head sheds decided it would be less costly to leave it all here and sell to the Belizeans by auction.

'The Ministry of Defence would acquire a modest amount of money by selling vehicles and equipment versus the considerable cost of transporting it back to the UK and then scrapping. So that's what they did, and the Belizeans bought all the old but usable equipment for next to nothing, which was all well and good but then a few years later, they began to get the hump.'

He paused when the sound of a vehicle's engine roared into life outside the office. They both looked through the window and saw Gareth behind the driver's wheel of the Land Rover; he was signalling to Lewis, indicating it was time to leave. Lewis held up a finger, implying one more minute.

'All right, Lewis, it looks like Gareth really needs to leave so could you cut to the chase, please,' Jack began to push him to move on.

Lewis ignored Jack's request and continued with the history.

'Two years after the British had left, vehicles and generators began to break down because they were at the end of their serviceable life. The Belizeans were pretty pissed but couldn't ask for their money back or get spare parts to repair anything because British Leyland had been the leading manufacturer, and it was far too expensive to have consumables like tyres, batteries, and camshaft belts delivered from their factory in the UK.

'Then everything went south; you see, the British had left Belize in a vulnerable position and without security or a trained defence force, so the Guatemalan junta ordered their military to cross the border and invade Belize.

'The Belizeans blamed Britain for leaving them unprotected and defenceless and demanded the British army return, regain their sovereignty and train and equip their army.'

Lewis paused, as Jack watched; his mouth opened as if in a momentary trance, then, using lightning speed, slapped the side of his neck. He stared into his hand, smiled and turned his palm to show Jack the remains of the squashed mosquito and a small splash of blood.

'So anyway,' he continued, 'the British Army returned to Belize, kicked Guatemala out and set up military bases in Belize again, shoring up the borders and defences and began training a Belizean Defence Force. That's when the Belizeans began to steal all the equipment to repair the vehicles we sold to them when we were here before.

'If a Land Rover was left out of sight for more than a few minutes, it would get stripped to the chassis, and I mean really stripped. Tyres, wheels, canopy, windows, engine, you name it. Basically, you would return to an empty shell or, on one occasion, just a steering wheel. This sort of thing was happening almost daily and was becoming a continuous headache to senior officers.'

The sound of a vehicle horn outside interrupted.

'I better finish off; Gareth really needs to leave for the delivery,' Lewis said, then continued; 'anyway, a soldier was posted here a couple of years ago; he originated from Jamaica if I remember rightly. So, for some reason he spoke to a couple of Belizeans in a bar in the city, and it turned out that these guys were two-bit criminals who arranged for British Army vehicles to be stripped and the parts sold to guys who couldn't get them elsewhere.

'To cut a long story short, he struck a deal with them. He told them he was able to get his hands on any spare part they wanted if they would offer the right price and could deliver tyres, gaskets, drive belts, batteries and whatever else they needed, which they could sell on the black market to anyone who wanted them.

'That was how the enterprise began. When I arrived four months ago, I was taken downtown and introduced to the contact, Baptiste, and the responsibility of the enterprise was passed on to me.

'I did the deliveries alone several times but soon realised it had become too difficult to do it alone. To be fair, I should have revealed the business to the other guys who worked in the section with me at that time. They would have appreciated the extra money to help make their stay in Belize more enjoyable and to have been able to afford to visit Mexico and all the other places.

'Eventually, about two months ago, I disclosed the business to Gareth and Stan and now there are just three of us involved, it's a huge money earner and because you are here now, you can be part of it. That's it, what do you think, Jack? Are you interested?'

Jack asked, 'Where do you get all the parts from? How can you supply so much equipment to him and so often?'

Lewis smiled.

'The parts we sell are what would be ordinarily scrapped and are at the end of their shelf life; we are just recycling stuff that's no longer in the public interest.'

He explained they search the vehicle compounds on the military base at the end of each day, looking for unserviceable or worn vehicle parts or spares. If they were challenged, they would say they were authorised to dispose of anything useless and would be taking them to the local refuse tip.

Soldiers almost always avoided mundane paperwork, so they were more than content to allow them to take the parts away.

The equipment would then be stored at the back of the Nissen hut under a tarpaulin and delivered to Baptiste each week in exchange for cash.

'All we do is recycle worn-out parts and prevent a load of rubbish being thrown on the tip.'

Jack frowned, 'I'm not convinced, Lewis; what about this guy Baptiste? Who is he? What's his background?'

Lewis responded, 'Baptiste is a nice guy, a bit of a loner really; he lives alone in a remote shack in the jungle and pays the same price for anything we take down to him, then presumably goes to town and sells the parts to scrapyards to be sold on; it's not as if we are striking a deal with a significant crime gang or anything, just a small-time guy doing a bit to earn enough to pay for his living.'

Jack looked at Lewis, who seemed too relaxed about everything, then said, 'Well, I'm a little uncertain about the logistics and how you justify the paperwork if it gets checked,

I have only just arrived here, and I don't want to get into trou ble; I need some time to think about the risks before I decide what I should do.'

Lewis almost choked, laughing.

'This is Belize mate! You left the real world when you got on that aeroplane, they don't keep records for anything out here, and there are no equipment inspections.

'Britain has an open chequebook for this place because the MOD and UK politicians felt guilty for leaving in the first place and allowing Guatemala to invade. Trust me; you will get a bloody good return for minimal effort or risk; think about visiting Miami, Cancún or Disney World!'

'Let me think about it first, Lewis; I must weigh the personal risks before deciding, remember I am taking over as the super-visor here.'

Again they heard the sound of the vehicle's horn a second time.

Lewis stood from the chair waving to Gareth through the window.

'Great,' he said, turning to Jack and smiling, 'why don't you jump in the Land Rover and travel to the city with Gareth? He's loaded up with spares to deliver to Baptiste. That way, you can see for yourself how easy it all is.

'Don't decide until you discover how straightforward the exchange with Baptiste is managed. Then you can let me know if you want to join the enterprise when you return. I know you will; as I said, it's an incredible earner, and I know that you will want to benefit from it.'

The constant and imposing heat and humidity were already beginning to take their toll on him; he felt lightheaded, and he was hot and sweating. Listening to Lewis had caused him to feel anxious and uncertain and felt he needed to find some space to think about all he had heard.

Without saying anything else, he left his chair, opened the door and walked towards the waiting Land Rover.

5

We had not expected paradise.
We had expected hardship.

Sue Burke

Gareth had removed the canvass canopy from the Land Rover, and the uninterrupted heat of the sun created a warm, intoxicating, and comfortable feeling, allowing the cool breeze to swirl around the vehicle whilst in motion. His hair tussled and stirred as the vehicle drove along the neglected, crumbling Belizean roads.

The scenery was stealing the show; he thought it was nothing less than stunningly beautiful. The roads had been bleached almost white by the constant rays of sunshine; short, crispy brown grass and dust skirted each side of the road, giving way to an overpowering display of the dense, deep green, and thick impenetrable jungle.

Periodically vibrantly colourful plants and flowers formed a surreal frame around the greenness of foliage. He was engrossed by the sight of frequent and lively glimpses of distant monkeys swinging by their tails amongst the trees, coupled with loud whooping calls of something larger. That ever-present stench of mould or rot was even more overpowering as the smell of the jungle permeated around him.

Between the trees and vines nearest the road, he occasionally caught glances of a very slow-flowing murky brown river bordering the thick foliage of the jungle. The river ran parallel to the road and, at times, met the fractured tarmac at its side, occasionally disappearing into the brown water.

He saw a muddy embankment on the opposite side bordering the river, which was sun-baked, and, to his astonishment, alligators or crocodiles, he didn't know which, were lazily basking on the mud banks in the warm sun. One thrashed its tail into the air as a bird, probably a yellow beak toucan, attempting to perch on its large head.

Gradually the thick foliage began to diminish, and the river started to take a different direction. Then, to his frustration, heaps of domestic rubbish appeared on both sides of the road, stacked beside huts.

Crudely built wooden buildings on tall stilts and the evidence of human life rudely replaced the incredible and stunning natural backdrop of fauna and flora.

Guessing they were probably entering the suburbs of Belize City, he watched increasing numbers of people of all ages, mostly young boys and girls, cutting wood, cooking, or repairing something on the sides of the road. Older people carried baskets full of fruit or vegetables or pushed wooden carts laden with rubbish or scrap; most looked poor and wore nothing on their feet and, unless bare-chested, were wearing washed-out and tattered shirts and ripped shorts or skirts.

He was surprised by how unnaturally thin most people appeared, the distressing sight of the impoverished and indigent disturbing him and reminding him of the disproportionate levels of the socio economic lower class that existed across Central America.

He remembered how before he began his arduous journey from England to Belize, he had read as much as he could about the country, its nature, people, politics, economy, and crime.

He recalled being surprised at the rapid expansion and proliferation of organised drug cartels and racketeering across Central America and how it unceasingly shattered the lives of people and communities. Years of ineffectual governance by the Peoples United Party (PUP), which had a reputation for scandal and corruption and providing too much to the over-privileged, increasing their omnipotence and wealth, while the underprivileged remained destitute and often had no choice but turn to crime, prostitution, or the drug trade to feed their families, often the only source of income available to the poverty-stricken.

When the Belizean Drugs Enforcement Agency swept up drug dealers during their infrequent and too often ineffectual operations, it was seldom the wealthy traffickers arrested, but the impoverished who mostly populated the prisons and were denied justice or hope with no money to pay for or bribe a lawyer, their families left alone to starve and fend for themselves without a financially supporting parent, sibling or child.

As they drove past the varying building structures, he was intrigued by the different and straightforward architecture; some were no more than hastily constructed wooden shacks built with rough-cut, recycled panels of wood. Most lacked windows or doors, just gaps, a curtain screening their privacy from the outside world and, of course, any blood-sucking parasites or insects, frequently resulting in diseases, malaria and occasionally death.

There was no evidence of trash cans or bins, and large piles of rubbish and waste surrounded most houses. Heaps of food packaging, pieces of plastic, discarded clothing and rusting bikes and car parts. Clearly, there were no local refuse and recycling centres in this city.

Packs of half-wild and feral dogs roamed amongst the rubbish, desperately searching and occasionally viciously fighting each other for scraps of discarded rotting food or rats, possibly their only daily meal.

'I think it's because of the bloody land crabs,' he heard Gareth shouting above the whining of the engine.

'Land crabs?' Jack asked.

'That's why the houses are built on stilts to keep out the land crabs, big buggers they are,' Gareth replied.

'They scare the hell out of me, and I've seen some as big as rats. On the way back, we might run over a few of them later; I usually see them on the road late afternoon. They are freaky critters, and have adapted to live on the land, away from water and burrow into the ground to keep out of the sun. I picked up a coconut once, and one bleeder was living inside the damn thing.

'They come out when it's cool in the evening time. The problem is, though, they swarm in their bloody hundreds, and the beggars are all over the place. Their razor claws can cut through the leather on your boot, so be careful if you are close to one.'

Jack shook his head, trying to comprehend the surrealness of his surroundings and felt a million miles from the familiarity and safety he had been so accustomed to most of his life.

He thought that over the next few months, he would probably crave all that he usually had taken for granted in his small, clean, orderly life back in England.

For the first time since his arrival in the country, and as he entered the city's central area, the pungent smell of the jungle started to taper off, and new fragrances, those of humans and the city, began to emerge. He smelled exhaust fumes, charred chicken, hot dogs and onions.

The widening roads began to generate more vehicles, most being driven around could only be described as historical wrecks from a bygone age. A Ministry of Transport test centre would have failed many of them, he thought to himself.

There appeared to be a total lack of road discipline by those driving the wrecked machines that were imitating cars. Indicators were seldom used or had broken optics. Cars and trucks turned corners and crossed junctions with perilous risk and often into the path of other vehicles, the drivers honking their horns and, occasionally, shouting angrily and gesticulating with their hands.

There appeared to be a complete absence of traffic light posts at junctions, and when he did see them, the glass lenses were often cracked or the post bare of any lights. Some posts had been cut down to stumps as if stolen and sold for scrap.

He looked at the once brightly coloured shop fronts but now faded and paint peeling, most advertising alcohol, roast chicken or chicken soup. A legion of hot dog carts occupied most street corners, and people queued to buy from them. He thought of the irony of the word hot 'dog' casting obvious doubt about the origin of the meat contained in the sausages.

Gareth saw him looking and confirmed his thoughts.

'Whatever you do, corporal, don't eat any hot dogs or the local chicken and never eat anything from the Chinese take-aways. Belizeans don't seem to want to eat anything else, and you can see how popular they are, I don't think they are too bothered about the type of meat they put in them or how old it was before being cooked.'

Observing the frequency of men who appeared drunk, standing or sitting on pavements, and drinking from a bottle disguised in a brown paper bag, he guessed probably home-brewed alcohol.

A disquieting prevalence of beggars and the homeless, occasionally stretching out a bony hand, hoping for some charitable offering, enabling them to pay for much-needed food, drugs or alcohol and assist in removing them from the pain and misery of life for a short time. Most were dirty, grubby, and appeared ill and disease-ridden.

'What a miserable hell on earth this place is Gareth,' then realising there were no females begging or drinking, asked, 'is prostitution a significant problem here? Lewis mentioned earlier that you frequently visit a brothel close to the army base.'

'It's bloody mental here, corporal,' he replied, 'but they tend to keep themselves to the safety of brothels; I think it's too dangerous to work on the streets.

'Don't worry, though; they're harmless and won't put you under any pressure unless you like one and fancy a bit; you'll meet a few of our regular girls in Raúl's Rose Garden; we go there most nights when we are not at the Moonshine bar on the camp, I think you'll like it there, most do, even the married blokes, it's only forty-one dollars for a full hour and if they take a liking to you, sixty-two dollars for the whole night; it's a great laugh, good music too.'

Leaving the degeneration of the city centre, the vehicle continued through the city's innermost residential and wealthier township.

Buildings became neat and more elegant and appeared to be sophistically and classically designed as if from some bygone ancient British colonial period. Some were constructed in brick and stone, others in wood, many of which appeared to be deserted condos with peeling paint and boarded-up windows.

'Look over there corporal,' Gareth said and pointed to a large, typically colonial building with far-reaching right-angled stairs on each side of the prominent entrance on the first floor. The facia cascaded with pillars and columns, and the sun reflected off every highly polished window. It certainly stood out over everything else he had seen so far.

'That's the Fort George Hotel, very nice it is too. Apparently, Queen Elizabeth stayed there in eighty-five when she visited Belize as part of her commonwealth tour; very nice if you can afford it.'

Eventually, the number of significant and affluent buildings dissipated, and the jungle once again dominated the sides of the dusty road. He felt the soothing warmth of the sun and the refreshing but musty, mouldy-smelling breeze on his face and closed his eyes. It wasn't long before the gentle vibrations and rhymical hum of the Land Rover's engine encouraged him to dose off into a comfortable sleep.

He awoke to the sudden jolt of the vehicle as if the shock absorbers were being tested to the extreme; Jack snapped his eyes open as he was thrust forward and thrown around in his seat. He quickly steadied himself by placing a hand on the dashboard in front of him.

Noticing they had left the main road, they drove down an

undulating, dusty dirt track. The jungle foliage was very close to the sides, and substantial hanging leaves slapped as they thrashed the vehicle. He watched as Gareth concentrated, tightly gripping the steering wheel, and attempting to keep the vehicle straight and, at the very least, on the track.

Thick vegetation overhead created infrequent shadows, causing a mild chill each time the vehicle was driven into the shade. Eventually, the width of the track reduced, and the surface became smooth, making the roller coaster ride a little less frightening as the jungle attempted to reclaim its territory and calmness returned.

Without any warning, they broke out of the dense and dank jungle and head-long into a bright clearing; rays of strong sunlight lit up in a kaleidoscope of natural colours in the clearing, and vines, young trees, and palms snaked the area like tendrils.

The clearing was almost circular and had been stripped of most foliage by humans; several trees had been cut down to stumps to create space. The most apparent evidence of a human presence was a dilapidated wooden shack with small outbuildings which stood almost centrally at the far end of the unnatural man-made area.

The building had once been painted, but the green flaking paint was almost gone, and the sun-bleached wooden panels faded with age and rot. On one side of the shack, a pile of rusting metal junk, mainly old vehicle parts, ripped tyres, dented body panels and a heap of vehicle batteries.

Standing proud amongst the debris was the front half of a British Army Land Rover, windows and wheels missing and only the bonnet and front end of what once was an impressive workhorse of the British Army, the remaining body panels still coated with the remnants of familiar green and black camouflage paint.

Around the once magnificent relic, six or seven hens pecked eagerly at the ground, searching for insects and grubs.

Jack's searching curiosity ended abruptly, and his attention turned towards Gareth, who was panting heavily and noisily; he saw that the Welshman was sweating more than he had noticed before, and his entire shirt was sodden with sweat and was steaming; then he remembered the purpose of their visit. He wasn't sure if his colleagues condition had resulted from the intense and energetic drive along the jungle track or if he had suddenly become nervous; he put it down to both.

Gareth continued to steer the vehicle slowly and completed a full circle, bringing the vehicle to a stop so that the front end pointed away from the shack and towards the track where they had entered the clearing.

Droplets of sweat meandered down his face when he spoke, spraying from his lips. 'This is the place, corporal; I always turn the vehicle to face this way, so when the exchange is done, I can leave quickly. Be careful when he comes out, don't take your eyes off him for a second.'

Gareth's explanation sent a shiver down Jack's spine, and suddenly, he became quite suspicious and nervous about the so-called enterprise with few risks. His eyes found the rear-view mirror and he scanned the shack looking for any movement or signs of life.

It was all quiet, and Gareth slowly opened the driver's door and then began to manoeuvre his large frame from the vehicle; Jack took it as an indication to do the same and watched Gareth push the driver's door closed stealthily and carefully until there was a quiet click as the lock engaged.

He sensed extreme cautiousness and anxiety from his driver, making him very feel quite uneasy. Gareth's demeanour surprised him, considering he had been here many times before and should be used to this unless something else was causing him to be suspicious and wary.

Jack inhaled deeply through his nose and smelled the familiar stench and humidity of the jungle. The baying calls of animals and the drumming sound of insects were more apparent due to the clearing surrounded by dense jungle and, usually, the lack of human presence.

The sound of someone shouting replaced the melodious sounds of nature.

'*Bonjou N'ap boule!*'

'*Bonjou Baptiste,*' Jack detected the nervousness in Gareth's reply.

The mesh door at the front of the shack swung open, and a man stepped out and stood on the wooden porch smiling at them. A large mop of dreadlocks spread over both shoulders, and he sported a scraggly wispy beard and wore a dirty red t-shirt ripped in several places and washed-out jeans cut at differing, fraying lengths below his knees.

Holding a dirty towel in his hands, he continually rubbed the material with his fingers. The towel had once been white but was now grey and ripped with dangling cotton threads. For a second, Jack imagined a weapon could have been concealed under the towel, then quickly dismissed the thought when the man began to wave the cloth above his head, wafting annoying flies away.

'Wellcoom my friends, and what geefts have yoo brought to us today, mister Engleesh' Baptiste said smiling, and focussing his eyes on Jack, then, with a toothy smile, said, 'ahh we have a new boy in toon; I am Baptiste, you have a name boy?'

'Can we just stick to business because we are in a hurry?' Gareth rudely interjected, 'we've got four tyres and two batteries for you. I don't want any messing about boyo, so check them and give us the usual, then we get out of here, let's make it pronto, we've got other things to do. *Ou konprann?*'

Jack was surprised at Gareth's terse response and the bluntness of his tone. Obviously, this was no more than a simple business deal, and they were not here to exchange pleasantries.

Baptiste's smile disappeared and then changed to a leering stare then following a short pause, began laughing loudly. He gave a broad smile and Jack noticed several gold teeth glinting in the sun as Baptiste stepped forward, jumped from the porch, and ambled towards them, still rubbing his hands on his towel.

He felt uneasy when Baptiste approached, then walked past them and, as they turned, saw him pause at the rear of the Land Rover. He whipped the towel over his shoulder and lifted the tarpaulin revealing the tyres and batteries underneath.

Seemingly satisfied, he dropped the tarp, unhitched the tailgate, and grunting, slowly removed each of the tyres and batteries and placed them on the ground at the side of the vehicle.

As Baptiste worked, Jack noticed Gareth glancing towards the shack and then scanning the edges of the clearing before looking at Baptiste working. It was obvious that Gareth was continually checking there was no one else in the clearing or waiting in the shack.

The suspicion heightened Jack's sensitivity and nervousness that something terrible was about to happen and remembering Gareth's instruction, he constantly observed Baptiste, all the time feeling trickling beads of sweat running down his face and arms.

Baptiste inspected the tread on one of the tyres and ran his finger along the rubber. Jack noticed the tyres were almost completely bald and smooth and were undoubtedly not road-worthy by any stretch of the imagination.

He expected Baptiste to say they were useless and not worth paying for, but he was wrong; after inspecting the batteries, Baptiste straightened and stretched his back, then gave a bellowing laugh which caused him to bend over at the waist, shoulders shaking, his towel falling to the ground.

When he stopped laughing, he picked up the towel and then, rubbing his hands in the material, smiled at them both.

'This is fooking good, Mister Engleesh. Is this man your new *jefe*' nodding to Jack. 'I hope so; this is much better tings than you brought to me last time.' Then he turned to face Jack and said, 'we do much business, mister boss man.'

Jack stared back at Baptiste and said nothing as he tried to hide the nervous tremble he was experiencing, then turned and glanced at Gareth, who was straight-faced and expressionless, watching every move that Baptiste made, eyes still darting to the shack and the edges of the clearing.

Baptiste turned and walked towards the shack, swinging the towel above his head and singing.

> *'I bet you're wondering how I knew*
> *Bout why you make me blue*
> *'Twas in my dreams of you.'*

Stepping onto the wooden porch, he disappeared through the tattered mesh door and into the shack.

A chance to check if everything was going to plan.

'Is everything all right, Gareth? You seem quite nervous about all this, is there something I should know?' he asked the other soldier.

'Everything is good so far, corporal; don't worry, after he has given me the cash and I have checked it, he will ask us to stay for a drink, he always does, but we will refuse and be out of here in two minutes, latest,' Gareth replied.

They were interrupted by the creaking mesh door being pushed open, and Baptiste stepped onto the porch. A bunch of crumpled green notes in his hand, the towel in the other.

'Yoo want to stop for drink and smoke, I can make yoo relax? I got some real good shit for you Engleesh boys; it came from Honduras and is the best; it cost you nothing today if you smoke it with me.'

Gareth replied, '*Pa kounye*, not now, mate,' then quickly walked to the porch and, without stepping onto it, reached out with a large hand and swiped the money from Baptiste's grasp. He stepped back a few paces and quickly counted the notes.

Jack was nervous and felt it would have been better to leave as soon as possible and count the money in a safe place later, but he was content that Gareth knew what he was doing and thought it essential to check that the money was correct before leaving. No receipts would exchange hands today, and no comeback if it was wrong.

Satisfied with the money, Gareth turned and quickly walked towards Jack. The eye contact and nod indicated that the deal was complete, and they were leaving, Jack turned and headed for the Land Rover followed by Gareth.

He reached the passenger door, climbed into the seat, and heard Gareth slam the tailgate closed. Looking through the rear-view mirror, he saw Baptiste sitting on the porch, smiling and singing while swinging the towel around his head, swatting more flies, then Gareth climbed into the driver's seat.

Turning the ignition key, the engine burst into life. However, Gareth mistakenly pushed the gear stick into reverse, and with an unexpected jolt, the vehicle shifted a short distance backwards.

Alarmed when they heard horrible and distressing squealing as the large rear wheel flattened a hen which had been scratching the ground for grubs behind the vehicle. Gareth immediately stamped on the brake as Jack looked through the side window watching feathers drifting in the breeze and a pool of blood on the ground at the side of the wheel, only the hen's head could be seen protruding from under the massive rubber tyre.

With little or no regard for what he had done, Gareth was in a hurry to leave and, following a gear change and brief wheel spin, accelerated the vehicle forward and drove at speed onto the exit track adjacent to the river and away from the clearing.

Again, Jack went through the process of being thrown around as Gareth drove back along the rough jungle track. Both sat in complete silence, unable to find the energy or will to talk following the stressful encounter. The incident seemed to have had the same equally traumatic effect on them both.

Jack wanted to try to understand how Gareth could find the courage and tenacity to go through the same experience alone each time he delivered equipment to Baptiste, completing that same routine each week must have caused him a lot of unnecessary stress and concern.

He watched him, gripping the steering wheel tightly and accelerating along the track crunching the gear stick up and down, expertly negotiating the potholes and obstacles.

It didn't seem to take long to get back to the main road, and approaching very fast and without slowing down, Gareth made a nerve-wrenching, tyre-screeching turn onto the tarmac road and then smoothly accelerated the vehicle towards the city. Relieved, Jack thought that if his timing had been wrong, they could have been sideswiped by a passing vehicle when they had launched onto the road.

They continued their journey in silence, and this time, Jack noticed Gareth's driving was clumsy and erratic. He jerked the gearstick hard, occasionally changing gears up instead of down, causing the vehicle to lurch forward as the engine screamed and the rubber tyres screeched on the tarmac.

Jack thought that if he continued to drive in the same manner, they would both suffer whiplash by the time they arrived at the army base.

Eventually arriving back at the city, he noticed the urban area had taken on a different character and appearance from what he had seen earlier, the onset of the evening bringing out the night dwellers and changing the city centre's appearance. Thankfully there was far less traffic on the roads but many more people standing and socialising on the streets.

Noticeably, more fried chicken stores were open, and hot dog carts were brightly lit by lightbulbs, plumes of blue and grey smoke swirling from their grills. People were standing around, mainly in groups, and laughing and engaging with each other.

Many people were holding glasses of drink, and some drank directly from the bottle, brown paper bags now gone. He could hear the music of differing genres, all competing, some tunes he recognised as jazz but mainly Jamaican mento or reggae, whilst people danced and laughed, eating street food and enjoying the evening.

After leaving the city and on the road to the base, Jack felt Gareth's driving had become slightly better composed, and although appearing to have calmed, he could still see uneasiness in Gareth's expression and his large knuckles tightly wrapped around the steering wheel, indicating his tension.

Still, he wanted to ask about the experience at the clearing and seek Gareth's thoughts regarding the enterprise. 'Do you usually do the deliveries alone, Gareth?'

Pause.

'Yes,' he replied, 'initially Lewis did the deliveries but passed the responsibility to me while taking on a coordination role. Anyway, doing it alone prevents mistakes, and I know these bad boys better than anyone else you see.'

'If anything were to go wrong, I would stand a better chance on my own. If someone else is with me, it means that I would have to think about their safety as well as my own, no offence, corporal.'

'No offence taken, Gareth, what do you know about Baptiste? I don't think you trust him, do you? Back there, you were constantly looking around the clearing as if there may have been someone else, we were unaware of, I sensed your nervousness, have you been there when there are others?'

Gareth slowly turned his head towards Jack, staring into his eyes in a weirdly uncomfortable manner. He suddenly regretted asking and began to feel anxious, particularly as Gareth was neglecting to watch the road ahead.

'They are murderous scumbags, corporal,' he replied.

Jack felt some relief when Gareth turned to look ahead again.

'Baptiste is harmless, but it's the others he knows who wouldn't think twice about cutting us up if ever they had the chance; I know better though and like to make them aware that I am tooled up and will use it if I need to.'

'Tooled up?' Jack asked curiously.

Gareth placed his hand into the driver's side door pocket and pulled out a long unsheathed machete. Eighteen inches of a shiny carbon steel blade glinted the headlights of a passing car. He held it in front of Jack's face and rotated the blade.

'Just a single move from any of the thugs, and it'll be good-night Vienna to anyone one of them who tries it first,' he said.

Then Gareth kissed the blade before sliding the weapon back into the door pocket, as Jack watched somewhat alarmed.

A full minute of silence passed before Jack asked, 'When you said others, I take it you've seen other people during previous visits. Why do you say they are murderous? Is that why you feel the need to have the machete Gareth?'

Gareth explained that during a previous delivery, he had met Baptiste outside in the clearing as usual but heard a sound from inside the shack as if someone else was walking across the floorboards.

Looking towards the shack, he noticed a man watching him from the window. He asked Baptiste who was with him, but Baptiste became defensive and denied anyone was there. When

Gareth looked back at the window, the man had gone.

'Do you think you could have been mistaken Gareth?' he asked.

'Not likely, I remember the size of this bloke, he was big, very big and insanely ugly as well. He had a stupid smile on his face that I would never forget.'

Gareth explained that during another visit, Baptiste had bent down to inspect the parts and he had seen the grip of a pistol tucked into the back of his shorts.

He had asked him why he thought he needed to carry a gun and Baptiste had said that some very bad people visited his shack but wouldn't say who or why only saying they were extremely violent and that he needed the gun for his own protection.

After the gun experience, he decided to carry the machete and to always keep it close just in case he needed to defend himself.

Jack remembered what Lewis had said earlier about getting quite a lot of money for minimal effort or risk but reflecting on the experience today and what Gareth had just told him, Lewis's comprehension and assertion of risk couldn't be any further from the reality.

It seemed that Lewis made all the arrangements, but it was Gareth who would be exposing himself to any threat or danger; it just didn't seem right; there appeared to be too much potential for things to go seriously wrong. At the end of the day, Baptiste was a drug user, and whenever drugs were involved, there would inevitably be high levels of risk.

As the sun began to set, Gareth switched on the Land Rover headlights, lighting up the road ahead, the lights surreally dancing off the jungle surrounding the road, glinting and reflecting startled eyes in the trees and flying insects in the air.

Jack had guessed that it would probably take another twenty minutes before reaching the base and settled back into the comfort of the seat. Even though the night was setting in and the sun had all but disappeared, it was still remarkably warm, and oddly, it felt like the humidity had been turned up a couple of notches. Resting his head to the side, he prepared for a short nap before they reached their destination and closed his eyes.

Then something he wanted to ask earlier came to his mind, and jolting upright, he turned his head to Gareth and asked, 'You counted the money; how much did Baptiste give you for the tyres and batteries?'

'Baptiste always gives the same amount of cash each time I visit. It's the same if I deliver four or ten tyres, so we try to keep to the minimum quantity if you see what I mean,' Gareth replied.

'How much?' he asked, persisting.

'It's always $800 Belizean corporal; that's just over $400 American.'

'That's weird, isn't it? I mean that he always gives the same amount of cash whatever he gets from you, even if the parts are junk and useless, just like those bald tyres we gave him today. So, what happens next? What do you do with the money?'

'I give it to Lewis, then he shares it equally between us.'

He recalled Lewis had mentioned a third person was also involved in the enterprise.

'Oh, yes, Lewis mentioned the name Stan when I spoke to him earlier,' he said.

'That's Stan Barnes, he's the other guy who works with us at the base; he helps search around the compounds for the stuff we take to Baptiste; you'll like Stan; he's a funny guy, nice but dim, and as thick as a barn door, I like to say, and yes, just the three of us until you join.'

Jack reminded himself that he had been sent to Belize as the section supervisor and had responsibilities and a duty of care for all the soldiers working in his section. Now that he had seen how the business was carried out, he felt the risk was possibly greater than the benefits and needed more time to decide whether to allow the enterprise to continue or to terminate it.

He settled back and closed his eyes enjoying the warm evening breeze.

6

*You cannot escape the responsibility of tomorrow
by evading it today*

Abraham Lincoln

The mobile prison abruptly stopped.

Jack opened his eyes, momentarily panicking and struggling to understand where he was and why it was so dark. It did not take long for hope and his heart to sink, remembering he was still in the cell.

Swinging his feet to the floor, he leaned back against the metal wall, steadying himself with his hands, trying to collect his thoughts.

He felt drowsy and tired and looked at the weakened hue of the hands on his watch, it was 3 am, and realising he had slept almost an hour. It was an hour wasted he thought, instead, he should have been trying to figure out how to end their predicament and was annoyed because of the lack of suggestions from the others.

It was intensely quiet in the cell while the vehicle remained motionless, the engine ticking over for a long time, and for a moment thought they must have arrived at the place they were destined for. Then he saw a red light piercing the darkness through the grill, red turned to green, and the truck suddenly lurched forward and drove on.

Rechecking his watch, again he tried to understand why it was taking so long to reach their destination. It just didn't make sense why the officers had been driving around the streets without taking them to the police station or city jail; perhaps it was normal in Mexico to keep prisoners until the end of their duty, but he doubted it. The whole thing reeked of something irregular and was already disturbing him.

He thought there had to be a reason for all this, he just needed to figure things out and felt he needed something obvious to transpire that would stimulate his thought process, some inspiration perhaps.

Satisfied the short but much-needed sleep had helped revitalise and stimulate his brain, and squinting his eyes, he saw Lewis, still lying on the opposite bench, and the two bodies had remained lying on the floor.

The sound of breathing in harmony with the engine's constant hum and the occasional grunt, along with snoring, confirmed that everyone was alive and well.

In the darkness, he saw a red light shine into the truck again and carefully stood up to take look through the grill. The mobile prison had been forced to stop at another traffic light on red and he pressed his cheek against the grill, allowing him to visually scan the buildings immediately in front of the truck.

Initially surprised and then strangely curious; it was there again, the Flamingo Plaza shopping centre on the right side of the vehicle. The same ornate pink carvings around the entrance doors. The traffic lights turned green, and the truck lurched forward.

Cautiously stepping backwards, he sat on the bench and rubbed his forehead with his fingers, the continuous routine reminding him of something that he had heard a long time ago during army training, then he recalled, "the secret of your destiny is hidden in your routine".

Prompting to again make an effort to try and understand why they had been driving around in circles for over three hours, their journey repeating itself over and over, like a broken record.

Then he thought of something which caused him to be even more curious, he hadn't heard the police officers make any calls on the police radio. Neither had he heard any transmissions or hiss from the radio set, indicating the device was not switched on.

Standing again, he carefully made his way to the grill and looked at the dashboard's centre. The radio set was there, but not illuminated; it was switched off; no voices or static crackle.

'That can't be right,' he said quietly then returned to the bench trying and think of reasons why there had been no contact with the police control room to update them.

The cops hadn't reported that either he or his friends had been arrested; therefore, no one, other than the two officers, knew they were being held captive and, more importantly, what their destination or fate would be. He began to suspect the officers were up to no good and were acting outside of their official duty.

He was suddenly relieved hearing Stan's voice in the darkness and returned to his bench, lying down.

'I've had enough of being locked up in here Jack, the whole trip has been a disaster, made worse by the fact the police stole our money at the hostel,' he said in a barely recognisable slurred voice, caused by his stiff and swollen jaw.

'Hi Stan, how are you feeling?' Jack asked.

Slurring, the voice replied: 'I've got a nasty headache, a swollen cheek and a cut on my lip, but it was worth it knowing I told the Welsh bastard what I thought of him.'

'Yes,' Jack said, 'after the beating, we received from the cops, I feel like I just did two rounds of boxing with Muhammed Ali.'

'You should be so lucky, I got one of Gareth's best uppercuts, I think,' said Stan.

'Could you check if you still have your passport, Stan? If we get a chance at the prison, whenever we get there, to call the British Embassy, we need to prove our nationality.'

'It's in my backpack; I checked it was there earlier,' replied Stan.

Stan became quiet and Jack continued lying on the bench. He was relieved that Stan was the one person sharing the cell he knew he could trust, then recalled, incredibly, that they had only arrived in Cancún, the day before, experiencing an enjoyable evening on the pirate ship, only to be followed by the debacle at the hostel, their cash being stolen and the first confrontation with corrupt Mexican police officers.

He thought that Lewis and Gareth had probably blown most of the money they had shared on alcohol and prostitutes. He still had most of his and most importantly, his passport which he needed to get back to Belize and out of this god-forsaken country, if only he could find a way to get out of this difficult situation.

Lying on the bench, his mind drifted back to the Flamingo Plaza and possible incentives the police would have in not making anyone aware they were being detained as their prisoners.

He opened his eyes when he heard a muffled voice in the dimness of the cell, the hum of the diesel engine, snoring and heavy breathing, reducing the sound to barely audible or understandable, turning his head, he saw the bench opposite, which Lewis had been lying on, was now empty.

Although having earlier slept, he was feeling tired and weary and had to make every effort to pull himself to a sitting position then swung his legs to the floor, trying to listen carefully for the voice again in the darkness.

The prison truck was still moving through the Mexican streets and gently rocked from side to side, the engine's hum soothing and the smell of burning diesel partially disguising the obnoxious smell drifting from the floor.

Then the sound of the voice again, this time more clearly.

'I'm telling you, Jack, it's like that Groundhog Day.'

It was the voice of Lewis who was standing and peering through the grill at the front of the truck. The blackness in the chamber was beginning to soften to a grey as the morning light began to reflect through the truck's windscreen, giving Lewis a ghostly silhouette.

Jack's eyes searched the chamber and he realised he could now clearly see the two soldiers lying on the floor, Gareth curled up sleeping, hugging Stan's bag, reminding him of the need to double-check and confirm the location of his own passport.

Realising he had not seen his backpack for hours, he looked at the floor around his feet then saw it but not in the place he had put it earlier and was again totally dislodged from under the bench.

Supported by his hands, he moved his hips forward and, using his right foot, firmly heel-kicked it, forcing it back under the bench.

Lewis heard a moan and turned from the grill to look at Jack. 'Oh, hello mate, I thought you were asleep. This is getting beyond a joke, we've been in here for bloody ages; there is something really strange going on because I've been looking through the grill and noticed they've been driving repeatedly around the same route; it's like that movie, you know the one where that weather guy restarts the same day again and again. I think it's called Groundhog Day, isn't it?'

Jack remembered the movie and accepted the similarity.

'Take a look at the centre console,' Jack asked Lewis. 'Can you see where the police radio is? Is it switched on or off? Are there any lights?'

Lewis turned and peered through the grill then turning back to Jack said, 'Hang on; it's switched off man, what can that mean?'

'Can you recall if they have made contact with their control station at any time during this journey?' he asked.

Lewis thought for a moment then replied 'No I can't, not at all, what the hell. What do you think? Are we being kidnapped? They're real police, aren't they?'

Hearing Lewis beginning to panic, Jack thought to reassure him.

'Everything appears to be genuine, their uniforms, batons, guns, and this truck, I can't see any of this being fake. I think they are up to something not quite legit, but I haven't been able to figure it out, they have been driving for almost four hours so we might find out before much longer.'

A voice interrupted; Jack was pleased to hear the Welsh accent.

'Are you all right Stan boy? I am sorry for knocking you for one earlier; you got on my wick, is all, like you usually do, and

I just lashed out; I'm sorry, boyo.'

A pause, then Stan replied in a croaky voice which sounded better than the slurring voice he had earlier. 'It's okay, you daft welcher, I've been hit by uglier and bigger tossers than you.'

Jack and Lewis smiled, realising they all felt a bit more cheerful.

Startled, Jack felt his backpack make contact with his ankles as if being forcibly pushed out from under the bench. He tried to think what could be happening and shaking his head with disbelief, forced it back under with his heel. A second later the bag was then pushed back against his ankle. Alarmed, he immediately realised someone must be concealing themselves under the bench.

'Stop, everyone, be quiet!' he shouted, startling the others, as they fell silent and stared at him.

Jack pushed the bag under the bench with his foot, then quickly lifted his legs and bending his knees, positioned his feet on the bench. They all watched in astonishment as the bag was flung from under the bench, colliding with Stan who was still lying on the floor next to Gareth.

They anxiously clambered to their feet and shuffled to the opposite bench while Lewis jumped to the far corner of the cell. Surprise and alarm spread across their faces, as they stared at Jack's backpack waiting for it to move again as if it was possessed like some sort of demonic poltergeist.

Then they heard a voice say: '*Mierda.*'

The voice came from under the bench Jack was sitting on, followed by a phlegmy cough lasting almost twenty seconds. They looked at each other in shock, realising that someone else was sharing the cell with them.

'What the…,' Gareth responded and quickly kicked Jack's bag towards the dark void from where he had heard the voice.

Jack, annoyed, glared at Gareth and bending over, grabbed a shoulder strap and lifted his bag while, quickly moving across the space and sat on the bench with Gareth and Stan, Lewis standing next to them.

Daylight had increased, and they all could see a bit more clearly in the cell. All eyes were fixed on the shadowed space beneath the opposite bench. No one dared to speak; until Lewis broke the silence.

'Who are you, and what do you want?'

Silence

'Whoever it is must have been there the entire time,' said Jack, 'I kicked my bag back under a couple of times because it became dislodged, and I thought it was the movement of the truck.'

'Has anyone got a stick? I'll flush the bastard out,' Gareth shouted angrily.

Jack thought how ridiculous that sounded as if anyone had a stick in the truck.

'Wait a minute, I've got it; let's tell the cops that there is someone else in here; when they come in, we can jump out the doors and make a run for it,' suggested Lewis.

Jack tutted thinking that was a stupid plan and added, 'Are you confident to translate into Spanish, a strange man has been hiding in our cell for the past four hours, Lewis?'

'Well, why don't you think of something smart arse?' he replied.

Stan stood and took two short steps, bent over, half looking into the darkness under the opposite bench.

'Hello, hello, *Hola*,' he said loudly, they all detected the nervousness in his trembling voice.

Silence.

'*Hola*, there is no need to hide. Are you hurt?' Stan persisted.

Startled when they heard the gruff voice again, '*Hombres, hombres*.'

A shuffling noise followed, and they watched, aghast, as two bare feet appeared and, in the increasing light, saw the body of a frail old man clamber out from under the bench.

Stan quickly stepped backwards and, sitting next to Jack, gripped his arm with both hands and leaned towards him. Jack could feel him trembling.

The dishevelled man pulled himself up and then sat on the bench opposite as the four friends watched in silence, unable to say anything, waiting for the man to make the next move.

Jack saw that apart from his bare feet, he wore a pair of crumpled grey trousers and a stained green shirt, rips on the shoulders and elbows poking through holes. He looked about seventy years old but was probably a lot younger.

'*Quien diablos eres tu?*' The man asked.

Lewis thought he recognised a couple of words and replied. 'We are English soldiers, do you understand, *Inglés soldados*,' hoping that saying they were soldiers might prevent the man from doing something hasty or unexpected.

'Ah, *soldados*, I was a *soldado* once, my friends, but that was a long time ago,' the man said and coughed again for what seemed two minutes, then spat onto the floor, adding to the fluids already there. 'Do you have a drink?' he asked.

'I have a beer in my bag,' Gareth volunteered.

The man cleared his throat, spat again on the floor, and said,

'I would very much like a beer if you have it, my *soldado* friend.'

Gareth removed his bag from under the bench he had been sitting on and pulled out a bottle, levering the metal cap off with his teeth, then spitting it to the floor and handed the bottle to the man. They watched as he grabbed it and gulped the entire contents without taking a breath. Then the man dropped the bottle, watching as it rolled across the floor in time with the vehicle's motion and at the same time releasing a deafening belch.

Staring at them and grinning, revealing barely more than a few teeth in his mouth, he asked, 'You have more drink, my friends?'

Ignoring him, Jack asked, 'Why did you just come out now, have you been there and listening to us all the time?'

Lewis replied before the man had a chance. 'Of course, he's been listening to us, he's probably a spy for those bent cops in the front, you idiot.'

Jack, irritated, cast Lewis an indignant stare, as the man released another loud belch, all turning their heads away and cringing as the stench hit them. Jack thought the obnoxious odour of urine and vomit on the floor hadn't smelled as bad.

'I am just a poor man, *amigo*; I live every day on the street,' he declared.

Lewis was suspicious and wanted to know why the man had been hiding all this time under the bench, waiting silently for his moment to reveal himself. He wanted to find out more, thinking that perhaps the old man could be a solution to getting out of the cell. 'Why are you here, old man? Did the police lock you up too?'

'I did nothing, my friend; I am just a poor man who lives

day to day on the street. I sleep and eat when it is possible, but the police do not like *vagabundo* because the city mayor thinks that we are not good and want the foreigners to spend their money, so they do everything to remove us from the streets.

'So, those are real police in the front of this van?' Jack asked, pointing to the grill.

'Yes, but they are not good; all the *policía* are very bad in Mexico; they steal money and make people disappear.'

'When did they arrest you? Was it during the night?' Stan asked.

Gareth tutted and said, 'For crying out loud Stan, can you remember him being put in here after we were locked up?'

Stan replied, 'If it wasn't for you knocking me unconscious, how would I know?'

The man gave a sickening, phlegm-cackling chuckle, then said, 'No *amigo*, I have been here for *tres* days and nights; they will not let me out; I will die here.'

'Give me a break,' interjected Lewis, 'there is no way you are still alive if you have been here for three days man, you wouldn't be able to survive without food or water? Look at you, you are like a stick insect.'

'That's because you know nothing soldier; I can live for many days without drinking or eating; the people locked in here are always desperate to leave and occasionally give me drink and sometimes food; the police make me stay here because I get money for them when I tell their prisoners how to get their freedom.'

The man looked in Gareth's direction and asked for another beer.

'No way, hobo,' he snapped, 'I am not giving you any…'

'Stop for a minute Gareth,' Jack interrupted holding the palm of his hand towards his friend and suddenly very interested in what the man had just said.

'Tell us again about getting money for the police, and how the prisoners get their freedom?'

Gareth wasn't offended by the response, and hearing Jack's sudden curiosity, said, 'Let me find you another bottle of beer, my friend.'

The man responded to Jack and said, 'I tell them how they can find freedom from this terrible place.'

Jack attempted not to be too obvious in revealing his enthusiasm and had become anxious to explore what the man had said earlier, leaning forward to get closer to him.

Lewis had also picked up on what he had said and quickly sat between Stan and Jack forcing all four friends to squeeze onto one bench.

'Okay old man, just explain how the police get money, and what the prisoners have to do to get out of here?' Jack asked.

'*Amigo*,' the man said, then gave a cackling laugh, 'I cannot tell you until I get a drink or food, after that, the *policia* will demand their pesos and you will be released, so give me what I ask for, then I tell you everything.'

Jack wouldn't let go.

'So, the payment for our freedom is food and drink to you; then you will tell us how to get released, is that correct?' The man's English was mixed with Spanish, and he found it difficult to interpret what he was suggesting.

'Yes, that's right, *amigo*.'

Jack's eyes darted from the man and then to the grill where he could just about make out the officers then he turned to his friends and spoke. 'Right guys get everything out of your bags; give him everything we can find, chocolate, chewing gum, anything. Gareth, give him your bottles of beer. This is sounding like we are getting out of here.'

Lewis was not convinced, as Gareth, Stan, and Jack began searching their bags for food and drink, he remained sitting on the bench staring at the man, and said, 'Hold on a second you guys, this bloke is a hobo, possibly a drug addict and certainly an alcoholic, and you believe he is telling the truth? If he is so desperate for food and drink, he would have come out from under the bench hours ago, but he didn't.

'I think he's lying and just wants anything we give him; he doesn't know how we can get out and is possibly spying for the cops. He's a liar and just another panhandler swept up from the streets, and I don't trust him.'

Gareth stopped searching his bag, stepped towards the man, and wrapped a long, muscled arm around his neck, squeezing gently and said, 'Listen to me, boyo, if you are lying to us, I will rip your head off and shove it up your arse.'

The man choked, making a gurgling noise as Gareth's arm slowly and gently squeezed his throat.

'Let him go, Gareth,' Jack shouted, punching the arm holding the man; Gareth released his grip.

The man coughed violently, then spitting on the floor, composed himself and looked across the cell towards the soldiers and said, 'Listen to me, *amigos*,' short gasps and coughs as he spoke, 'the police lock tourists like you in here every night because they know they have many pesos. They want me to ask for a drink and a little food; then I tell them to give money to the police in return for their freedom. It's the truth and it is as simple as I have explained to you, I was once in the army, and soldiers never lie to one another.'

The four friends looked at each other in silence, trying to make sense of what they had just heard and waiting for someone to be the first to respond.

When you kill a man, it costs nothing to be polite

Winston Churchill

Jack noticed the others looking at him in silence, obviously waiting for his response following what the man had just said.

He had already made up his mind about what to do next and felt that this was the best, if not the only, opportunity they had to get out of the dilemma. There was a risk, but he felt there were no other options, and they needed to act now.

'Like I already said, guys pull together what food and drink we have from our bags; anything will do; just find what we have and give it to him.'

Gareth placed three bottles of beer and a packet of cheese and onion crisps on the floor in front of him, and Stan produced a handful of nuts from his pocket and placed them with the other items.

'Where did you get those?' Jack asked.

'I emptied a bowl of nuts into my pocket when we were in the bar because I didn't know when we might eat again.'

Lewis put a bottle of beer and a half-eaten ham sandwich, wrapped in a serviette with the other items on the floor.

Jack held a protein bar, a half-eaten bar of chocolate and a bottle of water.

'All right, my friend,' he said, 'that is all the food and drink we have. Now, it's your turn, so tell us what to do next; what do we say to those cops without sounding like we are trying to bribe them? You get your food after you tell us, *comprendo?*'

'That is very wise, soldier; two nights ago, the tourists in here gave me very much food and drink, but before I was able to them, I fell asleep for a very long time.'

The man erupted into a sickening laughing cackle.

'You get nothing until you have told us what to do; otherwise, you will feel my boot up your arse, you stinking *sglyfath,*' Gareth responded.

Conscious that Gareth had started to move from the bench, Jack gripped his forearm before he attempted to take hold of the man's throat again, saying, 'Shhh… why don't you just calm down for a second, Gareth?'

Glancing at Jack he relaxed and slumped back onto the bench.

Stan said, 'You said you were once a soldier, old man; soldiers would never be disrespectful; they are supposed to look after each other.'

Lewis interrupted, 'Guys, sorry to spoil the small talk, but I need to get out of here. Can we just cut to the chase, please? I'm feeling a bit claustrophobic, particularly knowing freedom could be on the horizon.'

The soldiers impatiently stared at the man.

'All right,' he said finally, 'you are soldiers, as was I, so I will tell you. It is their game, *amigos*; the police already know that I will tell you. They have said to me that I must do it. I am just their puppet to get money from you. Later, they will replace you with other tourists. It is what they do. Why do you think this place is so bad? The floor is spread with urine from the people they keep in here all night.

'Sometimes they are here for many hours because they do not want to believe me, but I speak the truth. The police do not intend to take you to prison, they just want your pesos, and they know you will give it in exchange for your freedom.'

Jack was becoming restless. 'Gareth, if he doesn't explain what we have to do to get out of here in thirty seconds, do that throttling thing with your arm around his throat please.'

The Welshman smiled excitedly and leaned forward from the bench, obviously prompting the man to continue talking quickly.

'So, it is time, my friends, to tell you how to leave your prison,' he said nervously, glancing in the direction of the big Welshman.

'Halleluiah,' Lewis announced.

'They have already been waiting patiently for you to speak to them, as I told you, it is their game; they expect you to talk, and they are eager to release you so that they can search for more tourists when you have gone. They want your money to feed the mouths of their children and to buy gifts for their lovers.'

'So let us know what they are waiting for us to say, old man?' Jack said, pushing him.

The man continued, 'You must first know that they have been listening to you, they understand what you say and are waiting for you to tell them how much money you have in your pockets.'

Lewis quickly retorted, 'Screw you, *amigo*, don't trust him guys, I'm telling you, he's lying. If we try to offer money to the cops, they will charge us with bribery. We'd be better off sitting this out. It's a trap, don't you see it? If I don't trust the stupid hobo, how can you?'

The friends sat quietly, mulling over what Lewis said, and Jack could see that Gareth and Stan were staring at him, waiting for his response.

He turned to Lewis and said, 'Listen, mate, I know it seems like a massive risk, but it's obvious the cops are waiting for us to do something. You saw that the radio was switched off and that we spent four hours driving in circles, and you said yourself that corruption is prevalent in Mexico. On top of all that, they beat the shit out of us; they wouldn't have done that if it was legit.

'What the old man said seems to add up and I think that if we do nothing, we may end up exactly where you said earlier a rat-infested jail, and if we do something, we may still end up in a rat-infested Jail, but at least we tried. It seems the only way we can break this, what did you call it Lewis? Groundhog Day.'

Lewis sat and thought for a short while, then reluctantly nodded and whispered, trying to prevent being overheard by the police officers.

'All right, but if he is telling the truth, Jack, we simply don't have enough money, do we? At best, we have about five thousand pesos between us, and that won't be enough; they won't let us out for the price of a few bottles of tequila and a cheap bottle of perfume.'

The man, who was eyeing up the beer bottles in Gareth's hands spoke in a hushed voice. 'You are idiots; you have no idea? Five thousand pesos is much money to them, *amigos*; a man in Mexico can buy many presents for his lover with that money, but do not tell them you have all those pesos; you must say you have only two thousand. Then they will ask for more, but you only give more if you want to; remember, it is their game, and you must bargain with them.'

'There you are, Lewis,' Jack said, 'what are we waiting for?'

Then Stan objected. 'Hold on, all of you! Firstly, the corrupt cops ripped us off back at the hostel, and now we are going to give every peso left to these rip-off merchants; it's just not right. I will be skint after this and can't wait to return to Belize and sell some more stuff to Baptiste, I need the money.'

Jack tried to reassure him, 'Don't worry Stan, as soon as we get back to Belize, we can make a big effort to locate equipment around the camp, and then Gareth and I will deliver it as soon as possible to Baptiste. We'll be able to quickly replace what money we've lost, and more.'

'I am sorry, guys, it's too late, we can't do it anymore; Baptiste is dead, I killed him a few days ago,' Gareth announced.

Gareth's words hung heavily in the heat and humidity of the small space as Jack, Lewis, and Stan were stunned into silence and stared at the Welshman, not quite believing what he had just said.

'What did you just say!' Jack eventually found the courage and asked, barely recognising his own trembling voice, the words echoing around the chamber while Lewis and Stan looked on in silence.

Gareth slowly stepped across the floor, turned, and sat on the bench next to the man. Jack, Lewis, and Stan remained silent, shocked; sitting on the bench opposite, waiting for Gareth to explain.

The old man remained silent, understanding that there was about to be a fascinating revelation.

The man eventually broke the silence, having watched Gareth pick a bottle of beer from the floor, and holding a hand towards the Welshman, asked, 'May I have one, my friend?'

Gareth chewed the lid off a bottle and handed it to him. Again, the man drank the liquid in several gulps and dropped the empty bottle to the cell's floor.

'Gareth, you need to explain what you have just said, and start from the beginning; tell us everything and don't leave anything out?' Jack asked.

There was a long pause while Gareth composed himself, then began. 'Well, it's like this, you see,' he was visibly nervous, paused and continued, 'remember, after Jack made his first delivery, he made us all promise that if the enterprise was to continue, no one could do a drop-off alone.

'Well, last Thursday, we had a load of tyres and batteries stacked up, so Lewis told me to get it delivered to Baptiste. I looked around for Jack, but it was your laundry day, and you were busy. Stan was not around either, so I went alone; I didn't think it was a problem because it was the last delivery before we were travelling to Cancún, and I thought I would do a quick one, in and out, you see.'

Jack interrupted, turning to Lewis said, 'You jerk, I told you never to let him go there alone; it's just too dangerous; they're bloody criminals and you know what the rules are.'

'Steady on, Jack,' Lewis replied, 'we all needed extra money for the trip to Mexico; I didn't hear you complaining when you got your share of $800 on Thursday before we left, did I? Where else did you think I got the money? Please listen to what Gareth is saying before making any judgements.'

Jack, annoyed, looked towards Stan. 'Did you know about any of this?'

'It's not my fault,' Stan responded, 'I didn't know he was going down to the clearing. Honestly, Jack, I would have gone with him if I had known; this is the first I have heard of it.'

Jack squeezed his eyes shut, hoping to contain the anger welling up. He felt the pulse in his temple throb again.

'So, I loaded the Land Rover with four tyres, an old generator with a seized engine and four end-of-life dead batteries.

'Anyhow, I set off earlier than I usually do, and I'm thinking, get yourself down there, drop the stuff off, get the cash from him and get out quickly.

'So, I drive the usual way through the city and off the main road, but I get bogged in the mud a couple of times because of the rain on Wednesday night; remember there was a storm? Anyway, it's not too much of a problem, and I get to the clearing and put the Land Rover in the regular place just like I always do, facing the track for a quick exit.

'I did the same routine, just turned the engine off and sat in the vehicle for a minute or so, waiting for Baptiste to come out from the shack; I just thought I would see him come out rubbing his hands on his towel like usual. That's what happens every time, it never changes, and I'm used to it. Well, he didn't come out of the shack this time.'

Silence, waiting for him to continue.

'I sat there for a full five minutes, but Baptiste didn't show and at first, I thought he wasn't there and maybe was out somewhere because I was a lot earlier than normal and it was my tough luck for arriving early.

'Anyways, I kept looking in the mirror, thinking he might

be working out the back or was in the hen house, but the place seemed deserted, and I noticed something else, something was not right about the place because the front door was slightly open, and I could see wispy smoke coming out of the gap, so I just sat and waited, trying to think about what I should do.

'Anyhow, after about ten minutes, I decided to go and take a look at what was going on, especially with the smoke and all that.'

Jack interrupted.

'What the hell were you thinking, Gareth? You know how dangerous these people are. You should have just driven back, and we could have delivered another day; it's just not worth the risk man; how many times have I told you?'

Jack turned to Lewis. 'Did you put him under pressure to do this, for Christ's sake?'

Lewis remained silent, waiting for Gareth to continue.

'So anyway,' Gareth ignored the interruption. 'I get my machete and leave the vehicle, closing the door gently so there is no noise and pushing the machete down the back of my pants, then walk to the front of the shack, calling out 'Baptiste, Baptiste,' but there's no reply. While I'm walking, I check and look around the clearing to make sure no one else is there.

'Then I get a really strange feeling because the hens are huddled in the shed, not pecking around the clearing like they usually are. It's all too quiet; there are none of the usual sounds I'm used to. It's just a bit creepy like. So anyway, I get to the shack, step onto the porch, pull the fly screen back, and then push the door open.

'At first, I thought the room was full of smoke, but it wasn't and across the other side, the gas stove was on, and I could see a pan filled with boiling water and steaming like crazy. I look around the room but see no one. There's no furniture except a wooden chair and a mattress on the floor covered in a dirty blanket in the corner of the room.

'It's difficult to take everything in at first because there's rubbish all over the floor, tin cans, beer bottles and dirty clothes. So, I think the place is deserted and decide to turn the gas stove off and get the hell out of there.

'I begin to walk towards the stove when I suddenly felt something grab my ankle, knocking me off balance, and I fell onto the floorboards, face down amongst the rubbish. I was shocked and I rolled over, then saw that Baptiste had crawled out from behind the door. He's in a terrible way, sweating and shaking, and there is vomit all down the front of his shirt, in his dreadlocks and on the floor. His clothes are soaking wet, and his skin, normally black, has turned almost grey.

'Anyway, I go over to him, thinking that he is like, very sick and the best thing to do is to get him onto the mattress and so try to get hold of him, but when I put my hand around his upper arm, I felt something in the palm of my hand, there was a syringe sticking in his arm, and I have accidentally plunged what was left into him with my hand.'

Jack glanced at Gareth's hands; they were huge, and the description 'ham-fisted' described them too well.

'Then a few seconds later, he starts to explode and spasms all over the place. Foaming at the mouth, jerking, screaming, and shaking, I thought he would erupt in front of me, so I had to step back and watch. I'm thinking, what sort of drug was in the syringe that I've just pushed into his veins?

'I remembered the pan of water, so I went to the stove, switched the gas off, and noticed that there were syringes and needles in the boiling water. I went back to Baptiste, who had gone quiet by now and looked as if he was asleep.

'There was foam and blood all over his face and dripping on the floor, so I checked the pulse on his neck, but there was nothing. Baptiste was dead, then I realised that if I hadn't gone into the shack and tried to lift him to the mattress, he would still be alive. So, it was me who killed him.'

The soldiers sat, stunned and listened as the man asked, 'What did you do then?'

'I just panicked because I wasn't sure what to do; I could hardly call for an ambulance, could I? Anyway, I thought I had better pull him onto the mattress, so I dragged him across the floor, rolled him onto it, and then straightened his body to make him look decent.

'His eyes were open; the white bits were all yellow and red, so I pushed them closed with my thumbs; it just looked like he was sleeping. Then I pulled the syringe from his arm and threw it into the hot water in the pan.'

Only a chainsaw could cut through the thick, dense silence that followed. No one could find it in themselves to be the first to respond to the inconceivable account Gareth had just divulged to them all.

Gareth became quiet, remorsefully dropped his chin to his chest, and although Jack couldn't be sure, thought he saw a tear drop to the floor.

'I'm so sorry, Gareth, *(pause)* we all are, but it wasn't your fault, whichever way you look at it. Baptiste was an addict and had probably already injected enough shit to overdose and die anyway. You intended to help, not kill him. It sounds like a tragic accident, and there is nothing we can do now; what is done is done.

'We've just got to move on, and we don't need the enterprise; it's probably a good thing that we don't have to risk dealing with criminals anymore,' Jack said, awkwardly trying to reassure him.

Then he remembered something Lewis had said earlier which didn't quite make sense.

'Hold on a minute, Lewis, you gave us $200 each last Thursday; Where the hell did you get the money from, Baptiste's ghost?'

Lewis replied. 'Let Gareth finish, you will understand when he has told you everything.'

Gareth coughed as if annoyed at the continual interruption, then continued; 'So, I pulled the blanket over him and was just about to leave when I noticed something odd on the floor by the mattress. A square piece of wood was missing from the wooden floorboards and was leaning against the wall, in the hole in the floor were a few bags of brown powder, each the size of my fist.

'I just knew they had to be drugs, probably heroin, so I picked a bag up and underneath saw a stack of bundled notes of money, lots of money. I pulled a bundle out, and there it was, Belizean and US dollars.

'At first, I couldn't believe it and thought I was dreaming or something, and I just stood there looking at the money, then looked towards Baptiste, then back at the drugs, thinking about what I should do.

'I had a sudden urge to grab the money, get in the Land

Rover then cut and run, but then thought, what am I going to do with a load of drugs and money? So I just walked around the room thinking; I was confused and wished one of you guys had been there to help me work out what I should do.

'Then I pulled the blanket back and felt Baptiste's pulse again, but nothing; by this time, he was beginning to become cold, and I thought, this is really serious and decided to get out of there.

The old man suddenly cut in. '*Amigo*, please don't say you left without taking the fucking drugs and money!'

8

City life is millions of people together feeling lonesome
Henry David Thoreau

The coach abruptly stopped at a red light, and the engine began to tick over like a contented, purring cat.

The sudden loss of motion caused Jack to open his eyes as his subconsciousness abruptly shifted from the gentle, rhythmic movement of the vehicle into something motionless and lifeless.

In his attempt to pull himself up in his seat, he thrust both arms outwards and, in doing so, firmly punched Stan on the cheek, who had been in a deep sleep. Stan quickly jumped out of his seat, half awake and forgetting where he was, raised his fists to his chin and began to punch the air in a comical attempt to defend himself from his unintentional attacker.

He had been drinking bottled beer for most of the seven-hour journey and in a confused state, continued to shadow box in the darkened coach aisle.

A few passengers sitting close, who had also been sleeping, turned and stared annoyingly at the soldiers. Jack rubbed his tired eyes and, looking through the window close to him, and realised the coach had stopped at a traffic light.

It was dark outside, and he could see many buildings, tall

110

offices and hotels, suggesting they had arrived at their destination, the Mexican city of Cancún.

Checking his watch, he saw it was almost 7.30 pm and was instantly relieved and cheered that after almost seven hours sitting on a coach, the harrowing and arduous journey was almost over.

'Sit down, you daft sod,' Gareth said to Stan, who had stopped boxing but was still standing in the aisle of the coach, staring and confused. Further irritated passengers glanced at the soldiers, the unpleasant behaviour annoying them.

Jack was more interested in what he could see through the window. The city was very different from where he had come from. Only seven hours' drive behind them and the heat, humidity and jungle had been replaced by bars, restaurants, and casinos.

His brain tried to take in the complex and colourful display of bright fluorescent lights and recognised familiar hotel signs such as Radisson and Holiday Inn.

Without warning, the engine roared, and the coach lurched forward, as it continued along the wide roads. He saw more brightly lit signs as they passed Coco's nightclub, Congo bar and Marti Gran Plaza shopping precinct.

Feeling back in modernity almost made him tremble with excitement and anticipation.

For a Saturday evening, the roads were unsurprisingly busy, and a build-up of traffic frustratingly delayed the last few minutes of their journey but allowed him to take in the fascinating ambience he felt he had been denied for so long.

There was a buzz of excitement amongst the passengers, who became animated after so many hours cramped in an unbearably hot and uncomfortable thirty-year-old coach with a broken air conditioner.

Jack turned from the window and looked at his friends; Stan was thirstily gulping from a bottle of water while Gareth and Lewis, who had been asleep for the last half of the journey, were doing what they had done for almost all the time they had been awake, swigging from bottles of beer.

Within minutes, the coach stopped at the 'Central de Autobuses ADO,' the city coach and bus station.

Switching off the engine, the driver climbed from his seat and, standing in the aisle facing the passengers, forced a loud cough into his hand to attract everybody's attention.

'*Atención por favor...excuse me*' he shouted in Spanish and then English, pausing to check that the passengers could hear him speaking. 'The *autobús* will *returnaz* this *placee* on, how you say? Monday at 8 hours in the morning. It must stay for only three zero, how you say, minutes? *Pero* must leave then to Belize.'

He paused as if to check that everyone had understood, then continued; '*Gracias y que tenga una agradable estancia en Cancún.*'

Then reaching towards the driving controls he activated a switch; with a hissing sound, the doors folded open and in an almost frantic surge, passengers began filling the aisle, removing bags from the overhead racks, and hastily leaving the coach.

The foursome remained seated at the rear of the coach, trapped as other passengers disembarked.

Eventually, having waited his turn, Jack stepped off the coach into the warm and humid Cancún evening. He immediately thought it seemed a long way from Belize's savage humidity, heat, and stench. The smell of rotten and moulding jungle substituted by a fresh and gentle breeze.

Sucking in a lungful of air, he smiled realising the growls, hoots and squeals of jungle creatures had been replaced by the sounds of human laughter, chatter, and music as the city's animals enjoyed the bars and restaurants.

Then, lurched forward, startled, as Gareth landed a slap in the middle of his shoulder blades. He caught his balance and swung around, irritatingly annoyed then seeing his friends laughing, he relaxed and smiled.

'We are here, guys!' shouted Lewis, punching the air with his fist.

'They won't know what is about to hit them,' added Gareth.

'Let's get going, chaps; we only have two days to make this work,' Lewis said, shouldering his backpack and began walking along the pavement towards the city's bright lights, followed by Gareth, then Stan.

Jack threw his bag over his shoulder and followed his friends.

He was impressed at the orderliness and observed that the streets of Cancún appeared very clean and tidy. Palm trees lined the roads, set on trimmed grass verges and the bright street-lamps revealed colourful floral borders. Rotational water sprays active and nourishing the native flora's succulence and colour.

Expensive cars drove along the highways, and posters advertised pricey hotel rooms and lavish restaurants. He was a long way from the underdevelopment, destitution and poverty seen on the streets of Belize.

'How far to the hostel,' he heard Stan ask. The word 'hostel' sounded disheartening, probably made worse as they walked past the opulence of the Ritz-Carlton resort hotel.

Lewis pulled a crumpled piece of paper from his trouser pocket, unfolded it, and stopped under a streetlamp. 'I've got a map; I think the hostel is a few hundred metres further down here.' He unconvincedly traced a route on the map with a finger.

'Yep, this way,' he announced, then continued to walk.

A short while later, the soldiers approached three girls, smoking cigarettes and standing on the pavement outside a bar, loud music coming from inside. The soldiers were forced to step onto the road to pass the girls who were laughing and squealing, generally enjoying their lively evening.

As the soldiers passed the trio, one of the girls wearing a tight and flirtatious short white dress began to shout at the men whilst the other girls twisted their hips provocatively and blew kisses. '*Hola chico amante que quiere bailar conmigo.*'

Lewis firmly gripped Gareth's arm telling him to ignore the girls and continue walking without looking at them. In utterly comic fashion, Gareth complied and marched forward whilst throwing a glance over his shoulder at the girls. Jack and Stan laughed as they watched the comedy as the Welshman acted like a naughty child who had just been scolded by a parent.

After a hundred yards or so, Lewis stopped and examined his crumpled map again, then declared, 'We're here…I think.'

The others watched as he pointed to a run-down, neglected building on the opposite side of a busy road. A flickering, half-illuminated neon sign above the entrance door displayed the words '*Can Mook Hostel.*' The word '*Mook*' in darkness.

Together, they crossed the road and entered the hostel entrance door, and into the large reception area, the dimly lit room dominated by a sizeable desk-type counter situated in the middle of the room.

The desk seemed out of place due to its generous proportions and lack of any other furniture in the room. A large, centre ceiling fan spun around inconsistently, disturbing the silence with an intermittent clatter.

The only other notable feature in the reception was an arched doorway on a wall, half covered by a worn and faded maroon velvet curtain.

Behind the counter, a teenage boy with a vast crop of black hair perched on his head. He wore a grey string vest, which had once been white and had several tears across the front.

As the entrance door clicked closed behind them, the boy looked up from the desk, a broad smile spread across his face displaying a set of brilliantly white teeth. '*Hola chicos,*' the young Mexican said as they walked towards the desk.

Lewis took the lead and answered the boy. 'Hello, we have a reservation for two nights. Do you understand, *amigo?*'

The boy's unfailing smile remained, his crop of hair trembling and threatening to topple when he nodded, demonstrating he understood.

Lewis produced another piece of crumpled paper, handing it to the receptionist who spread it on the counter. He squinted, inspecting the English words. After a few moments, he looked up, still smiling and informed them, in broken English, that they must each pay five American dollars for two nights' stay at the hostel.

The soldiers searched their pockets and backpacks, and each added a share to a pile on the desk, then watched as the receptionist counted and inspected each note, randomly holding a few to the light as if checking for counterfeits.

When finished, he informed them, in barely understandable English, that they had reserved a shared room and stressed how important to leave anything valuable in the reception safe as the hostel would not be held responsible if anything went missing from their room should leave it unattended.

Lewis stepped close towards the others and said, in a hushed voice, 'Guys, don't give him anything valuable, or you will never see it again. We should hide our passports, or they'll end up in a Hong Kong printing shop before you can say enter the dragon.'

Then Gareth said, laughing, 'The only thing of value I brought is my beer and it's staying with me.'

Jack had been curious when he had earlier heard Gareth's backpack constantly making clinking noises, now realising that it was full of beer bottles and little else.

After Lewis informed the boy that they had nothing of value to place in the safe, they watched as he pulled open a desk drawer, extracted a door key with a fob and handed it to Lewis.

'You lose key, forty pesos. You stay *habitación tres*,' then said, 'room *threea*,' pointing to the maroon curtain over his shoulder, grinning.

The men picked up their bags and followed Lewis one by one, filing through the curtain leading to a narrow corridor stretching about fifteen metres with pale green doors symmetrically situated on each side. They squeezed along the passage until Lewis stopped outside a door, saying, 'I think it's this one, but that's very odd.'

They looked towards where Lewis pointed at the door, a number nine had been written using a black marker pen, then scribbled over and a number three written next to it.

'What do you think guys? The key has a three on the fob,' Lewis asked and looked at the expressionless faces of the others, then shrugged his shoulders and pushed the key into the lock and turned it. The door unlocked.

The room was in darkness and Lewis reached in and felt the wall until he located a switch. The light above the door suddenly illuminated the room and they followed him into what was to be their home for the next two nights in Mexico.

The room was small, probably two by three metres. A broken ceiling fan, designed to hold three blades, had only two causing the rota to spin lopsided and unevenly, the strained bearings made a clunking and ticking sound on every complete turn.

Jack, last to squeeze into the room, switched it off.

Two sets of metal bunk beds lined the wall on either side of the room, leaving a small floor space in the centre where they stood, cramped.

Each bed had an old, badly stained mattress and a single pillow and two sheets which had been thrown crumpled onto the bed. A window at the end of the room was covered with a grubby net curtain tacked to the window frame with pins, and black metal bars filled the frame, giving the impression of being in a prison cell.

The room itself was dusty and grimy, and countless previous guests had written their names, messages, and other graffiti across the walls. Most alarmingly, substantial and neglected spider webs hung from the walls adjoining the ceiling, each containing dozens of trapped dead flies, weighing the webs down. The bare floor was strewn with empty beer bottles, take-away containers, clothes, a shoe and litter.

Stan looked at the others and seeing disappointment, decided he would be the first to show some positivity. 'Well, I think we need to get as drunk as possible each night, so we don't notice this scumhole when we get back, eh lads?'

Gareth abruptly pushed past his friends and threw his bag on one of the top bunks, then Lewis immediately followed and did the same on the opposite bunk.

'Hey, why are you two keen to get top bunks?' Jack asked.

'I want to avoid yellow rain and getting wet if you two piss the bed at night,' Gareth said and laughed along with Lewis.

Reluctantly, Jack and Stan began to spread the bedding over their mattresses, while Gareth removed bottles from his bag and levering the caps with his teeth, handed everyone a bottle.

'Here's to a bloody good time,' he said.

Chinking their bottles together, they toasted their first night in Cancún City, drinking warm beer.

Stan suddenly pulled the bottle from his mouth, coughing, then announced excitedly, 'I almost forgot about the ship, guys, who's got the tickets? It's tonight, isn't it?'

Before they had left Belize, they had been advised by soldiers who had previously visited Cancún that they should reserve tickets to what they had discovered to be one of the most exciting attractions in the city and all spoke of highly, the Pirate ship, a rebuild of a sailing ship where tourists and visitors dressed in pirate costumes, acting and larking around as if real pirates.

To add to the drama, it had been explained that the ship sailed several hundred metres out of Cancún harbour, and high jinks would begin when guests received copious amounts of rum punch to drink, walk the plank and role-play as mischievous pirates. There was also a dance floor, music and lots of girls; they had all agreed to reserve tickets before they left for what they thought would be the highlight of their short stay.

'I've got the tickets and we better get a move on,' Jack said after checking his watch.

'I'll get the reception boy to call for a taxi,' Lewis said and left the room. A frantic scramble followed as the men used the limited space to freshen up, removing clean shirts and shorts from their backpacks.

Only Gareth decided there was no need to replace his sweat-stained clothes and opened another beer while belting out a terrible rendition of the Welsh national anthem, 'Land of My Fathers.'

'Taxi will be here in ten minutes,' Lewis informed them when he returned and began to change his shirt.

When they were almost ready, Lewis said 'Oh, I almost forgot, we need to agree about our passports and additional cash. I was told by guys who came here before that pickpocketing is rife on the pirate ship, and we can't trust the hostel staff either.

'The guys who stayed here previously said that they concealed their valuables in the room and ensured the door was securely locked, so I suggest we do the same and put the money in the bottom of our backpacks then stash them under the bottom bunk bed. We can conceal them using the rubbish from the floor; if someone were to get through the door, they wouldn't even know that our bags were in the room, what do you think?'

He dangled the door key towards them as if to suggest everything would be secure and safe.

Jack wasn't convinced. 'I'd prefer to keep my passport with

me,' he said.

'That's all right Jack, but what if you end up swimming in the sea or your passport gets nicked?'

Jack thought he was probably right and reluctantly agreed.

They were interrupted by a light tapping on the door, it opened, and a scruff of black hair poked through the gap, followed by the smiling face of the reception boy.

'Taxi', he said, then closed the door as he left.

The soldiers quickly concealed their passports and most of their money except for a small amount they thought would be needed to spend on the pirate ship and pay for the taxi, then smiling and back-slapping, excitedly filed out and into the corridor.

Lewis locked the door, pushing the key deep into his pocket.

The taxi driver knew exactly where these typical gringos were heading; the words 'pirate ship' was not a phrase in his tongue, but he knew that it was a popular attraction for American and English tourists staying in Cancún and had been asked many times to take fares to the ship.

He couldn't remember how many times he had taken passengers to the harbour but felt it had been countless.

There always seemed to be something consistent about the gringos he drove to the ship; they would normally only speak English, were often drunk before they began the night, and would talk with contempt for his people.

Even though he did not understand their language, he knew God had bestowed him with a gift, the ability to apprehend their constantly hurtful and insulting words.

Sometimes if they were polite and respectful, he would

charge the standard price for each mile, but if they were arrogant coupled with drunkenness, he was determined they would pay a lot more for the journey.

Most foreigners didn't understand the hardship Mexican people endured to make ends meet, the taxes they had to pay to the corrupt government, and the hardships imposed on them by the authorities, police, and politicians.

He glanced at the rear-facing mirror and recognised that these gringos were no different from hundreds of other fares he was used to; the big gringo with black hair and moustache was the worst of the kind. His accent differed from the other three, and something made him more obnoxious than the others, but he didn't care, they were all the same in the end.

Feeling belittled and disparaged, he had already determined that the charge for this journey would be much higher than it ought to have been.

'Look at the size of that mother,' Gareth said, slurring and pointing towards the ship moored at the harbour, as the taxi slowed at the harbourside.

The vehicle stopped, and they climbed out, leaving Lewis to pay the driver.

Stepping into the warm evening, Jack felt that it had become almost unbearably humid, and he felt sweat sticking to his skin, making his shirt damp.

They gazed at the inclined ramp stretching from the concrete harbour to the middle deck of the ship, which had the appearance of an 18th-century Spanish galleon. On the deck, three masts complete with sails, one supporting a jolly roger flag emblazoned with skull and crossbones.

Multi-coloured flashing lights glinted from the portholes

and entrance door, music blasted from speakers on the deck and a powerful and intense laser lit up and danced across the sky above.

A screech of the tyres, interrupted as the taxi drove away and then Lewis joined them, slapping Stan on the shoulder and saying, 'Christ almighty, that hardly cost anything; I can't believe how cheap the taxis are here, so I gave him a big tip.'

The four men walked steadily up the ramp to the entrance and were met by an attractive Mexican girl standing akimbo and dressed in a pirate's costume, striped bandana, and eye patch. She warmly greeted the four men.

'Bienvenido a nuestro barco,' she said and pointed to a sign displaying the rules of entry in several languages. After casting their eyes over the information, Jack handed the pre-paid tickets to the girl and in exchange, each was given ten drinks coupons along with a cheap plastic eye patch and a well-used pirate bandana.

The girl indicated they should choose either a plastic cutlass or a wooden musket from a nearby table. The soldiers looked at the uninspiring imitation weapons, some broken, and decided they were more excited to begin the evening without them, informing the girl they were ready to enter the ship.

The girl said, *'Aye aye, Piratas,'* and smiled, suddenly Gareth reached out, taking her hand and kissing it.

She Shrieked, cringing and quickly stepping away from him; then, laughing, they walked onto the main deck of the ship and Jack watched as Gareth and Lewis headed for the bar with haste; Stan walked onto the busy dance floor and began dancing alone to the music.

Jack was curious and decided to explore the ship. He removed his eyepatch and bandana and climbed wooden steps to the upper deck. There were fewer people around, and although he was always more comfortable when not in a crowd, felt it could get much livelier later.

He was fascinated at how authentic the ship had been dressed to appear like a pirate galleon, noticing metal cannons, boxes of imitation jewellery, and fake skeletons carefully placed around the deck. Metal cutlasses and muskets were added to the theatre. All were sensibly chained or bolted to the bulkheads or the deck.

Most guests on the ship were not dressed in pirate attire, only their issued plastic eye patch and bandana giving a half-hearted effort to mimic a buccaneer. The majority were couples, dancing, laughing, shouting, and generally having an extremely alcoholic fuelled evening.

Looking over the upper gunnel, he saw Gareth and Lewis dancing with two young mock pirate girls. Gareth gyrated his hips while holding a large plastic cup of green liquid, spilling onto the deck and annoyingly splashing people dancing nearby as he danced awkwardly.

Then the ship began to lurch and swayed from side to side as it moved, followed by excited screaming and laughing, Pirate-dressed crew members dropped anchoring ropes, and the ship slowly distanced itself from the harbour.

Returning to the bar, he exchanged a ticket for a glass of rum-infused pirate punch, then made his way to the highest deck, noticing a small alcove near the front of the ship, and sat on the deck and relaxed.

The volume of the music from the speakers was not as loud there and feeling the need for space from the others and all their boisterous activity instead enjoyed peace and solitude.

Tilting his head back, he took a long drink, tasting the rum and coconut mix and looked upwards; he noticed the extreme blackness of the night sky and the bright, glimmering stars. It had always amazed him how black and unpolluted the night skies were in the Caribbean and then watched in disappointment as the ship's laser scored a bright blue line across the night sky, reflecting off the moisture and dust in the atmosphere above him.

A warm breeze created by the ship's movement on the placid sea cooled the sweat on his face, arms and already sodden shirt, and he noticed how the humidity appeared to reduce the further the ship increased the distance from the dock.

Feeling an overwhelming sense of serenity, he thought how incredibly fortunate he was to be in Mexico and expected the next two nights he was about to enjoy would be the most amazing life-fulfilling experience, the memories would stay with him forever.

Then hearing a noise close to where he was sitting, he looked over his shoulder and saw a couple who were kissing passionately. They had partially concealed themselves behind a fake ship's wheel and were groping and fumbling with each other's clothes. It was obvious to Jack that their provocative behaviour would lead to something he really did not want to witness.

Smiling and knowing voyeurism was not something he wanted to be accused of, he decided to move away, then heard screaming from the deck below as the music changed to a popular dance floor filler.

The almost copulating couple quickly got to their feet, rearranged their clothing, and ran past in the direction of the stairs and to the dance floor without noticing him.

Finishing his drink, he placed the plastic cup in a bin cleverly disguised as a chest of stolen treasure, then smiling and feeling upbeat, followed the lovers towards the dance floor.

9

The less you trust, the less you get hurt

unknown

It was almost 11 pm when the pirate ship returned and docked in Cancún harbour.

As the foursome walked down the ramp leading away from the ship, they laughed as Lewis recounted how Gareth had caused a minor emergency by mischievously deciding to walk the plank from the lower deck. The set-up was supposed to be an imitation and had displayed a notice warning of the dangers and that it was for effect only. He had been so drunk; he'd fallen ten metres into the dark but calm sea.

The screams of those watching resulted in the music being turned off and emergency floodlights being switched on whilst crew members and security frantically threw life buoys into the water and searched for him, crowds running to each of the sides of the main deck, some laughing others concerned.

Eventually, Gareth was seen happily swimming around in the sea, singing a rendition of Tom Jones's, 'Green Grass of Home'. Finally, after some theatre, the Welshman succumbed to the rescue and was hauled aboard to everyone's laughter and applause. It had made an enjoyable night for all, the copious amounts of alcohol adding to their buffoonery.

After a short wait on the harbour side, they saw the same taxi which had brought them and hailed the driver.

During the journey to the hostel, the driver complained disapprovingly about their drunken and lairy behaviour. His grumpiness drowned out as they loudly sang together 'My My Delilah' for the entire journey.

Arriving at the hostel, the reception boy, who was still on duty, smiled as they arrived in reception but became annoyed when Gareth patted his head, flattening his crop of hair as the soldiers passed through reception.

The boy muttered something and then mimicked spitting on the floor as they walked through the maroon curtain to their room, upsetting him further when they ignored his insult.

Lewis turned the key, and the door swung open; he reached in found the wall switch and turned on the lights.

The foursome stood motionless in the corridor, speechless and staring in complete disbelief at what they saw in their room. Jack thought it was the effect of the alcohol causing confusion and they had opened the wrong door, then saw the equally shocked expressions of the others, confirming the devastation they witnessed in the room.

Lewis examined the door, double-checking the number, and then stormed to the reception.

Gareth entered and heaving a mattress from the middle of the floor space, gathered crumpled clothes which were lying in disarray amongst the clutter of discarded possessions and rubbish, throwing them onto the bare bed springs.

He discovered his bag and checked the contents then smiling, turned to his friends and said, 'Thank goodness for that, they've left the beer.'

Jack had seen his backpack amongst the disorder when Gareth had moved the mattress and pushed past Stan, snatched his bag, then sat on the rusting bed springs, desperately searching for his passport and money, already knowing they would be missing then he stared into his empty bag in disbelief.

All their bags had been ransacked and emptied onto the floor, and their money and passports had been stolen.

Suddenly feeling nervous and disorientated, alcohol exacerbating his confusion, he was brought back to reality when he heard a clink and hiss as Gareth opened a bottle of beer.

'The bastards have stolen our stuff, and all you can do is drink beer?' he shouted at Gareth.

'It's a little warm but otherwise not too bad; do you want one?' Gareth offered an unopened bottle as he swigged on another.

Jack ignored him and watched Stan, on his hands and knees, sorting through clothes, toiletries, and towels lying all around the floor, desperately hoping to find his passport or at least some money.

Then a high-pitched scream from the reception startled them. Jack ran from the room into the corridor and pushed the maroon curtain aside; he wasn't prepared for what he saw.

Stationery, papers and keys were strewn across the reception floor, and Lewis was lying face down over the desk, legs horizontal, attempting to balance himself and holding the receptionist, who was sitting on the floor, his left arm around the boy's neck, right fist raised, about to punch the boy in the face.

Lewis screamed at the young Mexican. 'You have five seconds to tell me who entered the room and stole our stuff, or I will smash your face in *amigo*.' Spittle flecked Lewis's lips and chin.

The boy was petrified and only able to shake his head slightly; choking, unable to breathe.

Understanding he was about to be harmed and knowing how much it would add to their growing problems, Jack held Lewis's legs, pulling him away from the boy and upsetting his balance, Lewis slid off the counter, clumsily falling to the floor.

He climbed to his feet and wiping saliva from his chin, walked around the counter to face the boy who was now half kneeling, and holding his neck, coughing and tears rolling down his face.

As the soldier approached him, the boy's expression again turned to terror, and he shielded his face against the expected punch.

Lewis bent at the waist, nose less than two inches from the young Mexican's face and said, 'I will ask you for the last time. Who did you allow in our room and has trashed our belongings? Tell me the truth and I will not hurt you!'

'*Nadie, nadie,*' he replied.

Lewis was becoming impatient. 'You don't seem to understand, my little hairy friend, we are being reasonable at the moment, you don't understand who we are.'

'*No entiendo,*' came the reply.

The maroon curtain was abruptly pushed aside; Jack rolled his eyes when he saw Gareth walk into the room, beer in hand.

Gareth scowled at the boy and then quickly walked around the counter, pushing Lewis to one side with such force that he fell over heavily and rolled across the reception floor.

The Welshman carefully placed his beer bottle on the desk, grabbed the boy by the crop of his hair, and pulled him upwards so that he was standing, then elevated his arm further until the boy's feet were dangling about an inch above the floor of the reception. The boy quickly raised his hands above his head and gripped Gareth's large hand to prevent his hair from literally being pulled from the scalp.

'Now then, boyo,' Gareth said, his Welsh accent adding further satirical theatre to the events as the boy swung gently held by Gareth's hand. 'I am going to give a second to think boy, and if you don't tell me who stole my passport, I'm going to rip your head off and piss down your throat. Then after that, I will burn this cesspit down with you in it, *comprendo*!'

By now, it had become unmistakable to the receptionist that the situation was not looking particularly good for him, perhaps way out of control, and removed his grip from Gareth's enormous hand, then slowly and carefully stretched a hand towards the counter.

He was obviously trying to reach something, and Gareth assisted by taking a step closer to the desk, lowering his hand as the boy's feet touched the floor.

They watched as the receptionist twisted his body, and stretched as far as he could, finger straight, then pressed a brass button mounted on the side of the wooden desk.

They stood motionless and glanced at each other wondering what would happen next.

After a moment of silence, Gareth asked, 'What does that button do boy?' At the same time releasing his hair, the Mexican collapsed onto the floor, turned onto his back and with tears rolling down his face, began to loudly howl. His once proud crop of waxed and preened hair now hung down the sides of his face like a pair of limp curtains.

The Welshman was unperturbed and began to search the desk drawers and removing a guest book, opened it and began flicking through the pages.

For a moment, it appeared as though he was searching for the names of other guests, trying to establish who else was staying at the hostel, a possible suspect, but instead, began to tear the pages from the book, crumpling them then throwing them at the boy.

Removing a cigarette lighter from his pocket, he tore another page from the book, flicked the flint wheel and applied the flame to the paper, then approached the sobbing receptionist surrounded by pieces of crumpled paper.

Jack and Lewis glanced at each other, realising Gareth was about to burn the pages lying around the receptionist.

'No, no, no…,' Lewis shouted, stepping between the receptionist and Gareth, as Jack rushed to the boy, taking hold of his arm and sliding him across the reception floor away from Gareth.

Then the sound of sirens in the distance prompted the three men to freeze, the sirens becoming louder as they realised the police were probably heading to the hostel.

Gareth dropped the burning paper to the floor, stamping and extinguishing the flame.

A few seconds later, screeching tyres could be heard outside the hostel as blue flashing lights glanced through the windows and reflected off the reception walls, the three soldiers stood in silence, knowing what was about to happen.

The reception entrance door suddenly flung open, and three Mexican police officers wearing pale blue uniforms, hands resting on their pistol holsters, rushed into the reception area and stood together, surveying the soldiers, the mess in the reception and the boy, lying on the floor who continued to sob and howl.

One of the officers, who had the most pieces of shiny metal on the lapels of his jacket, and a larger hat than the other two officers, shouted harshly at the boy, '*Lo que ha sucedido?*' he asked.

The receptionist wiped tears from his face, stood up then began frantically babbling to the officer, speaking fast and excitedly.

A heated exchange between the officer and boy continued, and for a moment, it appeared the police officer was berating him.

Then, after a while, the officer turned to his colleagues and spoke quietly, as if preventing the boy, and the soldiers, from hearing.

Suddenly, the maroon curtain abruptly swung to one side, and all hell broke loose; the three officers whisked their weapons from their holsters and pointed their guns towards Stan, who had appeared through the doorway and was holding four bottles of beer.

His expression turned to one of terror and he quickly raised his hands in the air. The beer bottles fell to the tiled floor making loud 'popping' noises as the glass shattered, bottles spinning and beer spraying across the room, soaking anyone standing nearby.

Then realising Stan was with the other three men, the lead officer slowly holstered his gun, indicating with a flat hand that the other officers should do the same. The tension in the room dissipated as they holstered their weapons. The only noise was fizzing and spitting beer.

The lead officer looked carefully at each of the soldiers and then said in broken English, '*Amigos*, you have not been good here; you must take your possessions and now leave.'

Jack relaxed, wiping beer from his face and chest, then glanced at Stan, and said, 'Just stay with it, don't say a word,' Stan nodded and slowly lowered his hands.

Turning back to face the police officer, Jack said. 'Sir, we have just returned to our room, and someone has stolen our passports and money. The receptionist had the spare key. He must have entered our room or given the key to thieves. We were only asking him before you arrived. We are British soldiers on holiday and are stationed in Belize.'

The officer looked around the reception at the disarray and then turned to his colleagues, whispering.

Jack thought he heard '*soldados británicos*', confirming he had understood him.

Turning to the receptionist, the officer asked '*Dónde están sus pasaportes y todo nuestro dinero?*'

Shaking his head, the receptionist replied, '*No sé!*'

Lewis interrupted, and shouted, 'He's a dirty scumbag liar.'

The lead officer gave a single nod to the two officers, who then walked to Lewis, took hold of his arms, and began pushing him back towards the curtain. Lewis resisted slightly but had no choice but to comply, then disappeared behind the curtain with the officers.

The lead officer looked at Jack and demanded, 'We will get your things and you leave this place now; you have done enough *amigos*.'

Gareth who had observed quietly pointed to the receptionist, saying, 'We aren't going anywhere mate until this little sleazebag gives us our money and passports; only then, we will leave.'

The officer stared at him, then they were interrupted as the two officers appeared through the curtain carrying four back-packs, Lewis followed. The officers walked to the centre of the room, abruptly dropping the bags on the reception floor and amongst the spilled beer and broken glass.

Gareth shouted, 'Hey, be careful boys; there are bottles in my bag.'

The senior officer took a step towards Jack, and said, '*Amigo*, tell your friends to go into the *calle*, how you say, street, I can return your *pasaportes* and *dinero*, you must trust me.'

Jack looked at the officer for a moment then said to his friends, 'Come on guys, collect your bag and do as he asks, we don't have any choice.'

Picking up his bag and shaking it free of beer and glass fragments, he walked towards the exit door. The others did the same, following him into the street, then stood in a group on the curb as an officer exited the hostel then closing the doors, stood officiously with his arms folded, obviously preventing them from attempting to re-enter.

Jack suggested they check their possessions in the bags and exchange anything misplaced, saying that they had no choice and would just have to hope that the officer could get their valuables returned.

Then Gareth said, 'Did you hear that? Listen to what's going on in the reception guys.'

The lead officer was shouting loudly. Then there was the sound of a slap, followed by a high-pitched scream and then silence followed by further screaming.

The soldiers looked at each other, not quite believing.

'I think they are kicking the crap out of that kid,' said Stan.

Then the hostel door opened, and the lead officer walked from the hostel towards the soldiers, readjusting his headdress and straightening his jacket.

'*Amigo*,' he said, 'I have what you want,' holding four passports and a bundle of notes.

'He informed me a criminal came to the hostel this very night. He was threatened by the thief who took the key to your room and stole everything. He dropped these before he escaped.'

Relieved, Jack took the documents and money, identifying each passport and handed them to their owners.

'That's utter bollocks,' Lewis said, not satisfied with the explanation. 'That's not enough, where's the rest of my money?' Pointing to the notes in Jack's hand. 'No criminal came here tonight; it's that lamebrain receptionist who robbed us.'

Gareth added, 'Hey Pedro, I had a hundred American dollars in my bag; there are just a few dollars there, so who has taken the rest? Either you or the receptionist, which is it?' The soldiers watched in disbelief as Gareth stepped towards the officer, his fists clenched.

The officer stared at Gareth; his expression turned from friendly to something more cautionary and smiling, leaned slightly backwards, and began withdrawing his police baton from his belt, as his two colleagues started running towards them, also drawing batons.

Jack quickly stepped between the officer and Gareth, knowing who would come worse off, and using both hands, forcibly pushed Gareth backwards and away from the officer.

'Knock it off Gareth! You will get us all locked up you idiot. Just calm down and accept our losses. We are finished here; let's do as the officer says and leave this place now.'

Jack looked at the others seeking agreement, Lewis adding, 'Jack is right, let's leave and find somewhere to talk about what we do next.'

Gareth gave a deep sigh and along with Stan shouldered his bags and began walking away from the hostel. Lewis looked at Jack, smiled, and said, 'That was a good call mate, the last thing we want is to land in jail tonight.'

Jack nodded to Lewis and watched as he began walking in the direction of the others.

Turning towards the officer, who was looking at him sedately, said, 'Thank you for returning our passports, it's a relief and we appreciate your assistance, do you know where the remainder of our money is?'

The officer's expression turned to one of arrogance and replied, '*Amigo*, we don't need your passports; no one is better than the Mexican people crossing borders without papers; ask the Americans; accept that your money has gone, and you are fortunate to get any pesos, but I am feeling generous tonight; this is how it works in my country. You must not return here; the boy has nothing now.'

The officer turned his back on Jack and walked to the reception, raising his hand and shouting, '*Adios amigo*,' without looking back.

'Thieving bastard,' Jack said quietly, then began walking in the direction his friends had gone.

After a short walk, he saw them in the distance assembling around a table outside the front of a dimly lit café bar and quickly catching up, placed his bag under the table and joined the soldiers as they sat quietly, in a sombre mood and patiently waited for the server.

When he appeared, Stan asked for four bottles of beer.

Jack looked at his watch; it was almost midnight, and it had been less than an hour since they had left the pirate ship in an upbeat and cheerful mood. Now, everything seemed to have very quickly turned sour, and instead, he felt miserable and dispirited, not helped by a disquieting pulse beating in his temple.

Gareth spoke. 'When those cops have gone, I'm going back to torture that little bastard, I'll get our money back from him.'

All the aggravation began to stress Jack who said, 'Shut up, Gareth, I think you and Lewis have done enough, and the kid hasn't got our money anyway, the cops have taken it from him. Take it on the chin and move on, there is nothing more we can do.'

Gareth ignoring him had become distracted when he heard a female laughing at an adjacent table.

Jack continued, 'What is important is that get home on Monday, thankfully, the coach is already paid for,' then looked at his watch, 'after our first catastrophic night, we have one more to get through, can we all just try to behave and get through this without any further trauma, please? I'm feeling really stressed with all this now.

'So, if anyone has any ideas on how we get through the next thirty-six hours with what little money we have left, I'm sitting here waiting to hear because, to be honest, I'm fresh out of ideas.'

They were interrupted by the server, placing four bottles of beer on the table along with the bar bill.

Stan suggested, 'We could go to the British Embassy and tell them we've been robbed. We are British citizens after all, and they might allow us to stay at the embassy or maybe arrange a hotel until our transport leaves.'

Lewis scoffed 'Yeah, all right, and they'll probably also pay for us to eat at Cancún's finest restaurants, perhaps give us some cash to visit a nightclub, and now you mention it, maybe sort for a couple of prostitutes for us; you imbecile Stan, I don't think so.'

Stan retorted, pointing to Lewis, 'It was your idea to leave our passports and cash in the hostel, wise guy!'

Gareth, who had half-listened asked, 'Do you think they would really arrange for prostitutes?'

Ignoring him, Lewis said, 'I think we should share all the money we have equally. The cash that the cop gave to us and anything we have in our pockets.

'It doesn't matter who had more or who had less, we share it equally, so we have the same chance to get through the time we have left here. We should also split up into pairs, things will be easier that way.'

Jack knew it made sense and warmed to the idea.

Stan asked, 'Hold on a minute, are we not better as a team? It's a bit risky out there, what with all the hobos and druggies on the streets, it's probably seriously dangerous in the city centre.'

Lewis replied 'Listen Stan; it's the peak of the American holiday season in Mexico and every middle-aged Yankee woman loves the English accent, and if you fancy buttering the biscuit, just say you are English and have met the queen and they will absolutely fall in love with you. A sure way to share the hotel room of a mature American housewife; do you *comprendo?*' Then winked exaggeratedly.

'I'm not going to sleep with anyone old enough to be my mother, American or not,' Stan replied.

Lewis slammed his beer bottle on the table, patience fading, 'Well that's your choice Stanno, go sleep with the hobos then, I don't really think you understand the predicament we have found ourselves in.'

The mood was becoming increasingly argumentative, and Jack felt it necessary to lighten things up a little; they were tired and had too much alcohol. He thought it might be safer together, remembering the phrase "United we stand, divided we fall".

'He could be right Lewis, it would be safer if we remained together, strength in numbers and all that?' Jack offered.

Lewis replied, 'Normally I would agree, Jack, but as I said earlier, four guys together could make things complicated, especially if you want to tap someone for a free bed for the night. I really think the next thirty-six hours will be more manageable in pairs.'

Of course, Jack knew Lewis was right and said 'Okay, if everyone agrees, that's the plan, we share the money equally then leave in pairs and meet up at the coach station on Monday. Does everyone agree?'

They showed their agreement, Stan reluctantly.

Jack placed the money the police officer had given to him on the table, and the soldiers added any other money they had from their pockets, as Lewis began to count the cash, dividing it into equal piles on the table.

'Okay,' he said, it's not too bad; we have just over five thousand pesos and five American dollars, about fifty quid each. Not enough to afford a luxury hotel or anything, but enough to comfortably get through the time we have left.' He looked at the others seeking agreement.

Stan remained silent.

'Look, Stan,' Jack said, 'why don't you hang out with me? We have enough money to get a cheap hotel, some nice food and a few drinks, what do you say?'

Stan looked up from the table, smiling and visibly relieved replied, 'Okay mate, that sounds great.'

'All right guys,' Jack said, 'I think that's it then; Stan and I will meet up with you two on Monday, agreed?'

Jack's fingers were crossed under the table, hoping for agreement, knowing with conviction, Gareth and Lewis would get into further trouble; the last few hours were evidence of that.

'That's good with me,' Lewis replied, 'I enjoy hanging out with Gareth but only he's sober, it's when he gets drunk, he's a bleeding nightmare!' Teasing and softly punching Gareth's shoulder.

Then put his bottle to his lips to take a drink as Gareth slapped him hard on the back causing him to spray beer across the table, soaking the money, and his friends.

'Before we go, let's toast to a safe few days.' Jack announced, and they clinked their bottles together.

Collecting their allocated piles of cash and wiping beer from the notes, Jack noticed Lewis had discreetly put the five US dollars on his own pile, knowing he had shrewdly increased the overall value of his share.

'Don't worry guys, I'll pay for the drinks,' Gareth picked up the bill from the table and added, 'good luck boyos, see you on Monday safe and sound, *adios,'* and walked into the bar to pay.

'Good luck Lewis,' Jack said, 'be careful and try to keep Gareth out of trouble. Don't forget, the coach leaves on Monday at 8 am and the driver won't stay more than 30 minutes longer,' Lewis nodded.

Turning, he saw Stan already walking away along the pavement as if he had a purpose and a place to head towards, which of course, he didn't.

Jack shouldered his bag and followed.

The streets were not as busy as they had seen earlier, but Cancún was a twenty-four-hour city, and even at this time, bars and nightclubs were still buzzing with nightlife and some late-night drinkers.

Occasionally, as they walked the streets aimlessly, a homeless person or a beggar, not always indigenous to Mexico, approached and desperately asked for something, anything.

Although sympathetic, neither felt they were able to offer anything without compromising their own limited finances for the next few days.

After walking some distance, they approached a busy tequila bar and restaurant, La Parrilla. Stan, suddenly excited, suggested they stop for a drink; he had been told the bar was world-famous for its tequila and mariachi music.

Jack was already finding that the endless walking was becoming tedious and eagerly agreeing, they sat at an outside table and ordered beers and tequila shots.

'I'm getting too tired walking around Stan,' Jack said, 'we can't just traipse around all night, and I don't feel like sleeping on the streets, so what do you say? We find a hotel, spend some of our money and get our heads down for the night. In the morning we can get a decent shower and a good breakfast, then plan for the next twenty-four hours?'

Stan enthusiastically agreed and downing their drinks, they paid and left.

Several minutes later, walking along a road leading away from the lights of the city centre, the area began to appear to be run down and poverty-stricken. Stan suggested they return to the busier streets suggesting it could be dangerous if they found themselves in the outer, poorer suburbs.

His concerns were heightened by the frequent sound of emergency vehicle sirens; the police seemed constantly busy, particularly during the last half hour.

Jack agreed, and they walked back towards the city lights.

Then, they saw a black *Policía* truck, siren wailing and lights flashing blue and red, appear from a side street and watched as the vehicle continued in their direction. As it neared, they expected it to go rushing past them, but to their surprise, screeched to a halt next to the curb where they stood.

The soldiers stepped back from the edge of the curb as the ignition was switched off, and only the hiss and clicking of the cooling and resting engine disturbed the quietness.

Neither of the soldiers were aware that they were about to enter a whole new episode of chaos.

Fortune does not change men, it unmasks them

Suzanne Necker

The soldiers remained on the bench and stared across the floor at Gareth, who was sitting next to the old man and gathering his thoughts before continuing.

Everything he had said so far had somehow seemed surreal, and there was an unconscious agreement not to interrupt and to allow him to continue when he felt he was ready.

He inhaled noisily, then releasing, continued.

'I kept looking around the shack and didn't know why. Then I looked through the window and around the clearing until realising that I was checking that no one else was there, and then waited for a full fifteen minutes before deciding what to do.

'I know this sounds stupid, but I checked Baptiste's pulse again, and nothing had changed; he was still dead, so I removed all the drugs and money from the hole in the floor.

'There were too many bundles to carry, and looking around I saw Baptiste's dirty towel, the one he always rubbed with his hands, lying on the floor behind the door where he had first collapsed.

'So, I took it and wrapped it around the drug bags and money bundles, then left the shack.

'At first, I walked to the Land Rover with the package, thinking I should leave but then realised returning to the base with it was a stupid idea, and I could get searched at the gate, it seemed too much of a risk.

'I can remember thinking that I should put it back in the hole, forget I had ever seen it and get the hell out of there and stood staring at the towel-wrapped package, wondering what to do, feeling my heart thumping in my chest and trying to keep calm.

'Then it just came to me; it made sense to hide the money and drugs somewhere safe until I could speak to you guys about what had happened.

'So, I quickly looked around the clearing and my eyes kept going to the front end of the old Land Rover next to the chicken shed and then I remembered how extensive the air filter housing was in that year's model, much more significant and oversized and without the filter, large enough to conceal the package.

'I quickly walked over and lifted the bonnet, unscrewed the centre locking screw with my fingernail and took the head off. The filter was still inside, so pulled it out, flinging it into the long grass, and then pushed the package into the housing, it fitted perfectly, so I replaced the head and screwed it back into place, closed the bonnet and walked back to the Land Rover.

'Then I realised I still had the equipment which I'd brought to sell to Baptiste in the rear of my vehicle and was the reason I had come to the clearing in the first place, also reminding me about money for our Mexico trip. I returned to the old Land Rover, opened the filter again and removed $800 from one of the bundles then sealed it up.

'Returning to the shack, I searched around to make sure I hadn't left anything behind and checked that Baptiste was still dead. Then went to my vehicle and removed the tyres, generator and batteries, stacking them by the chicken shed. Then left and then drove back to base.

'When I got back, I met up with Lewis and tried to act as if the exchange had been as expected, but probably due to me being in a bit of shock, he didn't believe me, so I told him everything.'

The old man asked, 'How much do you think was in the bundles, Gareth.'

'Erm, I have no idea, a lot, a mix of notes, some were Belizean, but quite a lot were fifty and hundred American dollar bills and from the size and number of bundles, perhaps tens of thousands of US dollars.'

The man explained to them that drug dealers usually concealed vast amounts of money from rivals, and the authorities, and because Baptiste was in a jungle location could be hiding it for other dealers too.

He added from the description of the drugs that it was possibly fifty thousand US dollars of uncut heroin, the street value would be worth ten or fifteen times more, and from the size of the bundles of dollars, he compared them to the size of Gareth's fists; possibly fifty thousand dollars or more as that would be the least a drug dealer would need for cross border deals depending on the level Baptiste worked at.

Jack was listening but had more questions for Lewis. 'Why didn't you tell us before we left Belize, do you not understand how serious all this is Lewis? Gareth could be locked up for murder.

'Oh, I have just realised and now I know why, you kept quiet because you intended to return to the clearing and get the money for yourself. Is that what the truth of it is Lewis?'

'No Jack, that's not true, of course, I was going to tell you, Gareth was in a terrible state when he came back with the money, and then he fessed up. I was so taken aback when he told me and didn't want to spoil our trip, I'm telling you the truth.'

A thick air of melancholy hung around in the truck then Jack responded.

'Fine, fine, I get it, first of all let me apologise to Gareth on Lewis's behalf because he allowed you to go to the clearing without backup, putting you in danger and at risk.

'You've had to carry a terrible burden on your shoulders, but to be honest, I would have appreciated being told about this earlier, especially because it was me that assumed responsibility for the enterprise and decided it should continue.'

Lewis felt the jab as Jack glanced at him disdainfully.

Jack continued, 'You did your best to help Baptiste and then put him at peace, oddly, I think he would have appreciated that but critically, we have a dead body and a load of evidence in the clearing pointing the finger at us, so we need to think about what we are going to do.'

Staring down at the floor, Gareth replied, 'Thank you, corporal.'

Pause

'Okay,' he said addressing the others, 'the most important thing is to get out of this truck right now, and the old man has told us how it can be done, we have no choice but to trust him, we need to make damn sure we all get on that coach on Monday, return to Belize and then to the clearing as soon as we can because, after Gareth's mind-blowing revelation, there is a lot of cleaning up we will have to do.

'We will have to start by destroying any evidence of us ever having visited the place, and that includes disposal of Baptiste's body. Hopefully, no one has visited the shack yet so getting there is a priority, only when we're satisfied it is clean, we can think about recovering the money.

'Gareth, I understand this is upsetting, because of what you have been through, but I want you to be strong because I need you to assist in sorting out this mess. Now, unless anyone disagrees, let's turn our attention to getting out of this sewer.'

Lewis was impressed by Jack's determination and how quickly it had taken him to devise a plan to destroy evidence at a potential murder scene. Still, the part that excited him most was the mention of recovering the money.

Standing, Jack walked to the grill and tapped on the frame with his knuckle; the police officer in the passenger seat looked over his shoulder and smiled as if expecting him.

He was determined they would be leaving the cell and was convinced that, if the old man was telling the truth, their ordeal would soon be over.

He spoke confidently, 'Excuse me, officers, we have many pesos, can we pay you to let us out of here?'

The passenger laughed and spoke in Spanish to the driver, who also laughed. Then awkwardly shifted his obese bulk in the seat and turning, asked, 'You must tell us what pesos you have gringo, and then perhaps we will decide.'

Jack turned to face Stan and Lewis and felt there was a shared sense of enthusiasm and excitement in the cell.

He remembered the old man had mentioned that initially,

they should offer two thousand pesos and spoke with a raised voice, intentionally allowing the officers to hear.

'All right, guys, the officers have asked us to hand over all our money and they will allow us to leave. They are being very reasonable, so let's give them all the pesos we have.'

'Bollocks', Gareth said in a hushed voice, 'they're thieving bastards.'

Jack stepped towards Gareth and placing his face very close to his, earlier empathy gone and whispered, 'If you had not been such a dickhead, Gareth, none of us would be here, so I don't really rate your opinion at the moment, just do as I say, or you will be staying in this stinking hole with the old man, *comprendo*?'

Lewis leaned towards Jack, whispering, 'Why don't you ask them how much money they expect? That way, we don't need to negotiate.'

Jack agreed it was worth a try and turned back to the grill. 'How much is it that want to allow us to leave sir?'

The officers laughed, replying, '*Todo, todo*, everything you have sir.'

Jack felt his shirt being pulled, then someone's mouth close to his ear; it was Lewis again.

'Look, these guys must be on minimum wage, and any money is a lot of money and as the old man said, we have enough for them to bribe themselves into a new life in America. As the old man suggested, tell them we have a total of two thousand pesos, and then we will still have enough left to see us through until we leave Mexico. It's worth a chance.'

Jack nodded and stepped back to the grill.

'Sir, we have put all our money together, and we have two

thousand pesos, that is all of it; so please take it and let us go, we won't do anything wrong again, and promise not to tell anyone.'

'We are British soldiers, and we will leave your beautiful country as soon as possible.'

The passenger spoke to the driver, translating what Jack had said then, following a serious exchange of whispering, turned back and said,

'That is not enough *amigo*, it is an insult, you give us three thousand pesos, or we take you to jail to rot with all the other bitches we have there.'

Jack turned to his friends. 'We have to give them three thousand pesos, and it's a done deal.'

They didn't have to be asked again; having all heard the officer, they were already subtly pooling the money, Lewis collected it together.

Jack located his backpack, removed his money and gave it to Lewis, who collectively counted all the money onto the bench, then, when satisfied he had the right amount, handed the notes to Jack.

He knocked on the grill and the passenger turned, looked over his shoulder and saw the cash then indicated that the notes were to be rolled and pushed through the holes in the grill.

Gareth and Stan stepped forward, eagerly assisting Jack by pushing the notes through the grill as the officer straightened them and created a pile on the dashboard. When the last one had gone through, he counted the notes, smiled then held up a thumb to the driver.

Having searched for a discreet place to stop, the driver slowed the truck, manoeuvring into a dark alley before abruptly stopping, causing those standing in the cell to lose their balance and lurch forward, flinging out hands to steady themselves.

Relieved, they gathered their backpacks and sat on the benches waiting in anticipation that, finally, the doors would be opened, and they would be allowed to leave.

The engine quietly ticked over, as the two officers remained in their seats, motionless and silent as if waiting for something more.

'You need to speak to them again,' the old man offered.

'Why, what is wrong? What didn't you tell us?' Lewis asked.

'They have instructions for you; this is how they want you to leave; it is how everyone leaves, but you must ask them,' he replied.

Concern spread amongst the captives, and Gareth moved from his bench, sitting next to the man, glancing threateningly at him as Jack stepped to the grill; he peered through, the officers looking forward in silence, then he tapped gently on the metal frame.

The passenger responded. 'Thank you for your pesos, but you must now do as I ask if you want to leave, only one gringo can leave each time, then the next gringo when we say, *comprendo*?'

'Yes sir, I think we understand; one of us will leave and then we wait for you to tell us when the next one can leave, is that correct?'

'That is how it happens *amigo*, let me say, we hope you enjoy Mexico, and hope to see you again, have a nice day,' he replied sarcastically.

Then to their relief, the vehicle slightly rocked as the officers opened their doors and began to climb out of the cab leaving the vehicle's engine ticking over.

Lewis asked the others to quickly give to him the remainder

of their money, saying, 'We don't know what will happen when we get outside, but we should share what money we have left, just in case we are split up.'

He quickly counted the notes into four equal piles on the bench and handed a small bundle to each of his friends while waiting for the doors to open.

Gareth said, 'If you don't mind boys, I'm going first, I'll see you around, eh?'

Picking up his backpack and shaking everyone's hand, including the old man, he stood at the rear doors just as they slung open and the soldiers watched him leave, doors slamming closed behind him.

They sat in silence, listening and trying to detect noises outside the truck.

Jack thought he heard raised voices followed by a shout, then a 'thwack' noise and further shouting. Annoyingly the purring of the vehicle's engine didn't assist, he couldn't be sure.

He looked at Stan, his expression confirmed that he had heard something similar. Then nothing, apart from the constant hum of the engine.

'If it's all right with you guys, I'll go next, please? I want to get this over as quickly as possible,' Stan asked.

Neither Jack nor Lewis replied as he stepped and faced the doors. After a few moments they were swung open, and he hesitantly stepped out; doors slamming shut behind him.

Jack and Lewis strained, trying to listen to any unusual sounds.

Nothing but the engine noise.

'Maybe I was hearing things after Gareth went out and perhaps wasn't what I thought,' he said to Lewis.

Lewis nodded, then with dread, stared at Jack when he heard

the scream, several thuds followed by another scream and then voices talking heatedly.

'The thugs are beating the shit out of each of us as we leave; what are we going to do?' Lewis asked.

'You go next, Lewis, try to regroup with the others, if we get split up, we'll have to meet on Monday.'

'I won't say no Jack, but I don't understand why you want to go last?'

'I don't, but this is my shout mate; if all goes wrong, at least I know the three of you got away. The cops may have to justify themselves and take at least one of us to jail, so I'll wait to see what happens.

'If I'm not at the coach station on Monday, promise you'll tell the military police what happened and where I am,' then pausing, added, 'don't wait for me and make sure you get the money from Baptiste's place as soon as possible, and you must remember to destroy all the evidence.'

Lewis gripped Jack's hand and shook it vigorously. 'Good luck, mate, don't worry, we are all getting out of here.'

'Just one last thing Lewis, let me have the five US dollar notes you discreetly kept back for yourself; if this goes belly up, I might need to bribe my way out. American dollars carry a lot of weight with these people.'

'Of course, mate,' he said, taking the notes from his pocket and handing them over just as the doors opened, then Lewis nervously stepped out into the morning light.

Jack waited, tensing, head in his hands, thinking about the past eighteen hours, and then he remembered the old man was still sitting on the opposite bench.

'I forgot to thank you for telling us how to get out of here,' he said, 'I'm sorry we couldn't give you more food, but it's all we had.' He held the dollars towards him 'take this as our gratitude, it might assist you.' The man snatched the money, without showing any appreciation, and stuffed the notes into his pocket.

'What is your name?' Jack asked.

'My name doesn't matter; it has no meaning to you.'

(pause)

'I am not Mexican; I am Argentinian; my wife was like you, British and moved to Argentina many years ago. We had a child, but he was conscripted into the Army and killed by the British in the Malvinas; he was sixteen.

'My wife could not recover from the loss of our child and joined the protest against General Galtieri's corrupt government. She never came home, and I never saw her again; she became a '*desaparecido.*'

'Then one day the police came to my home, and they took everything, my identity card, papers, and my existence and told me that I would also become a '*desaparecido*' if I did not flee.

'That night I left, I crossed the border into Brazil and then travelled north and then to Mexico. I have no self-pride but to survive and do what I must in the name of my wife and son. There are too many corrupt governments and many courageous people who disappear or die in the name of political arrogance.'

Jack felt utmost sympathy for the old man and held his hand towards him, the man touched it, weakly shaking. Then the doors opened, standing, and holding his bag tightly to his chest, he walked into the sunlight and saw the two police officers standing at each side of the steps, staring at him and beckoning him to descend from the truck.

Squinting in the intense light, he looked around and saw the morning sun rays glancing off buildings; there was no sign of his friends. Nervously, he slowly stepped down from the truck, taking one step at a time.

As his foot touched the tarmac road, the driver with the walrus moustache swept his shin into Jack's calf, causing him to fall clumsily and instinctively throwing his hands forward to prevent his face from smashing into the tarmac. Fortunately, his bag, still in front of him, cushioned the fall.

For a couple of seconds, nothing, then he felt the hurt as two police batons walloped down on his back and buttocks. He screamed in pain; his beating was relentless and knew it would not cease unless he did something other than lying on the ground taking the beating.

Sucking in as much air as possible, he pushed his bag to his side, and bending his knees, adopting a hunched position, then tried to push upwards with his hands. The batons found new areas to hit, and now felt blows to his sides and kidneys.

He knew he could not take any more pain and had to act fast if he was to survive without severe damage being inflicted. The constant strike of the batons made it too difficult to get to his feet.

Then just as he thought that the pain was too much and it would be easier to lie down on the ground and permit the beating to continue, they stopped hitting him.

Silence followed, no noise, no movement, and, most importantly, no more violence. Then he thought he heard someone speak, a gravelly voice, repeated the words '*Toma esto.*'

He crouched as pain spread across his shoulders and lower back, but the pause allowed him to open his eyes and turned his head towards the truck.

The old man was standing at top of the steps outside the cell doors, holding the dollars that Jack had given him, and waving the money towards the two officers. Jack realised that the old man was distracting them, willing to trade the money in exchange for Jack's release and possibly, his life.

Placing a foot on the ground, he was able to push himself to his feet; the pain was excruciating, and almost lost his balance but was damn sure he wasn't going to let them have another opportunity and gathering all his strength, he stood straight.

His instincts told him to run immediately, but instead, turned and watched the moustached officer climb the metal steps and snatch the notes from the old man's hand. He inspected them, smiling, then dropped to the tarmac and handed two of the notes to the overweight officer.

Jack looked at the old man and could just about see his grey, glistening eyes. The man smiled and gave a salute of solidarity then shouted 'Corre amigo corre,' then waved his hand, indicating Jack should leave, and fast.

Taking hold of his backpack, he returned a nod of gratitude and then began to stumble away from the truck and towards freedom. Eventually, the stumble became a clumsy jog, he didn't care if anyone was watching, just satisfied he was escaping from the sadistic police.

He ran along the sidewalk and then past the Flamingo Plaza, which he had become so familiar with, past bars and clubs which he had seen brimming with people earlier but were now closed.

He continued to run even though he was becoming breathless, almost barging into a couple walking together. He didn't care for anything or anyone other than putting distance between himself and the brutality he had just left. He ran along curbs, crossing roads and through the streets until he could run no more.

Then, when his energy was depleted and exhausted, he fell to the ground, rolling over several times, only stopping because of his backpack. His chest was heaving, his lungs gasping for air and felt his heart bursting from his chest.

He lay for some time until his racing heartbeat had begun to decrease, and his breathing returned to normal.

Feeling excruciating aches and pains across his back, shoulders and buttocks and a warm and intense pain in his kidney area, his head began to throb, a grinding headache setting in.

Then he realised how exposed he was, lying in the middle of the pavement. He wanted to move and rolled to his side, then shuffled to a short wall bordering the sidewalk, using his backpack as a makeshift pillow and support for his kneck.

He lay for some time and then either lost consciousness or slept, later, he would not remember which, but was instantly comforted as his sensory preceptors were relieved of the pain.

1 1

When a new day begins, dare to smile gratefully

Steve Maraboli

His back ached and he felt tenderness and a burning sensation around the area of his kidneys, which had probably woken him from a deep sleep.

Unsure of where he was and feeling as though had been drugged and had just surfaced from a profound hallucinogenic trip, he remembered the old man and the police beating him and the dollars the man gave them, facilitating his escape.

Lifting his head even slightly caused nagging pains in his shoulders and allowed his head to fall back to the soft support, guessing he was going to have to take things more slowly.

After a couple of minutes of lying with his eyes closed, he was disturbed by the sound of vehicle engines, people's voices, and the whistling trills of birds.

He didn't want to move; whenever he did, the pain surged, encouraging him to remain motionless, but he knew he would have to make a move soon.

Then, to his disgust, he felt a warm, slimy and moist object stroking and tickling his ear. He opened his eyes, and weakly waved and wafted a hand around his head, slapping something large, hairy and warm.

Hearing a high pitched whine, he lifted his head, staring into the eyes of a gaunt thin dog, its tongue flopping from the side of its mouth and dripping saliva.

The animal sat next to him as if waiting for a treat and he saw self-healed scars and evidence of mange on its body, bare patches of pink skin and sores amongst white fur. He thought that whatever he had been through, this poor animal had gone through far worse.

Smiling at the starving creature and gently unzipping his backpack, he removed a bottle of water and poured a little onto the pavement, creating a small puddle, then watched the dog lap at the fluid. Then, feeling thirsty himself, drank from the bottle.

He observed the dog using its wasting muscles to bend forward, licking the water, motivating him to find the energy and sit up. He slowly shuffled to a sitting position, supported against the wall.

After the dog had licked the pavement until almost dry, the animal sat and looked at him, panting. He held the plastic bottle towards the dog, showing that there was no water and was convinced the dog gave a gentle smirk of appreciation and then watched the animal trot away along the pavement.

He sat resting for a few minutes, then found the energy to move and using the wall as a support and carefully manoeuvring, he was able to climb to his feet.

The pain in his back had slightly subsided and when his legs held his weight, he felt his balance and stood, looking around.

In front of him was a fairly busy road and early morning traffic, people opening their shops, others walking along the pavement. Behind the low wall was a raised grassed area containing random palm trees and borders filled with colourful flowers and behind, a tall building bearing the words 'Radisson Hotel.'

He felt that it was beginning to get seriously warm, and checking his watch, saw it was 7.15 am and indicating he was already almost halfway into his holiday in Cancún and had just twenty-four hours to continue enduring the ordeal.

Picking up his backpack and carefully climbing over the wall whilst wincing in pain, he studied the building and then sighed, noticing the rows of hotel room windows, longing to be able to walk into any of the rooms, take a shower, order room service, and then slip between the crisp sheets of a comfortable bed.

His thoughts were interrupted by the sound of splashing water and he noticed a sign indicating a swimming pool on the other side of the grassed area. A gap in a hedge revealed a white sandy beach and the blue-green sea in the distance.

He walked towards it.

The swimming pool belonged to the hotel and was reserved for guests. Morning staff had already placed thick comfortable floral cushions on lounger chairs surrounding the pool, obviously setting the area for the early morning arrivals.

A man wearing a yellow waistcoat used a net to skim debris from the water's surface. The water was clear and inviting, and the loungers appeared comfortable, too comfortable.

He saw a drinking water fountain on the opposite side, and quickly walked around the pool, taking a long drink. The relief of the cool water soothing his dry throat was almost overwhelming. When he finished drinking, he splashed chilled water on his face then filled his water bottle, placing it in his backpack.

Looking around the pool area, his eyes eagerly searching, he saw an unassuming lounger chair, away from the others and alone in a corner.

The man skimming the pool shouted *'Hola,'* and waved towards him.

He replied, *'Hola,* I have finished breakfast and want to take my seat early,' then pointed to the lone lounger, confident the staff member would think he was just another early morning hotel guest.

The man replied, 'Sure, sit anywhere; there are plenty of seats this early.' Jack nodded and made his way to the other side of the pool.

Pulling the chair into the recline position and pushing his pack underneath, he lay down and stretched out on the soft cushion, relaxing his aching muscles; the warmth of the sun soothed him, and in moments he drifted into sleep.

He didn't know how long he had slept, but the sun was scorching, and it felt like he was in a furnace. Drips of sweat meandered across his brow to his temple and then found the quickest route to tickle his ear lobe, then hung, waiting for another drop to join it, creating enough weight to fall to the tiles below.

There was a burning sensation across his face but not enough to motivate him to change his position; he was tired but comfortable and enjoying the rest.

Sweat began to well around and leak into his eyes, causing a stinging sensation. He pushed his course, dry tongue between cracked lips and winced as the dry sores on his lips split, tasting blood.

Realising he had earlier chosen a lounger in the open and was probably beginning to experience the outset of heat stroke; he decided to overcome his tiredness and think about finding shade.

Mustering all his strength, he clumsily twisted and then turned his body in the lounger onto his other side so that his face was slightly shaded from the sun. The movement allowed him to smell his own odorous stale sweat and mustiness.

A high-pitched scream close by startling him, followed by the splashing of water, more screams, then laughter and then a man's voice spoke with an American accent.

'Corey! Keep away from the hobo; they can be dangerous.'

Jack didn't need a great deal of imagination to figure out whom the man was referring to and slowly opened his eyes, and rubbed them with his hands, the sweat causing his eyes to sting.

Moving himself to a sitting position supported by his elbows, he looked around, squinting in the sun's bright light, and waited a few seconds to allow his eyes to focus, hearing water splashing and sloshing against the sides of the pool.

A small girl and a boy supported by buoyancy aids were clumsily swimming in the water. A man wearing swimming trunks, and standing on the far side of the pool, talking to the children.

Behind the man, a woman with bright ginger hair and pale skin wearing a green swimsuit, lying on a lounger. She wore a massive sombrero on her head, so large, the hat created shade over her entire body. Her face, arms and legs were coated in thick layers of white sun cream.

The man spoke again, Jack saw his eyes darting towards him and back to the children.

'Just keep to this side of the pool, away from the hobo,' he said.

Gradually turning his wrist, Jack looked at his watch and saw it was almost midday, realising he had been sleeping in full sun all morning.

'*Señor quiere tomar una copa?*'

He heard the soft female voice close to him.

Turning his head, he looked into the dark brown eyes of a young girl, no more than eighteen years old, he thought, standing close to the lounger chair; she stared back at him. He didn't say anything; just studied her up and down, conscious but unbothered that she was watching his eyes.

She wore a tiny red bikini showing off her light olive skin and delicate curves. A gold badge dangled from the breast cup of her bikini; '*Radisson Hotel, I speak your language!*' He looked at her pleasant smile, displaying perfect white teeth, and thought she was the most beautiful thing he had ever seen in his life.

Then conscious of his body's odour, moved back in his seat, trying to create distance between them.

'Sir, do you want a drink?' she repeated.

Jack croaked, '*Agua por favour,*' attempted to swallow, coughed, then said it again, this time a little clearer.

'*Sí señor,*' she said, and he watched as she slowly turned and walked alluringly around the poolside to the wooden hut, then a short time later, after the sound of clinking glasses, returned holding a glass of cold water and ice.

He sat up and, attempting not to appear desperate, snatched the glass from her hand, then drank the water in several gulps, lumps of ice followed, which he crunched and swallowed as the girl curiously watched.

Water dripped from his cracked lips and chin, and he held the glass towards the girl.

'*Otra, por favour?*' he asked.

The girl smiled and nodded, and again watched her tenderly walk back around the pool to the hut, then returning holding the refilled glass of water, which he took from her as she swaggered away to attend to other poolside guests, offering drinks.

He removed the ice from the glass, rubbed the melting cubes across his face, and felt some relief from the stinging sunburn.

The pool was becoming busy and four other couples had arrived, setting up loungers, the children still in the water, laughing and splashing, while their father constantly watched Jack with suspicion as if he presented a danger to everyone.

Realising he was attracting too much unnecessary attention, he decided he should leave and allow the guests to enjoy their day and gently placed the glass on the tiled floor, awkwardly swinging his legs to the ground and twisting out of the lounger to stand upright.

Then, aware of the sudden silence, he looked around the poolside; everyone, even the children, had stopped what they were doing and were watching him with suspicion and alarm. The kids' father was busily fishing them out of the water, ready to run if he felt he had to.

Collecting his backpack from under the lounger, he smiled and mischievously called out, '*Adios amigos.*' Then stiffly walked along the poolside to the exit in the hedge, feeling everyone's eyes watching him, and left.

He walked across the grass to the busy road, then along the sidewalk but was unexpectantly saddened when he saw the dog, he had earlier given water.

The animal appeared to have been struck by a vehicle and was lying on the pavement, its head over the curb, touching the road.

It was motionless and still, blood dripping from its open mouth.

Walking closer, he stared into its dry black, lifeless eyes attempting to understand what could have happened and if anyone was in the least bothered. Sombrely stepping over the poor animal, he thought how wretched its life must have been and how an unexpected death may be a comfort, then continued his journey walking along the busy streets of Cancún.

He walked for almost an hour, feeling he wasn't achieving anything but passing time, then approached a small public park with a large lake surrounded by tended borders of richly coloured flowers; finding a bench facing the pond, dropped his bag on the ground, then sat and rested for a while.

Rubbing his sunburnt face, he felt stubble on his chin and thought he would do anything for a wash or take a shower. He could still smell mustiness and tried to work out how he could change his damp, sweat-stained clothes.

His mind drifted, and he began to recollect the events of the last twenty-four hours, their passports and money stolen, savagely beaten by police, the prison truck and then the shock of Gareth's admission, believing he had killed Baptiste.

Thinking of his present situation, he was now alone sitting on a bench, stinking as if destitute, abandoned and with little money, then he thought of the other soldiers and how they would be surviving their ordeal. More importantly, wondered if they had received the same beating as he had and if they were also like him, separated and alone.

He was fully aware Gareth and Lewis were experienced enough to look after themselves but was concerned about Stan, who would probably find things quite difficult being the most naïve of them all, he hoped he was managing to take care of himself.

His mind turned back to Belize and Baptiste, wondering if it was possible to completely destroy the evidence of their dealings with him; then there was the money, from Gareth's description, there was a huge amount and it seemed insane not to recover it if that was possible. It emphasised how important it was to return as they had intended and essentially, he needed to work on a plan of what to do when they got there.

Checking his watch, it was already 3 pm, indicating, the coach would be leaving Cancún in about seventeen hours, and just a little more perseverance was needed to get through the time he had left in Mexico.

His stomach began to rumble, and removing the crumpled notes from his pocket, counted what he had. He had enough to afford a good meal and alcohol, or the sensible option would be to use the money and to pay for a cheap hotel room where he would be able to wash, perhaps have a bath and then have a full night's sleep in a comfortable bed.

His stomach grumbled again, and he thought back to the comfortable lounger chair at the Radisson hotel; it was decided; he would spend the money on some traditional Mexican food and some tequila, then return to the Radisson poolside and sleep for nothing on the hotel lounger. After all, the nights were warm and it should be safe enough, probably watched over by the hotel security.

He pulled his bag onto his shoulder and, feeling positive and upbeat, the pain in his back decreasing, set off at pace towards the city lights and the smell of food cooking.

It was evening when had finished the sizeable portion of enchiladas in the restaurant, he had ordered enough for two people and had washed it all down with Corona beer and tequila shots.

Then found himself walking the streets and experiencing the cool evening breeze in the city centre and attempting to enjoy his final hours in Mexico.

Again, he passed the Flamingo Plaza, reminding him of being captive in the police truck and the sadistic cruelty of the corrupt officers, and walking through the café and restaurant area, watched tourists drinking in the bars until he noticed the shops start to close as the sun began to set.

As he passed a tequila bar, he heard shouting and swearing in English, and stopping to watch the commotion then witnessed a man being evicted from the bar by staff. He was very drunk and thrown heavily onto the pavement, where he lay motionless. Then he heard the sirens and saw a police truck approach.

Jack anxiously ran into a nearby street ally, watching from the shadows as the truck stopped outside the bar then two police officers carried the drunk up the rear steps and threw him into the cell, slamming the doors shut. He remained, concealed, heart thumping, only coming out when he was sure the police vehicle had long gone.

He began to realise it was getting late and aware that he had used almost all his money and decided to return to the Radisson hotel then following a short and casual walk in the dark, arrived at the poolside.

He was relieved, but not surprised, due to the lateness to find the pool deserted. The loungers had been tidily positioned in neat rows, cushions left on the chairs, presumably for any guest wishing to take an evening swim.

The lights around the pool were dimmed, and the lamps

at the bottom of the pool created a surreal blue celestial-like shimmering tinge to the water.

Noticing a pile of neatly folded towels, stacked on a shelf near the poolside hut, he went over and collected two to serve as blankets should it become cooler later, then located a lounger in the same spot he had slept earlier, this time dragging the chair so that it was positioned under the branching fronds of a palm tree to remain dry if it began to rain during the night.

He removed the remaining pesos notes from his pocket and placed the money into his wallet, then into his backpack along with his identity card and passport, pushing the bag firmly under the lounger.

Lying down, he spread the towels across his legs, in an attempt to shield himself against mosquitoes then lay back, staring at the clear and unpolluted night sky and taking in the brightness of the countless stars shimmering against the backdrop of the black night sky.

Within a short time, encouraged by the food and tequila, he fell asleep.

'*Maldito Gringo*'.

Initially, he thought he had to be dreaming, and the voice was in his head.

Then as if to confirm its existence, he heard it again.

'*Maldito Gringo.*'

The words were harsh and gruff and became a reality when accompanied by the rancid smell of stale smoke and alcohol.

Realising it is impossible to smell in a dream, he opened his eyes in panic, only confirming his worst fear, as the cold blade of a knife pressed into his throat, almost making him retch.

Without moving, he stared directly into the eyes of a gaunt, unshaven, and dirty face, no fewer than a couple of inches from his own. Studying the man's virtually black, dead eyes, he saw coldness, lifelessness and pain, the whites of his eyes jaundiced yellow and bloodshot.

The man's face was so close he could smell the revolting breath from a mouth which was scarce of teeth, those remaining, black and broken.

A string of spittle hung from hideous cracked and bleeding lips, threatening to drip onto Jack's face as he said, 'I want your money Gringo.'

Each time the creature spoke, Jack winced as the assailant increased the pressure on the cold blade, threatening to split the soft flesh on his throat.

He knew with desperation he needed to do something to escape but was prevented by the man, his total body weight on top of him; the feeling of dread, paralysing him and he didn't dare move.

'It's in my bag,' he said in despair, feeling the increasing pressure of the knife against his throat but realised that the man did not understand.

'There, my bag, my bag,' pointing blindly with a hand under the lounger. The man looked to where Jack was indicating and bent over, reached under the lounger, removed the backpack and placed it on Jack's chest.

'It's in there, money; you want money?' Cautiously pointing to the pocket where he had placed his wallet earlier.'

The man slowly unzipped the pocket and nodded to it, indicating that Jack should remove what was inside. He felt himself trembling, and the pressure of the sharp knife against his throat increased so much it was starting to sting, he knew that the tightened skin wouldn't be able to resist any more pressure from the razor-sharp blade.

The man began nodding impatiently, Jack understood and frantically rummaged around the open pocket, then touching, withdrew his wallet.

He held it towards the creature who released the pressure of the knife on his neck and slipping the blade down the back of his trousers, snatched the wallet and stood back from the lounger.

Jack gagged and coughed, quickly placing his hand to his throat, expecting to feel the warmth of blood, and watching the man search inside his wallet. The robber pulled out several notes, counted them, and then searched for more.

He expected the robber to become angry when he saw what little money he had and would surely pull the knife again, but thankfully he was wrong. The man counted the money again, then looked at Jack, gave a hideous tooth-rotten smile of satisfaction, and then threw the wallet over his shoulder, making a splashing sound as it landed in the pool.

He fervently looked around to check that no one had been watching, then pushed the notes into his pocket, turned and ran towards a low wall adjacent to the beach, jumped over and disappeared into the night.

Jack sat quietly on the lounger, both hands grasping his stinging neck, feeling a painful and angry weal across his throat.

He pulled his legs up to his chest and covered his knees with the towel, thinking about, with increasing disbelief, the distressing events he had endured; it had been a hellish nightmare at every level; frowning, he remembered it was supposed to be a relaxing break, but instead, had turned into a disastrous journey and was almost comical if it had not been real.

Any further thought of sleep was out of the question, and glancing at the rippling water, he saw a dark, blurry image of his wallet, illuminated by the lamps on the floor of the pool.

Standing, he walked to the water fountain, pushed the lever and placed his head under the cool streaming water giving him some relief.

Hours passed as he lay on the lounger but he remained awake, trying to count the flickering stars. Even the therapeutic sound of the waves from the sea gently crashing onto the beach was not enough to make him feel tired.

Each time he heard the slightest noise or movement of leaves, he would jump off the lounger and prepare to run, then, realising it was nothing, returned to the lounger, covering himself with the towel.

He knew he was finished with Mexico now and wanted the remaining time to pass quickly so he could leave, and eventually, and to his relief, the dark sky began to lighten and became grey, and then blue, as the brilliant orange glow of the sun appeared on the horizon of the Caribbean Sea, creating a natural sereneness and beauty across the water.

He noticed a growing number of hotel room lights being switched on and increasing noise as staff arrived to begin preparing for work.

Then he was alerted to children's voices in the distance, getting louder and approaching the poolside, probably for an early morning swim.

Hearing the laughter and squealing made him feel optimistic, accepting that others were happy and enjoying their holiday, but the pleasant thoughts shattered when hearing the familiar father's voice warn the children. 'Stay close children, the hobo was back at the poolside.'

Jack shook his head and rolling his eyes, muttered quietly, 'Give me a bloody break, it's him again,' then stood, shouldered his bag and walked along the poolside just as the father and two children appeared and were walking towards him.

The father suddenly stopped and pulled his children close as he approached. He was shaking and looked terrified as if Jack was about to do or say something unpleasant but instead, gave a cheeky wink and smiled. The children smiled and giggled, watching him walk through the palm trees away from the poolside and towards Cancún city.

Thirty minutes later, the sun's rays had gained strength, and sweating, he entered the coach station, walking around the tarmac parking area and attempting to identify the vehicle that had brought him to this place two days earlier.

Several coaches were either arriving or parked, engines running, exhaust fumes bellowing and ready to depart the station.

Then he recognised the coach that had brought him to Cancún and felt his heart begin to quicken with excitement.

The sense of contentment was almost overwhelming and only self-respect prevented him from running to the doors and hugging the driver.

1 2

The exit is usually where the entrance was

Stanisław Jerzy Lec

Impatient and annoying tapping on the glass door caught the driver's attention who opened the pneumatic doors with a hissing sound, Jack eagerly stepped onto the coach, smiling broadly, and the driver winked in return.

He felt an enormous sense of relief and he ambled along the aisle, hoping to would see his friends already preparing for their seven-hour return journey to Belize.

Noticing that there were a few, but not as many passengers as those who had arrived in Cancún, he was disappointed when he saw the back seats vacant. Nevertheless, he reached the rear row, threw his bag onto a luggage shelf, and slumped down in a window seat.

Looking through the window, his eyes darted around the station terminal, hoping to recognise one of his friends every time he saw someone on the concourse.

He looked at the clock at the front of the vehicle; it was already 8.10 am and hoped his friends would arrive soon, then began feeling anxious when he heard the engine roar, and the coach began to vibrate. He heard the air conditioning unit whine above his head as it kicked to life, a cool draught wafting around the cabin.

'*Está arreglado*, it is fixed,' the driver shouted to the passengers, smiling into the rear-view mirror.

Over the next twenty minutes, more than a dozen passengers boarded, and the driver began to walk up the aisle checking passenger names against his list.

Jack was becoming increasingly uneasy and began to accept that he may be returning to Belize without the others. Then the doors hissed open and to his utter relief, saw Gareth and Lewis step onto the coach.

A noticeable, collective moan from the passengers as the Welshman called out, 'Don't worry, boys and girls; we just made it in time!'

Both soldiers made their way down the aisle, squeezing past the driver, who fell onto the lap of an elderly lady. Lewis helped him back to his feet then joined Gareth, hugging Jack in the back row.

As well as being unshaven and smelling of stale alcohol, their clothes, the same he had last seen them wearing, were dirty and soiled and like him, they appeared exhausted and drained.

'Where the hell did you two vagrants spend the night? You look terrible,' Jack asked, conscious of his own grubby appearance. 'I'm so glad you made it; for a while, I thought I was going back alone.'

'We nearly didn't, we got so drunk last night, we woke up this morning in a gutter, you see,' Gareth said smiling.

The engine accelerated, and they settled in their seats to prepare for the long journey home as the doors hissed closed, followed by a grating noise as the driver engaged the gears, about to leave.

'Wait a minute, where's Stan,' Jack asked, perplexed.

'We thought he might be with you; didn't you meet up outside the prison truck?' Lewis asked.

'No,' he said, staring back.

Then the engine noise reduced to an idling purr, and the doors hissed open again. Stan stepped into the Coach.

Almost unrecognisable, the three soldiers stared in disbelief at his remarkable appearance. Throwing an exaggerated wink towards the driver, Stan strutted along the aisle, smiling at passengers as he passed each row.

He wore a clean white shirt with the words '*Life's a beach in Cancún*' printed across the chest, his hair appeared recently washed and trimmed, a pair of ray-ban sunglasses propped on his head, the only item out of character was the dirty and crumpled backpack hanging by a strap from his shoulder.

Stan continued to saunter along the aisle, then, placing two fingers to his lips, blew a kiss towards the old lady the driver had earlier fallen on.

The passengers erupted into laughter when she blushed and blew a kiss in return, then reached out into the aisle, stroking his leg when he squeezed past her. The comedy ended when he made it to his friends, smiling.

The lingering essence of strong aftershave drifting around the cabin, aided by a draught from the air conditioning.

'Jeez guys, you smell like you slept in a toilet last night,' Stan said, disapprovingly.

Gears scrapped and engaged, and the coach engine roared, then lurched forward beginning its seven-hour epic journey to Belize, as Stan stumbled ungracefully falling onto Lewis.

Stan stowed his backpack saying that he was eager to tell them how he had spent his time. Jack thought it was obvious if anyone had an interesting story to tell of their past twenty-four hours, Stan's appearance and apparel indicated it was something worthy of being listened to.

Gareth and Lewis were content to relax following their alcohol-fuelled venture, while Jack didn't feel it necessary to explain the details of his own unmitigated ordeal.

They remained quiet, allowing Stan to chatter excitedly, until the sound of police sirens wailed nearby and, worse, the coach began to slow down.

Nervously, he watched the police car, displaying flashing blue lights, drive alongside the coach; he turned back to look at his friends and saw that Lewis was crouching in the footwell, while Gareth had pulled his shirt over his head in a comical attempt to hide his face.

With absolute dread, he thought the police were possibly looking for Gareth and Lewis, who had, in all probability, been misbehaving the evening before.

Turning back to the window he watched the police car accelerate and disappear into a side street, and then the speed of the coach, along with other traffic, increased.

Sighing with relief, he looked at Stan, who was still babbling away, oblivious to what had just taken place.

'It's gone, for a minute, I thought it was for us,' Jack said as Lewis stood from the floor and settled into his seat and Gareth pulled his shirt from his head.

Unsurprisingly, his friends no longer appeared tired and had become alert and conscious of their surroundings and unexpectedly Stan's encounter seemed remarkably more interesting than sleeping, at least for now.

He began by describing the events after walking through the police truck doors, ready to descend the metal steps.

One of the officers had slammed the metal doors closed while the second waited for him, baton in hand. As he stepped onto the tarmac, the obese officer swung his baton upwards and brought it down towards his shoulder, screaming, he held his backpack forward; the baton struck the bag.

Then twisting around, he watched the second officer swing his baton but, ducking low, found himself under the steps. The baton hit the metal, the impact resulting in vibration shock, causing the officer to shout out in pain. The officers seemed confused and disorientated, which gave him time and allowed him to crawl on his hands and knees, dragging his backpack behind him, and under the truck to the front end, then standing, ran as fast as possible in the direction of the city lights.

He ran for a long time and only until he gasped for breath, eventually finding himself walking along private beaches in front of hotels. He walked fast, continually checking that the police were not following, and then came across a grassed embankment with a cluster of bushes.

Crawling into the foliage, and allowing himself to be completely concealed, he used his backpack as a pillow and rested.

He recalled seeing the sun rising over the sea to the east but that didn't stop him from falling asleep, the bushes concealing and providing much-needed shade from the sun.

When he woke, the sun was high in the sky and feeling hot, sweat-soaked and incredibly thirsty, he crawled out of the hiding place, then walked in the direction he had come in the hope of finding his friends.

The sun was hot, and his sodden shirt clung to him with sweat, he removed it, tucking it into the waistband of his shorts. After a while, he saw a very lavish hotel; it was different from the others because of its opulent Art Deco styling and watched staff, wearing uniforms, attending to guests lounging around the pool. The hotel sign confirmed it was the Ritz-Carlton which he knew was one of the best and most expensive hotels in Cancún, evident by the appearance of the people sitting on the loungers, only the wealthiest could afford to stay there.

He walked along the hotel's private beach and was about to reach the boundary when he heard a woman's voice call out. He opened the gate to walk through, but the voice called again, this time a little louder.

'Hey, young man, I say, young man.'

Curious, he stopped and turned around. An older woman wearing a floppy sunhat and large dark glasses stood behind a waist-high wall that separated the hotel pool from the white sandy beach.

She must have been in her forties or even fifties, and was quite slim, her tanned body shapely and attractive in a tightly fitting lime green bikini with gold buckles. Her fingers flaunted numerous gold rings dotted with precious stones of varying colours.

It was clear she was calling Stan and waved to him. When she had his attention, she asked in a southern American accent.

'Young man, can you help me, please.'

Stan wasn't entirely convinced she was talking to him and looked around but there was no one else, so he walked towards her, stopping in front of the low wall.

'I've lost my wrap; it's blown over the wall and it's there, near the water. If it gets wet, it will be ruined; it's pure silk,' she said, sounding distressed.

Understanding she was asking him to get it for her, he walked to the water's edge as the sea gently trickled closer to the colourful silk wrap. Then lifted it and held it to his nose, smelling perfume; probably expensive he thought.

'Oh, thank you so much, young man; I must give you a well-deserved reward.'

Stan replied, 'Oh, it's all right, lady, don't worry about it.'

Then he saw her raise her sunglasses and smile as she looked at his trim waist and toned stomach.

'Oh, good God, do you work out? You are British, aren't you? I love the British accent and adore your Royal Family.'

She paused, causing him to feel slightly uncomfortable and self-conscious when her eyes glanced at his torso again.

Stan walked to the wall and handed the wrap to her; she smiled a little too adoringly, pausing before taking it from him.

'You simply must allow me to reward you properly, young man; the least I can do is get you a drink, follow me, and we shall drink together.'

She wasn't going to accept rejection, then turned and walked towards the hotel outdoor terrace whilst wrapping the silk material around her shoulders.

Stan paused when Lewis began annoyingly patting his head, Jack laughed and Gareth winked at him.

Knocking Lewis's hand away, combed his hair with his fingers then continued.

Stepping over the low wall onto the terrace he saw the woman talking to a waiter who was holding a tray of drinks.

She then walked to a set of lounger chairs and a table he

guessed she had been sitting at earlier, a classy, branded hand-bag on the tiled floor under the table, and without looking at him, settled into a lounger.

'Now you just come here and sit, young man, real close, and tell me all about England and all your adventures in Mexico.'

The waiter set two colourful cocktails on the table with small bowls of olives and pastries and Stan walked to a lounger opposite her and was about to sit down, he was startled when she said, 'Don't you dare sit over there; you get your butt in this chair,' patting a seat very close to her with her hand.

'You have been my hero today, and I want to know everything about you; now, what is your name, young man?' Then without allowing him to reply, she continued to speak as if not listening, or caring.

'Now you drink your cocktail, sweetie and let's toast you being the hero and saving my lovely silk wrap, it's a genuine Belmond you know.'

The glasses chinked, and he drank greedily through dry lips, cringing slightly when the rum stung his throat, then realising he was hungry when he felt his stomach rumble, reached over and took several olives from the bowl, sat back, relaxed and listened to his new female friend.

'Well, my name is Chrissie, young man, and I am from the state of Louisiana in the great U.S. of A, if you didn't guess already from my accent,' pausing, then called, 'waiter, waiter, fetch us two glasses of Dom Perignon; oh, just bring a bottle please.'

She didn't attempt to look at the hotel waiter as if expecting him to be present and waiting for her every demand.

179

Fortunately, he was and turning, disappeared into the hotel to deal with her request.

Chrissie asked if he was staying in the same hotel and what his plans were for the next few days. He was relieved when the waiter interrupted before he could reply, giving him a little more time to think about what to say.

The waiter placed two Champagne flutes on the table and struggled to pull the cork from the odd-shaped bottle, a loud 'pop' sounded. Chrissie squealed and giggled when the flutes were filled with the fizzy liquid.

'Come now, a spunky young man like you must have had a lot of fun here; please tell me, I promise I'm not shy and won't be too embarrassed.'

He felt a little too comfortable, the alcohol making him feel lightheaded and tipsy. The whole experience relaxed him, and the drink and snacks were free; why would he want to be elsewhere anyway? He thought, and it wasn't as if he had somewhere else to go.

He remembered what Lewis had said about older American women and looked at Chrissie; he thought she was old enough to be his mother. Taking a deep breath, he leaned forward, picked up the champagne flute and took a long drink then sat back in the chair.

'Well,' he replied, 'as you have been so kind, I'm going to tell you something that may find disturbing.'

Chrissie shrieked and sat upright in her chair, clapping her hands excitedly. 'Waiter, waiter, quickly bring more hors d'oeuvres,' she shouted, eager to hear his exploits.

Stan told her everything from the long journey from Belize to Cancún, the pirate ship, discovering their passports and money stolen at the hostel, the police beatings, being held captive in the prison truck and the escape then how he had found his way along the beach.

During the entire account, she continually laughed, gasped, frowned, and occasionally shrieked, moving around in her chair and waving her arms with animated excitement.

'Oh, my goodness,' she said and clasped her face with both hands, 'waiter, waiter,' she shouted, 'please recharge our glasses.'

The irritated waiter shuffled over and poured more champagne.

'Oh, you are a poor dear; please remind me of your name?'

Then she reached over and provocatively stroked his thigh with a finger sending a slight tremor up his spine. He began to say his name, but she interrupted, seemingly uninterested.

'My dear, this is one of the best days of my life; I simply adore English Soldiers; you are so brave, oh I can't believe my luck finding you. I am so happy; fortune has certainly walked into my life today.'

His flow was interrupted when Lewis spoke suddenly bringing him back into the coach. 'I told you when we were in that bar, remember what I said about Yankee ladies in Cancún? They love British accents and are always up for a little bit of red velvet treatment while on holiday away from the old man. Did you tell her you had met the Queen? I bet you did?'

They all looked at Stan, waiting for a reaction; he smiled and winked.

'You did, didn't you? You little babe magnet Stan, and top marks for taking my advice,' Lewis said, slapping him on the shoulder.

Stan continued, 'So, then she began to tell me about herself and said she was in Cancún on holiday. She came to the same hotel every year, initially with her husband, but had divorced ten years earlier, so now travelled with a friend whom she said was her companion, no, consort, I'm sure she said consort or something.

'She wasn't in a relationship; he was just a guy she hung out with on holiday. His name was Bertie, and she said she would get him to join us so I could meet him.'

'What kind of boyfriend is he,' Gareth interrupted.

'No, not like a boyfriend; they weren't in a relationship or having, you know, sex or anything; they were just friends.' Stan said, continuing with his account.

'I've got it!' Chrissie laughed and put her hand on his arm, stroking, and causing a nervous tremble,

He was already feeling the effects of the alcohol, and Chrissie was slurring, not surprisingly after all the champagne she had drunk, he guessed.

'I've thought of your reward for saving my wrap; After all, you have been through, I can get you some new clothes at the Plaza Caracul shopping centre. I will not take no for an answer, sweetie; it's all decided; we are going shopping. Now you wait here and finish your drink; I'm going to freshen up and will be right back with Bertie. You must promise to be here when I return; I won't be a minute, sweetie.'

Standing up from her chair and taking her handbag, she kissed two fingers, leaned forward and gently placed the moist fingers on his lips; he tasted lipstick.

He watched as she turned, wobbled, almost lost her balance, stood straight again, and then stumbled through the hotel doors, supporting herself by holding the door frame.

'Wow,' Jack said, 'what an amazing story Stan, that's incredible, so what happened next?'

'Well,' Stan continued, 'I just sat there, ordered a beer and some more snacks on her room bill and then twenty minutes later, she was back, all dressed up with some guy I guessed was Bertie.

'The first thing I noticed about him was that he was properly grumpy and acted as if I shouldn't be there or talking to Chrissie.'

'He's a gold digger,' Lewis interrupted.

'So, I followed them through the hotel, and a cab was waiting for us at the front. They got in the back and told me to sit next to the driver, and then we went to the shopping centre.

'First, she made me go to the hairdresser and told me to have my hair cut and styled. Then, I had to go to the men's clothing store and was told to choose anything I wanted.

'She pointed out a shirt and jeans, insisting she would pay, which was just as well because I only had the money Lewis gave me in the prison truck. All the time, Bertie never said a word; he just stood with folded arms and a sour face as if, at some point, he would find his moment and tell me to bugger off.

'Anyway, we visited a few shops, and she bought a new handbag and perfume then afterwards, some sunglasses and aftershave for me.

'Then in the late afternoon, we got in a cab and returned to the hotel. Bertie disappeared to his room while I sat with Chrissie in the lounge, and she ordered coffee and sandwiches. I just laughed and was enjoying listening to Chrissie, telling me how fantastic America is and how good they are at everything.

'Later, Bertie returned with the same grouchy face; he was

wearing different clothes and told Chrissie to go to her room and get changed for dinner. When she left, he sat with me but didn't say a thing; just ordered himself a scotch whisky and stared around the room.

'I asked him a couple of questions, but he ignored me. Then a short time later, Chrissie returned, she seemed really drunk and was wearing a different frock.

'We were shown to the table in the restaurant; I couldn't believe it; three waiters just for us. The courses kept coming, one after the other, we had wine and champagne, Bertie just sat there, like a wet fish, the whole time, passing a few comments to Chrissie but ignoring me as if I was invisible.

'After dessert, we went to the bar, and Chrissie ordered Cuban cigars and Whisky for Bertie and me.

'Anyway, it was late and getting dark, and I said to her, I've had a great day, but I'm a bit drunk now, so I am off to sleep under a bush for the night, but Chrissie insisted that I spend the night in her room with her.'

Gareth immediately became excited. 'Here we go, boys, here we go,' throwing his arms around Lewis and Jack, 'he's going to tell us the best bit now!'

Stan continued, 'I repeated that I would be fine sleeping outside, but Chrissie refused and insisted that she would not allow me to sleep on the streets and because I had been such a hero, demanded that I was to stay with her for the night.

'Then she told Bertie to go and prepare the bed settee in the lounge in her room. Bertie wasn't happy with that; I could see his face crease up, and he gave me a proper stare, but she shooed him away to go to her room and make up the bed, so he did.

'When he left, she told me that Bertie was jealous whenever she entertained a new man but would get over it. He had a room to himself which she had paid for, and it wasn't as if they were married or anything.'

'Come on, boyo, what happened next? Did you give her one? Did Bertie join you for a threesome?' Gareth excitedly asked.

Stan ignored him 'She ordered me a brandy saying it would help to digest my dinner, and then I followed her to her room, a huge place it was, and had a separate furnished lounge. Anyway, the settee had been made into a bed, and while I sat on the bed, Chrissie went to the bathroom, got undressed, and came out wearing a slinky nightdress.

'She walked over to me, I got nervous, and I think she noticed it, then gave me a sloppy kiss on the cheek and thanked me for being a hero and giving her a lovely day, then walked to her bed, climbed in, and fell asleep and within seconds, started snoring her head off.

'I went to the bathroom, showered, shaved, and brushed my teeth, all courtesy of hotel extras, then wearing a hotel bathrobe, climbed into the clean sheets of the bed settee.

'The next thing I know, I was awake and it was light outside; Chrissie was still asleep and snoring, I didn't know what time it was, but knew I needed to get to the coach station.

'I quietly dressed into my new clothes, sneaked out of the hotel room, and then ran to the station; the coach was about to leave when I got here.'

There was no reaction after he had finished talking, then Lewis began to laugh and said, 'Wink, wink Stan, we know what really happened; you can tell us the truth over a beer later.'

He replied, 'In your sordid dreams Lewis, it's what you wish happened; not everyone is as vulgar as you.'

Jack laughed and said, 'Glad you had a good day mate; for a while, I thought something terrible had happened to you; I'm just relieved we are all safe and on our way home.'

Stan gave an appreciating smile.

Suddenly, as though someone had flicked an imaginary sleeping switch, they moved around in their seats, trying more comfortable positions.

Nothing further was said as Gareth and Lewis tried to sleep. Jack and Stan stared through the window, watching the scenery as the vehicle trundled through Mexican states and municipalities and continued the long and exhausting journey towards the Belizean border.

In the furthest reaches of their imagination, the soldiers would never have predicted that someone so intensely sadistic and homicidal was planning their painful and agonising death on their return to Belize.

13

Hate traps us by binding us too tightly to our adversary

Milan Kundera

Having to stay at Baptiste's shack for even a few days made Mikel bored and restless; his endurance was waning, and he began to wonder if the soldiers would ever return.

He would rather drink tequila and waste some of his hard-earned money in the *Mañana Añejo*, his favourite brothel. His girlfriend, Anjeli, knew he visited the brothel to undertake his desires, but to him, she was only convenient for washing clothes and preparing food during the rare times he visited.

Like many men in Belize, for lust, the *Piruja* brothel girls were preferred over wives and girlfriends. Anyway, his *Piruja* was much prettier than Anjeli who he knew enjoyed the generous money he gave her, in return for her loyalty.

Sighing, he thought of where he would rather be instead of Baptiste's shack, although understood the importance of their presence and the obsession that preoccupied Satan.

His thoughts of the brothel disappeared when the hen he had been slowly stalking stopped, its head buried in wing feathers, trying to peck at the annoyance of a mite.

Moving quickly, he quickly grabbed the unsuspecting bird and, turning it, gripped the legs, then walked to a chopping tree block, smiling at his achievement.

Placing the hen on the block, he put his foot on its upper body close to the neck while its wings frantically flapped, the creature sickeningly squawking as if knowing what was about to happen.

He pulled the machete from his belt and swung the razor-sharp blade down with a single movement, completely severing the head from the body, then watched, curiously, as the head slipped from the block, followed by blood spurting from the neck cavity.

Two hens approached and began pecking hungrily at the lifeless eyes and gaping neck. It disgusted him when they did that. It just didn't seem right that they ate their own kind.

He plunged the headless hen into a pan of hot water he had earlier placed on the porch, waited, then removed it from the water, and began pulling feathers from the sodden body.

Becoming disinterested, and before completely plucking, he slit the stomach open and removed the innards, throwing them towards the other hens to eat, then pushing a wet stick through the carcass, walked to the small fire and placed the meat on the makeshift spit to roast.

Satan appeared from the shack. 'Ah, Mikel, you are preparing our dinner for tonight?'

Mikel nodded, knowing he needed to do everything possible to keep Satan content, reducing the chance of his behaviour becoming volatile and irrational; he knew from experience that no one should be anywhere near him when he wasn't in a good state of mind.

Besides, the heroin he had seen Satan inject into his vein a few hours earlier probably heightened his placid mood, that and the smell of roasting chicken.

Satan clumsily stepped from the porch, walked to the edge of the clearing, unzipped his trousers, and urinated onto the grass, exhaling and gasping with relief. Mikel noticed that he was urinating in the same place Baptiste's lifeless body had been dragged earlier.

He recalled how difficult it had been to move Baptiste and how a human seemed more cumbersome to move when dead.

In the past, he had moved several bodies following untimely or unexpected death and learned different techniques depending on how far they had to be moved. The centre of weight always seemed imbalanced and was made worse by flopping arms, legs, and head.

Baptiste needed to be taken quite a distance, and he had used the blanket to drag him along the uneven ground; pulling a dead body in a blanket or a piece of plastic was an option he frequently preferred.

When he had dragged Baptiste's body to where it needed to be, he pulled the blanket upwards and watched the corpse roll into the grass, then folded the blanket, it would prove useful later when the night chill settled in, and anyway, Batiste would not need for it now, he was dead.

Mikel was suddenly dragged from his thoughts hearing a sickening scream and saw Satan flapping his arms while jumping up and down near the grassed area.

Pulling his machete from his belt, he ran towards his *jefe* and then became confused when Satan began to laugh uncontrollably, pointing towards the grass where he had urinated, his penis flopping from the opening of his trousers.

Mikel looked down and saw a swarm of rats feeding on

Baptiste's remains having become agitated as urine had rained down on them.

'The rats will become drowsy when they taste the heroin in Baptiste's blood and my piss,' Satan said, laughing, pushed his penis into his trousers and walked to the old Land Rover, smacking the bonnet with his clenched fist.

'Why did Baptiste keep this trash, Mikel? He once told me he could build an entire vehicle from all the junk he bought from the British soldiers.'

He unclipped the hood and pushed it upwards, then supported the heavy metal while inspecting the engine. 'Hey Mikel, come and see.'

Mikel had returned to the fire, more interested in tending to the roasting chicken but then reluctantly walked over to discover what Satan thought was so important about the old engine.

'There are many strange pieces in this, Mikel, do you think you could remove them and make our vehicle work better?' Pointing to the engine.

'I don't think so; our vehicle is too old, and they probably do not fit.'

Satan ignored him and dropping the heavy hood with a shattering crash, walked to the shack, and shouted, 'Let me know when we can eat, I am hungry, but for now, I will sleep more.' He pulled open the door and entered the shack, the door making a loud slam behind him.

Mikel knew the effects of the heroin were making Satan irritated and sluggish. Getting the chicken ready for his *jefe* to eat would help calm him; afterwards, Satan would want to sleep, leaving him alone, and he looked forward to that.

Sitting down on the porch, the pleasant smell of the cooking chicken flesh wafted around; he took a fresh marijuana joint from his inside pocket, lit it, leaned back while taking a long suck, and inhaled the musty and dank smoke.

It was not long before for the cannabis to have an effect, it was good quality, and the feeling of mental relaxation was almost instant as he watched smoke wafting from the fire and spitting chicken, swirling upwards and beginning to form into little clouds in the shape of his *Piruja*, oh, how he wanted to be with his *Piruja*.

He felt happy and then became aroused by the dancing form of his lover, then suddenly, to his horror, the swirling smoke shape changed from *Piruja* to the hideous and tormented one-eyed glare of the monstrosity he served. His empty eye socket was crudely stitched, and disgusting puss trickled down his cheek.

Very slowly and deliberately, Mikel began to tilt backwards until the back of his head touched the wooden boards, and there he lay, the smoke clearing and his thoughts gently drifting to the shocking occasion when Satan lost his eye.

He had suspected one of his couriers had been stealing money from the proceeds of his heroin distribution. Satan was outraged when he counted the takings and realised that one courier was returning less than the others, deciding to challenge the courier at his home.

He had called Mikel and told him there would be a body to dispose of and to bring another trusted lieutenant, Nardus.

Meeting outside the courier's home, Satan kicked open the door, confronting the courier, witnessed by his wife and young daughter. The old man denied stealing money, but that was not enough for Satan, ordering Mikel and Nardus to hold the man's arm across the kitchen table.

Both had shown reluctance because the man was old and sick, but Satan gave them a pernicious stare, causing them to fear that if they didn't carry out his demand, his attention would turn on them and promptly did as they were told.

The old man continued to deny stealing money and cried out for forgiveness while his wife and daughter sobbed and wailed in the kitchen corner. The mother clasped her hands over the girl's eyes, warning her not to watch what was about to be inflicted on her father.

The man gave a guttural wail and watched the machete swing down with a thud, separating his hand from the wrist. An agonising and intense pain shot up his arm, and the old man gave a sickening, gurgled moan and was released by Mikel and Nardus.

Then as if in a confused and surreal hypnotic state, he lifted his arm and examined the blood-pumping stump. Satan watched and smiled with fascination at how the blood spurted intermittently through the exposed ulnar artery. To heighten Satan's grotesque humour, the man picked up the limp greying hand from the table and held it to the bleeding stump as if trying to reconnect his hand.

The freakish yet dreadful spectacle captivated Satan and his accomplices; but no one had noticed the man's wife had left her sobbing daughter and was creeping across the kitchen holding a small kitchen knife.

Sidling up to Satan, and with one swift movement, she swung the knife into his face, the sharp blade slicing his left eyeball cleanly in two. Grey vitreous fluid mixed with blood began to pour from the socket. To her horror, Satan's reaction was not to cry out or double over in pain; incredibly, he smiled at her and, with a swift and unexpected movement, buried the machete blade into the top of her head, her body instantly falling limply to the floor, dead.

He stood on her neck to assist in easing the machete from her skull.

Meanwhile, the old man, who was howling in pain from his unexpected amputation, dropped his detached hand onto the dirt floor and, moving to his wife's body, held her lifeless head, rocking and sobbing.

Satan walked around the table, picked up the old man's hand from the floor, then approached the little girl, crouched down and held the hand towards her.

'*Hola pequeña*, your *Madre* is dead, and your *Padre* will die soon; he is bleeding to death. Your *Padre* was a thief and has crossed me, but you have been released from them now.

'You should be happy now because I can find work for you in one of my brothels; it will stop you from starving and will put much money in your pocket *niñita*.'

The girl, sobbing, looked at him, the kitchen knife still protruding from his eye socket and the remains of his eyeball, blood and grey fluid dribbling down his face.

Taking her small hand, he placed her father's hand in it and squeezed her fingers tightly around the cold limb. 'A gift to you so that you will remember me, my name is Satan,' then stood and left, followed by his two henchmen.

Outside, Satan ordered Mikel and Nardus to take him to a doctor he knew and a member of his criminal syndicate, receiving illicit drugs for his surgery.

The Doctor, without administering medication, removed the knife, which was lodged into socket bone, stuffed the cavity with sterile cotton wool, and then roughly stitched his eyelid shut and eventually, over the next few weeks, the upper and lower eyelids sealed together.

Satan refused to have the stitches removed and although making him look even more hideous, he was proud to show his injury as a warning to others who may try to steal from him.

Soon after the amputation, Mikel had established that the old man had not stolen anything, Satan had miscounted the money, but it was not something he would discuss with the *jefe*; what was done was done.

He had slept in the shack longer than he had hoped, and hunger caused him to awaken, opening his single eye, he noticed the sun was beginning to descend and accepted that it would soon become dark.

Sucking deeply through his nostrils, he winced at the acrid stench of burning flesh, then twisting off the mattress and standing, he walked to the porch.

Mikel was asleep, lying on the wooden boards and quietly snoring. He looked around and through his single eye saw that the fire was now just glowing embers, and the chicken on the spit had been left unattended, its carcass black and burned.

Enraged that his meal was spoiled, he turned to Mikel and gave him a hefty kick in his kidneys, causing him to shriek out in pain then rolled off the porch and onto the dusty ground, and lay moaning, sharp pain spreading across his lower back.

'Mikel, find me some food now!'

Mikel tried to ignore the intense pain and hurriedly scrambled to his feet. He knew the consequences of allowing Satan to become hungry and thought of what he could do to calm him, then made pathetic attempts to grab a hen as it squawked, jumped, and flapped its wings to escape capture.

Meanwhile, Satan walked to the fire and inspected the embers. He pulled the charred carcass from the spit and, using his machete, scraped the black charred flesh, then smiled when he saw the overcooked white flesh underneath, biting into the dry tasty meat.

He sat on the porch and watched the entertainment as Mikel attempted to grab a hen, only to fall ineptly to the ground.

Satan laughed loudly, pieces of chicken meat spitting and falling from his mouth.

'Mikel, I think you will go hungry tonight; the hens are more cunning than you, he laughed.

Watching Mikel prompted him to recall their purpose at the clearing and reminded him of his intense hatred for those in authority, particularly the British but especially the soldiers. The British had controlled his government for longer than he could remember, and the time had come for his people to rise and turn against them.

They had been allowed to become too powerful because Belizean politicians, the army and the police had ignored their presence to cover their own criminal activities.

British army patrols on the Guatemalan, Honduras and Mexican borders complicated and disrupted his drug and people smuggling activities which were made even more difficult on the Guatemalan border where the heroin was better quality and the purest.

If it were not for the British soldiers' presence, he would already be very wealthy. Most were already aware that the politicians and police had their own illicit drug trade with Guatemala, and it was happening under the noses of the British, who looked away in the name of colonialisation.

One day they would leave his country, enabling him to expand his business, making him wealthy, influential, and honoured by his country's pathetic and weak people.

For now, though, he would ensure the soldiers responsible for stealing his property would feel the overwhelming sensation of extreme pain for their wrongdoing.

Then his attention was caught by Mikel, lying on his back on the ground. He was exhausted and panting and had failed to capture a single bird. Satan continued to laugh and threw the chicken carcass, cleaned of meat, to the ground next to his tired lieutenant.

'Don't go hungry tonight, my friend; I have a feeling that soon we will need much energy. I think the soldiers will visit here, we must be prepared and will inflict pain and torment on them.'

Mikel turned to his side and reaching out, grabbed the bony carcass, nibbling and chewing at scraps of chicken on the bones.

'When you have finished your meal, find wood and build a fire again, I'm getting cold,' Satan demanded.

Older men declare war,
but it is the youth that must fight and die

Herbert Hoover

The soldier standing at the gate was on sentry duty and saw the headlights in the distance; it wasn't yet dark but late afternoon, and he sighed knowing there were four hours of his duty left to go before he would be relieved and was already bored.

The approaching vehicle induced mild excitement because it would mean he would have to check the identity of whoever wanted to be allowed into the base. Then if granted access, he would signal to the guardroom to raise the red and white barrier.

Doing anything was better than doing nothing, and although he detested his twelve-hour duty, understood the importance to maintain security; then mild excitement was followed by disappointment when he realised the vehicle was a civilian coach probably making a drop-off outside the base.

The vehicle stopped, and he observed four passengers step off and walk towards him as the coach, turned, then drove back towards the main road. The soldier squinted to get a better look at their appearance, three of them appeared dishevelled, unkempt, and unshaven, hardly what he expected to see if they were soldiers.

'Well,' he said quietly, 'checking the identities of this lot should be challenging,' then rubbed his hands together, thinking it could be the highlight of his day.

After passing the cursory security checks at the gate, the soldiers continued walking to their accommodation and agreed that, firstly, they would unpack, shower, change into fresh clothing, and then meet in the base Moonshine bar to discuss what Jack had planned to do about the body and the evidence in the clearing.

Gareth could barely disguise his excitement and marched at a pace ahead, eager to shower and change then head to the bar for a drink of his favourite Belikin beer.

Twenty minutes later, Jack stood in a shower, his hands against the tiled wall, head bowed and refreshing, tepid water splashed over his head and helped him relax.

He thought of the last couple of days of chaos and violence and as the water streamed over him and he gently touched the bruises and sores on his stomach, hips and legs.

His thoughts turned to their situation and the risks around what they were about to do, knowing it had been temptation which had got them into this chaos in the first place. If it had not been for the financial enticements of the enterprise, he wouldn't be in this predicament. Now he felt that it was his duty to find a way out of the crisis and prevent their illicit activities from being discovered. After all, if they pull it off, it would potentially make them all quite wealthy. The others will depend on him to deliver a plan; they always did.

Understanding that since Gareth had last visited the shack, a few days earlier, the situation may have changed, and things could be less straightforward if someone else has been to the clearing and discovered the body.

For all he knew the whole place could be a crime scene crawling with police, examining the body, removing evidence and looking for suspects, but then he doubted the police in Belize were actually all that smart.

Hopefully, everything would still be undiscovered, after all, there was no suggestion that anyone frequently visited Baptiste.

Gareth had said, on a previous visit, he had seen someone in the shack, but he couldn't be sure. Any visit they intended to make, would have to be carried out with extreme caution should someone have discovered the body and were waiting at the shack.

The friends gathered around an unassuming table in the corner of the Moonshine bar, making it difficult for other customers to overhear their hushed conversation.

Stan, who had not spent any of his share of the money he had received before leaving the prison truck, paid for the drinks.

When the four soldiers were seated, each with a glass of rum and coke, Lewis raised his glass, and they followed, chinking their glasses together and drinking.

Lewis wanted to be the first to make an announcement, 'Whatever happens after tonight, we must never share it with anyone and has to remain our secret; we cannot allow anyone to know about the enterprise or what we are about to do, agreed?' he said almost solemnly.

They all agreed, then fell silent as Jack irritatingly felt their eyes looking at him, waiting for him to explain the details of what he had planned. He finished what was left in his glass, refilled it, and taking a large drink, began.

Firstly, he insisted they should understand that the priority was to destroy all evidence linking them to the clearing, which would include, if not already discovered, Baptiste's body, to which they all agreed.

Then said extracting the money would be secondary to the destruction of the evidence, and must not be their main focus, again they agreed.

Stan quietly asked, I'm not quite sure we should be doing this, Jack, I mean, it's pretty serious coving up murder; it was Gareth who killed Baptiste, if we destroy the evidence, aren't we all implicated?'

Gareth moaned loudly and began to rub his forehead.

Jack placed his glass on the table firmly, trying not to appear angry. 'No one has been murdered, Stan. Baptiste killed himself because he overdosed on drugs; Gareth tried to save him, the drugs killed him!'

'What is crucial to remember is that we have all been there and are all implicated in selling army equipment, our fingerprints are all over the place. So, if Gareth goes down, we all go down, don't ever forget that. We must work as a team; do you understand?' he waited for Stan to agree.

Lewis spoke before Stan could answer, 'I think we all understand that, Jack; so can we get to the detail please? If we do get our hands on the money and drugs, we can hardly bring it through the base security, can we?'

Jack topped up all their empty glasses, then explained that after the briefing, they were to leave the bar separately and meet at the rear of the radio store, there they would collect all the equipment that they would need to destroy everything in the clearing and load it into the Land Rover that evening and ready for an early start in the morning.

He specified what was to be loaded into the vehicle, including four cans of petrol to burn the evidence, body and buildings, a lighter for the fire, rags to assist the fire, an ammunition box to secure the money and two machetes should they be confronted by anyone unexpectantly.

'You have obviously spent a lot of your time thinking this through Jack,' Lewis said, 'but I have a question; you mention burning the parts with petrol, some of them are metal, the generators for example, how will petrol destroy those?'

He curtly replied 'Firstly, whilst you and Gareth were enjoying yourselves during your last night in Cancún getting drunk and sleeping in a gutter; along with being robbed at knifepoint by a hideous drug addict, I used my time trying to work out how we all get out of this dilemma.

'Secondly, we will spread as much petrol as we possibly can, with enough, it will be a raging inferno, assisted by the pile of rubber tyres and wooden buildings.

Although the charred remains may be recognisable afterwards, there will be no way of identifying the serial numbers and if ever discovered, they will be assumed to be parts that have been previously stolen from military vehicles parked in the city.'

'Why only two machetes Jack?' Stan asked.

'That is because tomorrow, and you may be pleased to know, only Gareth and I will be going to the clearing, you and Lewis you have another important role back here at the base which I will explain.'

Lewis exhaled noisily, seemingly relieved and attracted their attention.

'What's wrong with Lewis,' Gareth asked, 'are you too scared to go down there anymore?'

Lewis remained silent, and Jack continued, 'Gareth and I will meet at the radio store at 7 am tomorrow morning, and I expect the whole round trip to the clearing will take about three hours, so should return here at about 10 am. We need you two to be waiting for us near the Royal Engineer's disused fuel tank, at the top end of the base.'

'I don't understand why we have to wait for you at the old fuel tank, am I missing something?' Lewis queried.

'If you had ever been in the guardroom, you would know there are no security cameras along that part of the perimeter fence, it is also the lowest part of the boundary,' Jack replied, then continued to outline the plan.

On return from the clearing, Gareth would drive the vehicle around the perimeter fence adjacent to the fuel tank. They would then throw the ammunition box containing the money and drugs over the boundary fence where Stan and Lewis would be waiting to catch it and would take it to the radio store office, remove the contents and secure it all in the Chubb safe.

Gareth would drive the vehicle to the front gate and pass through security without having anything suspicious or incriminating should the vehicle be searched.

'That's it guys, I know it sounds simple and straightforward, but things may present themselves differently when we get down there, if they do, Gareth and I will deal with whatever we find. Do you all understand and are there any questions?'

Lewis was first to ask, 'What if someone has been there already and the body has gone?'

'Good question Lewis; we recover the money and drugs but still burn the evidence if that is possible.'

Gareth's turn. 'What if the police are there when we arrive?'

'Let's all hope it has not come to that yet, Gareth,' he replied, 'hopefully when we get there in the morning, it is still undiscovered, and we continue with the plan and can get away with a great deal of money.'

Stan asked, 'You didn't mention any communication. Are you going to take a radio set so we can contact you, especially if something goes wrong and you need assistance?'

'I already thought about that Stan,' he replied, 'we have to do this in strict radio silence; we can't afford radio transmissions to be picked up, this is our secret, so no radios.'

Looking around at his friends and with no more questions he finished by saying 'Okay, then I suggest we finish our drinks and leave a few minutes apart then meet at the store. It's crucially important we get this right, and if all goes to plan, tomorrow night, I will be buying the drinks in here.'

Standing, he left the bar and headed for the radio store.

An hour later, they had finished loading the Land Rover with all the equipment, satisfied everything was set for the morning. Jack locked the store and joined the others standing outside the front of the Nissan hut.

Gareth said, 'That's it guys, you won't see us two until we get back at about mid-morning tomorrow so make sure you are waiting at the fuel tank when we return.'

'Don't be late,' Stan replied, 'I'll be paying for the bacon sandwiches at the Moonshine bar when you get back.'

Initially, Jack was about to shake Stan's hand but it became a hug, they all followed and did the same, understanding that a certain, "brothers in arms" comradeship developed between soldiers in the same team just before going into battle, this seemed no different.

They quietly walked together to the soldier's accommodation, knowing they would probably all suffer a nervous, sweat-soaked and troubled sleep that night.

Today is the most important day of our lives

Nhat Hanh

Early morning calls from an abundance of howling monkeys and chirping insects woke Mikel from a deep sleep. Wincing, he touched his aching back and hips, recalling the painful kick to the area of his kidney.

He felt cold, noticing the blanket had slipped away and lay abandoned on the porch.

Turning on his side, he looked at the trees where the untamed lived and watched the morning mist permeating the lower parts of the vegetation.

He was morose and thought too many days and nights had already been wasted. Incensed that Satan was too stubborn about remaining until the soldiers or anyone else for that matter, visited the clearing. He was becoming increasingly anxious about being alone with the sociopath whose mood had become increasingly irrational and unstable.

Satan could be psychotic on a good day. It wouldn't take much for him to quickly deteriorate and become deviant and murderous when troubled, intensified by his determination to exact revenge on those he seemed convinced had killed his cousin and stolen his drugs.

Then became aware of his *jefe's* presence when the door swung open. Satan stepped onto the porch, stretched and yawned then jumped from the low elevation and walked to the water barrel, bent forward, his head disappearing into the algae-imbued water.

Mikel assumed the water would be putrid and infested with mosquito larvae, then watched as Satan's head reappeared, swinging from side to side, spraying water droplets and other debris in all directions.

Wiping water from his face, he said, 'Ah, Mikel, today is a good day; I can feel it,' then walked into the shack and ordered his lieutenant to follow.

Climbing to his feet, and ignoring the pain in his side, Mikel dutifully followed his *jefe* through the doorway, then stopped and watched as Satan approached the machete-damaged wall at the head of the mattress.

Using the tip of his machete, he began to score and etch words into the wooden wall, Mikel watched.

'I am leaving them a message, my friend; when they arrive, it is polite to let them know their fate, I will allow them to see.'

Satan continued to scratch his message into the wooden planks, as Mikel frowned, accepting his *jefe* was becoming increasingly dangerous and was beginning to lose self-control. Cutting a message into the wall was meaningless and futile, they had been there three days already; no one would be visiting the shack.

He wanted to make Satan understand that the money and drugs had gone forever but knew if he tried to tell him, he would almost certainly go into a meltdown and become even more malevolent and decided to let him work it out for himself.

Satan finished etching his message then stuck his machete into the wall, walked across the room, slamming the door as he left.

Mikel knew his *jefe* would adopt the same position he had since they had arrived, sitting on the porch, carefully listening for the sound of an approaching vehicle.

Waiting for the soldiers constantly dominating and preoccupying him, only hunger, sleep or the need to take heroin disturbed his daily pattern.

Squinting, he stared at the words etched into the wall and when realising their meaning, rolled his eyes and shrugged at the absurdity of it all, then left the room to join his *jefe* to offer him a reefer.

At that very moment, Gareth slowed and steered the vehicle from the main road, causing it to bounce and jolt onto the uneven track leading to Baptiste's shack; he had visited enough times to realise that it would take no more than ten minutes to reach the clearing.

Jack held his seat belt with one hand and gripped the door handle with the other in a vain attempt to prevent being thrown around in his seat.

As the vehicle bounced, he suddenly remembered the jerry cans that had been placed in the rear and glancing over his shoulder, saw them sliding around.

He shouted above the noise of the whining and revving engine.

'Slow down, Gareth, I'm uneasy about the jerry cans moving around in the back. Anyway, remember when we get to the clearing, if anything is different from when you were last there, we turn around and get out fast, okay?'

Gareth gave him a quick glance and nodded while gripping the steering wheel, attempting to gain control as the vehicle jolted along the track, dangerously close to the swollen river.

Satan sucked deeply on the long joint, taking a prolonged and deep inhalation, then slowly exhaled thick blue smoke simultaneously through his nostrils and mouth.

Meanwhile, Mikel stepped off the porch and gently kicked the fire ashes in the hope of finding a piece of uneaten chicken meat.

Then, he stopped and listened.

He wasn't sure if the whining and droning noise in the distance was the sound of an approaching vehicle; he looked at Satan, who was also standing motionless, hand raised to indicate that they should both be still and listen.

Satan said, in a hushed voice, as if trying to avoid someone overhearing, 'You can hear it too, Mikel? It's them; it's them, I know it is; they have come, now let us do what we have rehearsed for so many days!'

Satan ran into the shack, pulled his machete from the wall and returned to the porch, then taking his handgun from his waistband, checked it was loaded, jumped from the porch and joined Mikel, who was spreading ashes across the ground trying to conceal evidence of the fire.

Both men ran around the side of the shack, hunching down behind a rusting oil barrel and adjusted their posture to get the best view of the clearing entrance.

The sound became more distinct and recognisable, convincing them both it was almost certainly a vehicle approaching; Mikel saw droplets of sweat running down Satan's face, dripping into the dust and noticed he was trembling, presumably from being super excited that his snare was set and waiting for the kill.

Satan had talked of this moment so many times since they had arrived; he planned to wait until the soldiers were in the open and vulnerable, then surprise them and, using their machetes, hurt but not kill them until they said where the money and drugs were. Then would enjoy torturing them.

The morning sunlight delicately lit up the clearing, creating grey and green shadows as the light bounced off the slow-flowing river and shiny foliage and vines dangling above the two soldiers.

The vehicle rocked gently as Gareth negotiated the gears and expertly slowed its pace, almost stalling, to walking speed, then eventually stopping the large chunk of iron in the middle of the clearing, enough for them to get a good view around the open space and shack.

Jack whispered, 'Switch off the engine so we can listen.'

Gareth did as asked, and both sat quietly, looking and listening for anything different or unusual that would prompt them to drive away hurriedly.

Jack spoke again, 'Have you noticed anything, Gareth? If there is anything that you are not happy with, we are not going in; we just leave, okay.'

Both the soldiers' eyes searched the clearing looking for something that was not quite right or any unusual movement, anything out of place.

Jack reached over and gently touched his friend's forearm without taking his eyes from the shack.

'Let's just slowly turn the Land Rover around, facing the track, just in case we have to make a quick exit.'

Slowly manoeuvring a wide turning circle so that the front of the vehicle was facing away from the shack, Gareth reversed a little, stopping the vehicle in the middle of the clearing and switched off the engine.

After observing for a full five minutes, neither moved nor said anything. They just concentrated on any unusual sounds or movements in the clearing, shack, and chicken shed, using the large wing mirrors to observe the area behind them.

When he thought it safe, Jack said, 'Does everything look the same as when you were last here Gareth, yes?'

Gareth nodded, then said, 'Except for the hens, they were hiding in the shed.'

Jack had already briefed Gareth during the journey but decided to cover the main points again. He wanted him to complete his tasks as quickly as possible; they were both uncomfortable and nervous.

He reminded him that when they leave their Land Rover, he was to assist Jack in carrying the jerry cans to the shack, then return to the vehicle, remove the ammunition box and take it to the old Land Rover bonnet, and it would be his responsibility to extract the drugs and money, place them into the box and return it to their vehicle, while Jack poured petrol around the shack, soaking Baptiste's body.

When that was complete, together, they would pour the remainder of the petrol over the chicken shed, Land Rover bonnet, vehicle parts and tyres.

Gareth would drive their Land Rover and park it near the exit track while he ignited the petrol using the rags and then run to the vehicle and both leave the clearing.

He noticed that Gareth had begun to tremble and sweat dripped from the tip of his nose. 'There's no reason for you to go inside the shack, don't worry, I can do this, you stay in the vehicle for now.'

Gareth looked at Jack, his face pale and said, 'No corporal, I need to see him one last time, just to make sure he is dead. That's if you don't mind.'

He nodded and indicated they should get on with it, and climbing from the cab, quietly walked to the rear of the Land Rover, watching and listening.

The tailgate was dropped, and four jerry cans were removed. The metal cans were heavy, petrol sloshing noisily as they were slung to the ground.

Taking one can each, they slowly walked towards the shack, carefully placing the first two on the porch, then, without speaking, returned to the vehicle. At the same time, Gareth extracted the ammunition box from the rear, and Jack opened the passenger side door, removing two machetes.

Gareth put the ammunition box on the ground and Jack handed him a machete, watching him push it into his trouser waist, he did the same, and then both walked to the shack.

As they stood on the porch, Jack quietly asked, 'Are you ready for this mate?'

Gareth nodded, Jack pulled open the door, and they entered.

Mikel and Satan had remained crouched in silence behind the oil barrel; the soldiers had done precisely as Satan had hoped and were nearing the centre of his spider's web, he was enthusiastic to get on with it.

It was going to be an exciting day, he thought, feeling himself trembling, something he always experienced when someone was about to die.

He had curiously observed the two men awkwardly carry the fuel cans to the shack and then watched the big man remove a metal box from the rear of his vehicle, then saw the glint of shiny metal caught by the sun when the smaller soldier removed the machetes.

It pleased Satan that the soldiers had brought weapons and knew how easy it was to overcome weak men and watch the pain and anguish on their faces when removing their weapons from them.

He had become excited when recognising the tall, burly one with the hair on his lip and whom he recalled had visited Baptiste before. The small one he had never seen, and he had no concern for either of them; they would both feel the pain of his vengeance.

Both would be held responsible for stealing his money and killing his cousin, and he was not in the mood for showing any mercy. He thought they would now have seen that Baptiste's body had been removed and would be reading the message carved into the wall, setting the scene for the impending blood-bath and carnage he was about to discharge on the thieving soldiers.

Turning to Mikel, he instructed him to capture the small soldier whilst he secured the tall one.

'Do not kill him until I say so, Mikel; I want to make them tell me where my drugs are, and then we will make them weep for their mothers, do you understand?'

Mikel warily nodded and tensed himself in preparation for the signal.

It's better to die on one's feet than live on one's knees

Emiliano Zapata

Jack, followed by his friend, stepped slowly to the middle of the room, his hand firmly and reassuringly gripping the handle of his machete.

The repugnant smell of decay and rot was overpowering, both men placing a hand over their nose and mouth as if applying a mask, hoping it might shield them from the stench. It smelled of a mixture of faeces, vinegar and mould, burning their throat and nostrils.

Chicken bones littered the floor and were on most surfaces; Jack's mind raced, attempting to work out why it didn't make sense.

Then when he realised Baptiste's body was not there, it became apparent someone had recently been living in the shack, he glanced at Gareth for a reaction, seeing that he was already staring at the empty mattress.

'He was there, on there, I swear it, he was dead on the mattress,' Gareth uttered, pointing.

Jack saw that he was physically shaking; beads of sweat ran down his face, dripping onto his shirt.

'He must be alive, Jack; he's been eating chicken; look at all the bones. We better get out of here before he gets back,' his voice trembling with uneasiness.

Jack held his hand up, instructing Gareth to be silent while he continued looking around the room. He didn't see things the same way as his friend, something was very wrong in this place, and it didn't quite make sense.

He understood that Gareth had been convinced Baptiste was dead and had checked his pulse several times. The body had been removed, and someone had been staying in the shack.

'He's dead Gareth, so stop thinking he just got up and walked away. Calm down for a second and let me think. I guess someone else has been staying here. Anyway, Baptiste would never eat his own hens, they were his pets, the only dead hen I ever saw was a flat one under your vehicle tyre, remember?'

'No, he would never kill them,' the Welshman confirmed.

'Take a long, hard look around the room, Gareth and tell me what, if anything is different from when you were here, that is except for a missing body and a pile of chicken bones on the floor?'

Gareth kicked the mattress and then looked around.

'Well, it looks the same, except I can't remember all that chopping and scratches on the wall though.'

Jack stared at the damaged wall and noticed the words scratched into the wooden planks. Stepping onto the mattress, he walked across to get a better look. The words were in Spanish, and each letter was badly etched into the wood.

Recalling Gareth spoke decent Spanish, he asked. 'Gareth, you understand Spanish better than I do, can you work out what it says?' Then slowly read each word aloud in the hope that Gareth would understand. '*La selva devorará tus gritos cuando mueras,* any idea mate?'

The Welshman stared at the floor, rubbed his head, thinking, then stepped on the mattress and walked nearer the wall to read for himself.

He spoke the words aloud then said, 'Shouting, screaming, will eat the Jungle or something. I don't know; it doesn't make sense.'

'Think back to when you were last here, Gareth, are you sure it wasn't here then?'

'No, definitely not Jack, I would have remembered seeing it, anyway; look on the floor, the bits of wood from the wall; they are fresh, it's been done recently.'

Jack looked at the small chips of wood that could have been confused for chicken bones. He knew something odd had happened here, and it was now more important than ever to finish what they came to do and then get the hell out and fast. 'Where are the keys for our Land Rover Gareth?' Jack asked.

'Where I always put them, behind the sun visor,'

'All right, can you go and get them and keep them in your pocket? I don't want anyone to remove our only means of transport if we need to leave in a hurry.'

Gareth nodded and left the room; Jack followed and stepped onto the porch and looking at the two jerry cans, decided to pour petrol over the pile of tyres first as Baptiste's body was no longer there.

Lifting a can and straining, he stumbled as he walked, the jerry can was heavy, and the weight caused his arm to ache as he gradually made his way to the tyres.

'Someone has had a small fire going here,' Gareth shouted.

He set the can on the ground and turned, looking at Gareth, who was kicking black charred dust in front of the shack.

'The ashes are warm and still smoking, and there are some burnt chicken bones here too.'

Jack had begun to get increasingly unsettled and wanted to finish the job then leave the clearing in a hurry. Mustering all his tiring strength, he began to drag the jerry can across the dusty ground towards the tyres.

Then the distinctive and overpowering fetor of decaying flesh caused him to stop, and he looked around. The smell appeared to be coming from an area of grass near the tyres.

Leaving the fuel can behind, he tentatively walked towards the stench. The closer he got, the more pungent it became and pulling up his shirt, covered his nose and mouth in a vain attempt to mask the foul smell.

Realising he might have been about to discover Baptiste's rotten body, he paused to see what Gareth was doing and looked over his shoulder, he saw him walking towards the Land Rover.

Slowly and carefully, Jack advanced towards the stench, then stopped when he saw a large shape begin to emerge in the long grass.

He grimaced when he recognised the rotten head of a man amongst the green undergrowth, bloated and misshapen, with tangled dreadlocks, sockets devoid of eyes and an open mouth displaying white and gold teeth.

Leaning closer and clenching his shirt tightly over his mouth and nose, he saw ribs pointing upwards like fingers, then something moving in the hollow chest cavity.

Without warning and probably due to his presence, the movement quickened and swelled, and he realised the corpse's chest was full of rats, eating and chewing the flesh. The swirling bodies spilled out of the cavity and darted, scattering in every direction; as one ran across his foot, he panicked and screamed.

Gareth had just placed the vehicle keys in his pocket and was about to lift the ammunition box when he was disturbed by the scream, quickly turning and running towards his friend, he pulled his machete from his waist belt.

'I'm coming Jack, what is it,' he called.

Jack was still shaking with disgust when Gareth reached his position, every hair on his body seemed to be standing straight. Gareth began swiping the machete like a fly swat as a couple of straggling rats ran across his path.

'It's Baptiste; he's there,' Jack pointed to the half-eaten corpse, realising his hand was shaking.

Gareth's eyes searched the grass area, and recognising the remains of Baptise, he bent over, threw down his machete, coughed and then vomited on the ground.

It had become clear to Jack that someone had discovered Baptiste dead, and dragged his body from the shack before dumping him in the undergrowth. Then had remained in the shack for some time, lighting a fire, and eating Baptiste's hens.

Thinking that whoever it was, may return any second, he didn't want to be there when they did.

'All right, Gareth, finish puking, we have to work fast now. Let's get the job done and get out of this purgatory before whoever did this comes back and gets pissed off with us.'

Gareth was still bent over, coughing and spitting out what little remained in his stomach. Hearing Jack, he paused, turned his head and stared with bloodshot eyes then nodded in agreement.

'Just go and get the drugs and money; we will stop on the way back to base and put them in the ammunition box; it'll be quicker that way. I'll get the other petrol and rags out of the Land Rover; it's time to torch this place and leave as soon as we possibly can.'

Gareth stood half straight, hands on hips taking deep breaths, while Jack walked quickly to the Land Rover.

Satan had become impatient and decided to take the soldiers captive earlier than initially planned. Both were facing away from him, which afforded him and his lieutenant valuable time to pounce without alerting either until the last second.

Even more pleasing was that the big one looked like an injured animal and had thrown his blade to the ground.

Slapping Mikel on the shoulder, he indicated that it was time to grab their game and using the oil barrel to pull himself to his feet, eagerly began running towards the unsuspecting soldiers.

In a matter of seconds, Satan was on Gareth, who thought he had heard the pounding of feet but didn't have time to turn before his assailant grasped his thick black hair.

His head was painfully and forcibly yanked backwards; shock and surprise overcame his ability to resist. Before he could raise his large hands, the cold, eighteen-inch steel machete blade, held by Satan, was already pressed firmly into the Welshman's exposed neck. Gareth had no choice but to comply, knowing that resistance was useless.

At the very moment, Gareth was apprehended; Jack had placed the ammunition box into the rear of the vehicle and had begun pulling out the rags, then heard one or maybe two people running fast. Instinctively reaching for his machete, he swung around with the blade raised above his head, but he was already too late.

He was shocked at the scene before him, and his heart sank with dread.

Gareth was on his knees no further than fifteen meters away. He was motionless and facing him. A man gripped his head backwards, clenching his hair and revealing his large and bulging larynx.

The man looked strong and was completely overpowering his friend. Jack was startled when he saw he was holding a machete and was pushing the blade against Gareth's throat, who began to gurgle as his trachea stretched and compressed.

He could hear his friend gasping for air, and each time he flinched or tried to resist, his captor jerked his head back even further.

It was a standoff, and there was nothing he could do; lowering his machete, he looked at the man restraining Gareth, squinting to get a clearer view of his face which he saw was weirdly contorted.

The man appeared to have one eye stitched closed, the other open and glaring back at him. He could barely believe what he was seeing, he displayed a horrid grimace across his face as Jack realised, he was actually smiling, making the situation seem even more terrifying.

Gareth gave a half-muffled, spluttering cough, and it was clear he was gagging for air; his head was so far back, Jack thought that if pulled any further, his neck would snap.

Then he saw someone moving behind Gareth's assailant; there was another man, who was panting and holding a machete above his head, slowly walking towards him. Even though out of breath and sweating, he appeared just as threatening as the man who held his friend.

Jack wasn't sure what he could do then took a couple of steps forward on the offensive and raised his own machete, hoping he could buy some time to think about what to do next.

'Come any nearer, and you'll get a piece of this,' he shouted at the assailants.

The second man stopped walking.

Then the man holding Gareth shouted. 'You have what is mine, soldier and it is time to give it back.' His English was not good and further complicated by his crackled and gritty voice. Then he spat on the ground,

Jack was confused; what did he have that he thought belonged to him?

'I don't understand what you mean mate; we haven't got anything belonging to you and I don't even know who you are, just let him go,' he replied.

'Oh yes, you do, *amigo*; this big maggot came here last week and removed my property. He also killed my cousin,' he looked down then spat in his face as Gareth's eyes bulged and he gasped for air.

Then it suddenly dawned on him, the drugs were not Baptiste's after all, and instead, belonged to this man. He must have visited the shack to collect them on the day Baptiste died and discovered them missing; it was all beginning to make sense.

'Let my friend go, he didn't kill anyone,' he replied.

Satan had no time for small talk.

'Do not test me, you piece of stinking shit; return what is mine, or I will slit his throat and feed him to the rats that are eating my cousin.'

His retort was repulsive and so unsettling, it made him feel anxious and scared, he wanted to drop his machete, then turn and run from the horror of it all and realised that if he had not asked Gareth to remove the Land Rover keys, he could jump into the vehicle and drive out of the nightmare, but that would have meant leaving his friend to the fate of these people just to save his own skin.

More terrible sounds interrupted the silence as his friend gulped and fought for air and possibly his life, bringing him to his senses. He had to find the courage to concentrate on his predicament, knowing his gasping friend would choke to death if he didn't do something soon.

Then he looked at the old Land Rover and where the drugs and money were concealed. Understanding that Gareth's life was much more important than money, he knew he had no choice but to trade the drugs in exchange for his friend's life.

'Okay, okay', he said, 'your stuff is over there; I'll show you where it is; just let him go, and you can have it.'

A sickening smile spread across Satan's face, and he said, 'That was easy gringo? You will excuse me if I keep this big man as insurance until you show Mikel exactly where it is.'

Satisfied, Satan slightly relaxed the tension on Gareth's head, allowing him to breathe a little easier. Jack saw the movement and the gurgling eased as he was allowed to suck in much-needed air.

Gareth then spoke throatily, pausing between each word. 'Don't... do... it... Jack.'

Satan reapplied pressure to the sharp blade against Gareth's neck, splitting his skin and causing a small trickle of blood to run down his throat.

Jack realised he had to move quickly, or his friend would feel more pain.

Lowering his machete, and pointing to the old Land Rover hood, said, 'I need to walk over there and show you where it is. We hid it to keep it safe and because we didn't know it was yours, and thought it belonged to Baptiste.'

Satan despised excuses, and Jack's response made him even more venomous. 'Of course, it is mine, you fucking parasite. I am Satan, the life and breath of the people of this country. I only allow those I choose to live and take the lives of others for my pleasure; you colonial intruders are nothing but dirt on the sole of our shoes.'

Jack stared at him and began to believe that the man had to be insane, or at the very least a narcissist judging from his commentary. Their situation now seemed to be as serious as it could get, and he understood that they might not get out of this one alive or at best, together.

He looked at his friend who was being slowly choked to death by the beast. Whoever he was, he thought he had heard the word *Satan,* he was undoubtedly enjoying his own sick and violent behaviour.

'Please take the pressure off his neck, I already told you, I'm going to show you where your stuff is. Can you tell your mate over there to lower his machete, and stay where he is?' Jack pointed to Mikel, suddenly feeling apprehensive and acid reflux filling his throat.

'Mikel, do it,' he replied, releasing the blade's pressure against his captive's throat.

Jack slowly walked towards the old Land Rover, while glancing between Mikel and Satan. He was nervous but knew, if forced, he would bring his blade down hard if any one of them tried to grab him.

Eventually passing them both, he slowly and cautiously turned around and then began carefully stepping backwards, occasionally checking for obstacles behind him while trying to watch them both.

Satan pulled at and twisted Gareth's hair, forcing him to shuffle awkwardly around on his knees and face Jack.

Eventually, he stopped in front of the Land Rover bonnet, relieved that he had put some distance between himself and the assailants but felt he had now cornered himself as he was so far from his vehicle, but knew that without the ignition keys, was useless.

He knew the safest option would be to give them what they demanded and hope that they would release them both and allow them to leave.

'It's here, behind me,' Jack said.

'Where? You need to explain, *amigo*,' Satan tightened his grip on Gareth's hair, placing further pressure on the blade.

'It's inside the vehicle behind me,' he said, twisting and patting the bonnet with his hand.

'You are fucking with me, *amigo*; you think I am stupid? I will send your friend to his grave for wasting my time.'

Then realising he was preparing to slide the machete across Gareth's throat as more blood dripped onto his already blood-stained shirt, Jack shouted.

'Stop, stop, it's here inside the engine, just stop!'

Satan responded, 'Show me, or he dies,' then spat in Gareth's face again.

At that moment, Jack understood that any hope of getting

out of this ordeal was probably useless and the maniac intended to kill them both whether he got his drugs back or not, Gareth was far less likely to escape. He knew his own chances were not great, but at least he was not being restrained and the jungle was a short distance behind him.

'All right, but I need him to help me get it out,' pointing his machete towards Mikel.

Satan watched cautiously for a moment and was reassured when Jack lowered his machete and pushed it back into his waistband.

'Assist the piece of scum, Mikel.'

Mikel pushed his machete into his belt and walked towards Jack, then stopped and turned as Gareth discharged a sickening cough and muttered in a distressing and croaky voice, 'The jungle… the jungle… it will… it was a warning to us, Jack… devour your screams… when you die…, it was the message on the wall, the bastards intended to kill us from the start…, run Jack, run.'

Satan looked down at Gareth's face, tightening the grip on his hair and pulling his face close to his own. He laughed, spittle spraying in the Welshman's face.

Gareth had just confirmed to Jack that the message on the wall had been intended as a warning to them but hadn't understood when they first saw it.

It was now clear they had always intended to kill them both and Jack stared at his friend with complete dread, saddened by the pain and suffering he was having to endure.

Remembering that a cornered rat, when outnumbered, would come out fighting, he decided that he may as well go down with a fight.

Then an idea of a possible escape came to his mind but would probably be at the cost of Gareth's life. He looked at his friend, blood seeping across his chest and the monster holding him grimacing and enjoying the torture. His mind was made up, he was leaving.

Turning to the wrecked vehicle, he pushed the heavy bonnet upwards, holding its weight. 'It's there, Mikel there, do you see it?' he said and nodded towards the rusting engine.

Mikel, standing nearby, stepped forward beside him and leaned over the grill to get a closer view, his eyes quickly scanning the engine.

'It's there, look, at the back, reach in and pull it out; quickly, the hood is very heavy, I can't hold it for much longer.'

Mikel couldn't see anything but metal and rubber hoses and stretched his legs, leaning further beneath the bonnet, his eyes darting around, looking for anything resembling money or drugs.

It was when he heard Jack whisper behind him, he realised something was not right, but his body weight, leaning so far forward, wouldn't allow him to pull himself back from his position quick enough.

'This is for Gareth, you bastard,' Jack whispered before using all his strength and weight to forcibly slam the metal plate downwards onto Mikel's head and shoulders.

Hearing a muffled grunt and seeing that Mikel's body lay limp, he lifted the bonnet and slammed it down again; then he did it again and again.

The was no need; the first impact had caused severe head trauma and concussion to the rear of his skull, cracking his cranium and several ribs; the second impact snapped his cervical vertebrae and tore his spinal cord. Mikel's limp, dead body lay on the rusting engine block.

From somewhere, Jack had found the inner strength to kill him and now felt mentally and physically exhausted. His arms ached as he supported the bonnet, looking at the body lying across the engine. The blood was mixed with bone fragments on the back of Mikel's distorted head, the disturbing image making him feel the need to vomit, but he knew he wouldn't let that happen because there was more he needed to do.

Deciding not to wait for Satan's reaction and dropping the heavy bonnet on Mikel's lifeless body, he ran towards the jungle, and higher ground, as fast as he could. He had noticed earlier a track leading from the side of the shack and into the foliage and knew it was his only chance to escape and reach safety.

In less than fifteen seconds, he was enveloped by the jungle, panting, and pushing through thick vegetation and hanging vines. He stopped moving through the foliage when he was satisfied he was concealed from Satan in the damp, dark, and humid jungle.

Then he began walking at an angle, trying to circle around and get in a position to watch the fate Satan would surely inflict on his friend as punishment for what he had just done to Mikel.

He dropped down to his hands and knees and crawled to the edge of the foliage at a different place from where he had entered.

A sizeable thick fern at the edge of the vegetation gave good cover and creeping forward amongst the leafage, concealed himself, providing a view over the clearing.

Gareth was still on his knees being restrained, the machete

blade pressed against his throat, blood now soaking his neck and shirt. He wasn't sure how Satan would react and had already realised earlier that Gareth was not going to walk away.

When his friend had told him to run, the Welshman must have already known he was about to die and must have accepted then that only one of them had a chance to get out alive, knowing it wouldn't be him.

Lying on the damp, stinking ground, he waited for Satan's next move.

He didn't have to wait long.

'Well done,' Satan shouted, scanning the jungle edge with his single eye, 'you have impressed me gringo, Mikel was an idiot and very strong, but your friend, he is weak.'

Jack's eyes darted towards the position of the Land Rover bonnet, Mikel's body still underneath the metal plate, only his bottom half and legs exposed.

'Do you know what I am going to do now in return for what you did to Mikel? I think you say, a life for a life, yes?'

Jack remained silent, not wishing to say anything that could give away his position, then watched in absolute horror, as Satan violently jerked Gareth's head back until it could go no further, larynx bulging, and with increasing pressure, slowly slid the length of the sharp machete blade across his neck, creating a gaping slash, blood gushing down his chest and splashing onto the ground in front of him.

Feeling horrified and nauseous at what he witnessed, Jack quietly said, 'You've got to be fucking kidding,' then heard a hideous gargling sound as the air was released from Gareth's lungs and escaped from his open throat.

Still holding the machcte, Satan pulled Gareth's hair upwards allowing Jack to see the expression of sheer terror as his friend's life ebbed away. His eyes bulged, and his tongue stuck out in what looked like a sickening hallucination of suffering.

Jack continued to watch, in utter disbelief as his friend's life faded away in such a hideous and disgusting way, while Satan laughed, then to his astonishment, looked on as the savage dropped to his knees behind Gareth and, supporting his limp body, placed a hand over the slit across his neck, blood gushing between his fingers, and holding Gareth's head, placed his cheek next to his then spoke to him, auditable enough for Jack to hear.

'Go slowly and peacefully, my friend; you will die now; let it go, accept death, she will take you gently. Shhh…shhh, think of peace and your mother, don't fight against it.' Then he gently kissed Gareth's cheek, released his grip and allowed his body to slump forward, falling face down onto a pool of his own deep red blood where he lay awkwardly, no movement, no sound, just stillness as he succumbed to death.

Satan stood up and placed a foot on Gareth's lower back, bent forward and wiped the blood from the blade of his machete on his shirt, then tucked it into his belt.

'There you are, soldier, we are equal now, don't you think? Now come out, and we can talk like, how you say? Gentlemen. Let us get this stupid business over, and we can both go home to our *amantes*.

'You have my property, and I have your freedom; the *selva* is not a good place for you; it is dangerous there, so come out and let us drink and talk. What do you say, *amigo*?'

Jack did not answer and had not heard Satan speak; after seeing him clean the blood from his machete, he had slowly lowered his face into the softness and moistness of the decaying vegetation and was quietly sobbing.

Man should forget his anger before he lies down to sleep

Mahatma Gandhi

'It is very dangerous in the jungle, *amigo*; things there will eat you or lay eggs in you; they may have already begun, my friend. Come out, and you can take your vehicle. All I want is what is mine.'

Satan's words rebounded around the clearing.

The horror of what he had witnessed repeatedly played out in his mind while he lay on the ground, the sound and constant drone of insects, reminding him of where he was as he recalled Gareth's last words before being gruesomely murdered, then he recalled the message scratched into the wall, put there as a warning to them.

'*The jungle will devour your screams when you die*'; they intended to kill us from the start, '*run Jack, run.*'

Even with a blade at his throat, he must have been thinking and trying to translate the message all that time; when he had figured it out and realised he was about to die, he was still able to find the strength to summon his final words and tell Jack to leave him and save himself.

No human should ever be forced into that position he thought.

Feeling tears welling in his eyes again, he remembered the first time he had visited the clearing with Gareth and recalled how his friend had been so cautious and guarded, he had carried a machete for his own protection.

Gareth had always known how dangerous these miscreants were, and that's why he always appeared nervous and afraid whenever he visited the clearing.

'Let us negotiate like men, you give me my property, and you can go to your home,' Satan yelled.

He lay still, quietly thinking about what to do next. To trust Satan would be foolhardy, and he didn't believe, for a second, he would allow him to leave, especially after what he had seen.

Once again, he found himself on the back foot with few options and knew he wouldn't be able to stay in the jungle much longer, especially unequipped to deal with the dangers.

He was trained for jungle survival, but only with a section of eight professionally trained soldiers, machetes, maps, compass, water and survival equipment. This was very different; it was raw and, with no equipment to support him, would become food for animals to feed on and a host for insects to lay their larvae.

Slowly raising his head, he looked through low-hanging leaves; Satan paced backwards and forwards in the clearing, obviously frustrated by his silence.

He watched him swing his machete around and realised, he was trying to strike a hen, then, alarmed, began to tremble, aware that something was slowly stepping along his arm.

Slowly moving his head, he watched the huge black tarantula casually but gracefully stepping from his elbow and towards his wrist.

His hands were on the ground in front of him, so the direction it walked was towards his face, and it was getting closer.

He remained motionless, and beads of sweat began to trickle down his face. On a typical day, he would flick it off and jump away, but that would give his position away. Fortunately, he was aware tarantulas rarely bite humans unless aggravated, and felt that keeping perfectly still would not alarm the creature.

Nevertheless, the eight-eyed arachnid still terrified him; he wouldn't die if it became aggressive and bit him but would be in agonising pain for a very long time.

The spider continued its journey and then stopped about an inch from the tip of his nose, raising its pedipalps towards him, trying to detect movement. He held his breath, and then with the perfect balance and grace of a Bolshoi ballet dancer, the beautiful creature stepped off his hand, making its way across the jungle floor and allowing him to breathe normally again, feeling the thumping of his heart in his chest.

Satan shouted, 'Come out, and you can keep all the money; I just want my drugs. I offer no more. Let us do this, then you leave with your vehicle.'

Jack sighed, knowing Satan was lying and just trying to get him to come out of the jungle, which he would not do unless to find a way out of all this mayhem, then gawped when he felt something crawl across his cheek, using a finger to flick it off this time, a red fire ant fell to the leaves in front of him.

The ant's fat body was almost an inch long and walked awkwardly. He held a reasonable knowledge of dangerous insects and recognised the unassuming ant was one of the fiercest insects in the world, whose bite was something he didn't want to experience; obviously, the jungle inhabitants were getting active and hungry and decided it was time to move.

Satan was still walking around the clearing in front of the chicken shed, grunting, randomly chopping with his machete.

Jack slowly and carefully rolled over and sat on the ground, then turned onto his hands and knees and cautiously crept deeper into the foliage. Conscious that the river should be to the right of his position and could hear the distant sloshing of water, he continued in that direction.

After about ten metres, he was confident that the vegetation concealed enough to allow him to stand up and continued to force himself through the foliage, using his hands to push vines and low-lying branches aside.

To begin with, it wasn't easy, but he persisted, the river became louder, and then he found himself at the edge of the vegetation, facing slow-moving brown water.

The warmth from the sun was a relief after the cold shadows of the jungle and he sat on a large smooth rock close to the river. Cupping his hands and placing them in the water, he felt its coolness and drank, then quickly stumbled backwards when a large object floated to the surface, no further than a couple of metres from where he had been sitting.

The diagonal and rigid scaley back of a young crocodile broke the calm waters, slapped its tail on the surface then elegantly swam away from him.

Looking at his watch, it was 12.30 pm, and he remembered that they had arranged to meet Lewis and Stan at the fuel tank hours ago. He wondered what they would be doing now, still waiting at the old fuel tank or sitting in the bar having a cool beer.

It was impossible to alert them to what had happened and

remembered that Stan had asked about taking a radio; too late now.

Anyway, he thought, there was little time to think about Stan and Lewis; he needed to focus on survival and get out of this nightmare before Satan decided to write the final chapter.

He felt for the handle of his machete, and, shuffling backwards, putting some distance between himself and the water's edge, should the crocodile decide to come over for a chat and watched as the reptile meandered across the water's surface, searching for its next meal.

Patience had never been one of Satan's better qualities. He was now increasingly displaying signs of frustration and anxiety, grunting and cursing, swiping the machete at anything close to him. He knew that shouting at the soldier was useless because he refused to listen to him.

Looking down at Gareth's lifeless body lying on the blood-soaked ground, he had always been fascinated to see how far blood spread after a throat had been cut. Even when the ground was absorbent, the blood would still spread quite a distance; today was no different, he thought.

'Mikel', he called, 'move this piece of shit near to Baptiste,' then, remembering his first lieutenant was no longer at his call, he turned and looked at the legs hanging down from under the bonnet and walked to the vehicle. Curious, he lifted the hood with both hands, then dropped it suddenly, quickly jumping backwards as Mikel's body fell awkwardly to the ground.

Vivid red blood had spread across his contorted face and chest, and pink foam stained his nose and mouth. Satan bent down and looked closely at Mikel's face. Then, he dipped his finger into the blood on his collapsed chest and painted the word *muerto,* Spanish for dead, on Mikel's forehead.

He felt disadvantaged without his lieutenant, especially when more bloodshed was about to begin, but was confident he had the upper hand and knew the foreigner would become a lost child in the jungle. It would be a strange and uncomfortable environment, especially in the dark, when the night creatures came out to feed.

He was convinced that before much longer, possibly when the sun's warmth began to weaken, the crying child would feel most vulnerable and would run from his hiding place and beg for his life. Of course, he would promise him safety; he would allow him shelter, let him eat and feel comfortable, then after he was reunited with his property, he would take pleasure in painfully bringing an end to the miserable and pathetic life of the soldier.

First, he thought, he had to remove any possibility of the soldier's escape and searched Mikel's pockets, removing the keys to his own vehicle, then walked towards the dead soldier, intending to search him but as he approached, saw rats chewing at the skin around the gaping slit in his neck, lapping the blood and decided to allow them to finish their meal, he would search his pockets later.

Feeling that his day had been merciless yet successful, with only a minor issue that would soon conclude in his favour, he walked to the shack and began looking for firewood. Soon it would be time to light a fire and allow some delicious roasted chicken odours to drift into the air; that would certainly entice the soldier to come out of the jungle, he thought.

When in danger or in doubt, run in circles, scream, and shout."

Herman Wouk

'Shut up, Stan,' said Lewis, annoyed.

'No, I won't,' he replied, 'it's half past eleven, and Jack said three hours, so they should be back now. Something must have happened to them to cause such a delay.'

They were sitting on the ground, leaning against a pillar supporting the storage fuel tank.

Stan, standing, walked a couple of paces and turned to face Lewis.

'They wouldn't be late unless something's gone wrong, Lewis; we have to do something, they could be in trouble and need our help.'

'Shut up, I said we should wait a bit longer; everything will be fine, they should be back soon.'

Stan paced frenziedly back and forth, making grunting noises, then stopped and spoke again. 'Let's take a Land Rover and go and see if they are all right; it won't matter if they are on their way back; we'll meet them on the way, let's just make sure they are safe.'

Lewis picked up a stone and threw it hard at the perimeter fence. 'Shut up Stan, they both know what they are doing; we didn't exactly discuss what to do if they didn't return on time and you told him to take a radio set, but he refused.

'We are not leaving the base, otherwise, we won't be here when they arrive with the money. Just chill out and enjoy doing nothing; before you know it, they will be back here. I am going to get a drink; do you want one?'

Stan didn't reply, and Lewis walked along the road and headed to the bar.

It was early, and there were no customers in the bar area, he could smell something greasy, but delicious, remembering that they were supposed to meet for breakfast after Jack and Gareth had returned from the clearing. A large ceiling fan spinning, attempting to clear the air of smells and creating a refreshing draught, then he heard clinking and walked to the bar; the barman was crouched down, stacking bottles into a cooler fridge.

'You all right, Pete,' Lewis asked.

The barman turned suddenly, standing upright.

'Bloody hell, Lewis, don't go sneaking up on me like that again, you nearly give me a heart attack.'

'Sorry Pete, can I have a couple of cokes, please.'

Pete opened the fridge, removed the bottles and placed them on the counter.

'What you up to now, Lewis? Didn't you just get back from Cancún? I saw you in the corner over there last night with Stan and Gareth... *pause*... and that other bloke. We don't see him in here very often, what's his name?'

'That's Jack,' Lewis replied.

'Yeh Jack, the quiet bloke, keeps himself to himself and seems half decent. A better bloke than you or me Lewis, we should all do better, don't you think?'

Lewis ignored him. 'How much for the coke?'

Pete continued.

'From where I was standing, it looked like you lot were planning something a bit surreptitious last night, all that whispering and looking around at everyone, making sure no one could hear you.

'Are you still up to your old scheming, Lewis? I've known you too long and never known you not to be doing something on the side, mate.'

Lewis fumbled in his pocket, removing coins.

'Just a bit of friendly advice, mate, I'd be careful if I were you because one day one of your scams might come back to bite you on the arse.'

Lewis slammed the coins on the counter and picking up the bottles, leaned towards the barman.

'Well listen to me Pete, people in glass houses shouldn't throw stones, and selling cases of military discounted Copalli rum to the pimp who owns Raúl's Rose Garden is not exactly legit and yes, mate, we all have secrets so take some advice from me, just stay out of my business, and I'll stay out of yours.'

Lewis turned and walked towards the door then heard Pete say, 'It doesn't make it right, even if we're all doing something not quite legit, and remember, nothing is illegal until you get caught, see you later Lewis.'

Regardless of the draught from the fan, he was already sweating before he walked into the glaring hot sun.

Lewis walked towards the fuel tank but in the distance saw that Stan was no longer there so changed direction and headed to the radio store office instead.

Stan was pacing the office floor when he walked through the door.

Slamming the bottles on the desk, and sitting, he opened a drawer, removed a pack of cards and began laying them face up on the desk.

'Lewis, do you have a moral conscience or what?' Stan asked, 'it's now half past twelve, and all you can do is play cards. Does it not register with you that they are almost three hours late now? Something has almost certainly gone wrong, and they might need assistance.'

Lewis ignored him and continued turning cards.

Stan was tired of Lewis's ambivalence and began to think he may know something more sinister was happening, perhaps supporting his indecision. He remembered the previous evening when he had appeared relieved when chosen not to go to the clearing and wondered if he was afraid.

'All right, I'm uncertain if there's something you're not telling me, but if you are just going to sit there and do nothing; hand me the Land Rover keys from the drawer, because I'm going to look for our friends.'

Lewis continued to ignore him.

Frustrated, Stan shouted, 'Give me the keys NOW! Lewis.'

Lewis stood quickly, throwing the cards onto the desk, his chair pushed backwards with such force, it fell over and slid across the office floor. He felt his blood surging, his cheeks beginning to feel hot.

He walked towards Stan, who adopted a defensive stance as if he was just about to be struck.

Lewis raised his hand and pointing a finger, struck Stan hard in the chest.

'Listen to me, you vacuous moron, I'll put this in plain English because you haven't got the brains to work it out yourself.

'You have no idea about what really goes on down there, and there is something evil connected to that place that you would never comprehend. You don't know half of it and if we risk going there, we will probably both end up with our throats cut and dumped in the river.

'Now do me a favour, stop your whining and do something constructive like getting your arse over to the bar and get some beers and a sandwich, this could be a long day.'

Stan allowed the tension to dissipate then replied.

'You do know something, don't you? If you have let them go down knowing there would be trouble, I'll break your neck, you treacherous bastard.'

Lewis walked to the chair and setting it upright, opened a drawer and removed a half-full bottle of Caribbean rum, then filled two coffee mugs, holding one to Stan.

'I've really had enough of all this now, Stan; it's all gone too far; it wasn't even my idea.'

Lewis slumped into the chair and took a long drink from the cup while Stan quietly sat in the other chair, not wanting to interrupt what was sounding like an admission.

'I have never spoken to anyone about what I am going to say now; if I had told the truth at the beginning, none of you would have dared to get involved, leaving me to shoulder all the risks.

'When I was handed responsibility for the enterprise, I received the same brief as I gave you, do you remember? The only person involved was Baptiste, a small-time criminal who traded in stolen property helping towards a solitary life. A great deal of money was received in return and there were no known risks.

'It had already been going on for about eighteen months before I got here, so it was well-established and worth continuing because the financial rewards seemed incredible.

'The truth is, I didn't want anyone taking the spares down to Baptiste but me, and of course, the less anyone else became involved, reduced the risk of me being found out. In a nutshell, I was overwhelmed by the temptation and too greedy to share it with anyone else and enjoyed all the money to myself.'

Lewis paused, looked at Stan for a reaction, saw nothing, drank from his cup then continued; 'So, at first, I couldn't believe the amount of money I was pulling, but it was hard work trying to locate the parts around the base alone and then taking the deliveries down to Baptiste's on the quiet was time-consuming.

'I did most of the work after the other guys had finished for the day and while everyone else was having a night relaxing and drinking, I was scouring the base for equipment and then loading it ready to be delivered the next day.

'If anyone asked, I would just say I needed to visit one of the other army bases and would leave with a load of parts in the back of my Land Rover, visit the clearing and sell them to Baptiste, get my $800 and then do it all again a week later.'

Lewis stopped talking and finished his rum, then refilled the cup, offering a top-up, Stan refused, placing his hand over the cup.

'I remember the first time I met Baptiste. I was quite nervous, but he wasn't what I expected and was really friendly, inviting me into his shack for a drink and something to eat.

'I was reluctant, to begin with, but he seemed okay, so eventually, I did and then I enjoyed it, him telling me about Belize and me telling him what it was like to be English.

'I think he liked the company, and I can remember, on one occasion, staying there all afternoon and we drank a whole bottle of rum. He asked if I wanted to share a marijuana joint, but I refused, of course, and I suppose that made him understand there were differences between us that weren't going to change.

'After that, it was the same routine every time I took stuff down to the clearing. I would go into the shack or sit on the porch and would share a bottle of rum with him and he would smoke dope.

'Baptiste would ask me about England, the Queen, our history and culture; he had a fascination for our royal family and wanted to know what snow felt like because he had never seen it except in pictures.

'He told me about his upbringing, the poverty, the hardships, and the abuse. I was fascinated, and the more I delivered parts to him, the more we talked and the more I wanted to know. In a way, although we were worlds apart, we became friends.

'Things were going great, and I looked forward to visiting Baptiste every week, not only to take money from him but to spend some social time which I enjoyed and after all, I didn't have any friends back at the base. Then something happened, and everything changed.

'One day I drove into the clearing and felt something was different; I didn't know why; I just had a feeling. I had brought the usual stuff and stopped the vehicle in front of the shack. Baptiste came out, and when I saw him, I knew something was wrong.

'He didn't give me the usual smile and handshake as he always did when he would meet me, and seemed nervous, and he didn't invite me in to drink like usual, instead, just asked me to unload the parts, take the money and leave.

'I genuinely felt hurt and asked what was wrong, but he insisted I go. I became worried and said I wasn't going anywhere until he told me what he was so nervous about.

'Eventually, he reluctantly asked me into the shack but said it was dangerous and that I couldn't stay long.

'He poured us both a glass of rum; and said what he was about to say could never be shared with anyone, saying it was dangerous for a foreigner in his country to possess the information and made me swear not to tell anyone else.

'Then told me he had a cousin who was involved in the Belizean and Mexican drug cartels. He was called Satan, apparently the name had been given to him because he was evil, people really believed him to be the devil or a demon.

'Satan organised all the smuggling of cocaine, heroin and people across the borders and provided drugs to the middle then lower-level dealers who sold it on the streets.

'He was head of the Sinaloa drugs cartel, which has the reputation of being the most ruthless, violent, and murderous group of criminals in Central America. Baptiste told me that he disapproved of the exploitation of hard drugs and was satisfied with his marijuana, which he felt was customary for all Belizeans to smoke.

'All of Satan's family knew of his position leading the cartel and his passion for violence. They were all God-fearing people who recognised he was evil and understood it had always been his destiny.

'Then Baptiste told me a story following his cousin's birth, saying that while his mother lay sobbing from the pain of childbirth, the father of the newborn baby, looked down with intended affection, but instead of a crying baby, which would have been expected, the 'thing' just lay there and looked back at the father in silence. The father frowned and leaned towards the baby to take a closer look but was instantly horrified at what he saw lying in the wraps.

'The father was an intensely religious man, and his faith was more important than life itself, but when he looked into the eyes of the grimaced face, he saw pure evil and an entity which, in all his years of being devoted and dutiful to his religion was the very thing that he had been warned against and was convinced that demons possessed the creature.

'Then felt his faith was calling him to do something for what he believed was a monster and had to act quickly, he wrapped the baby in the sheet and rushed from the house as the mother wailed and could only watch in horror as her child was taken to its fate.

'He got his horse and cart and transported the baby through the village and into the jungle for several miles, even more convinced it was evil when the child made no sound during the entire journey or even tried to move.

'Eventually, he arrived at a relative's home; he begged them to take it, or he would take an axe to its neck if they refused. Shocked and with sympathy for its poor mother, they accepted the child to the relief of the father, who, before leaving, made them promise that they never reveal to the child who its birth mother and father were.

'They agreed, and before the father left, they asked if the child had been given a name. The father nodded and told them it was Satan.'

Stan stood up and walked to the desk, grasping the rum bottle, refilling his mug, and then sat down again, waiting for Lewis to continue.

'Baptiste told me that as Satan grew, he became unsettled and showed intense hatred for everyone around him. It wasn't long before he began to tell his surrogate mother and father that they were not his true parents.

'They were surprised as they had held their promise and had raised Satan as if he had been their child.

'As years passed, the boy established an intense dislike for authority and discipline and developed a hatred for anyone who told him what to do.

'When he was only five years old, he told his surrogate parents that he intended to find his father and mother and kill them for abandoning him at birth, which shocked them because they had never told him of his birth parents.

'Six years later, his natural father, mother and four sisters were killed in a ferocious fire which raged through their wooden shack on the north side of Belize City. Satan had gone missing from home four days before the fire and the fire department could not determine how the blaze had started.

'When Satan eventually returned to the home of his surrogate parents, they questioned him as to who may have started the fire that had killed his real family, but the boy became mute and never uttered a word to anyone for several years afterwards.

'Everyone, including his adoptive parents, thought that his silence was a form of physiological shock which would soon diminish, but the silence lasted until the age of eleven when one day, he packed his possessions and walked out of his home to make his own way in life. At the age of twelve, he entered a brothel in Belize City to begin work as a pimp, and within two years, he took over after the owner of the brothel mysteriously went missing.

'Baptiste told me that Satan grew up and continued his teenage years in a world amongst prostitutes, drugs, and gangs, developing a hatred for law enforcement and the government and his reputation and position in the Belizean and Mexican criminal underworld quickly accelerated and no one, especially family, wanted to be connected in any way.'

'What you are saying is unimaginable Lewis, are you suggesting this deranged animal is somehow responsible for the reason why our friends have not returned?'

'I think so, but I wanted you to understand how demented and unhinged he is, and here's an important part, Baptiste also told me that Satan was the main financer paying for the equipment we exchange for the money. Because of the remoteness of its location, Satan has been using Baptiste and his shack as a front to conceal the money coming in from major drug exchanges with the Mexican and Guatemalan cartels.

'The shack had several things that appeals to him, it was remote and unknown to the authorities, and there was no direct connection to him.

'Because Baptiste spent most of his time in the shack, he was effectively the 'caretaker' for all the drugs and money coming in and out of the country, an ideal place to store drug consignments from the Belizean drugs enforcement agency.'

'Can you just go back to what you said about Satan and his drug cartel being the main financer for the enterprise? I thought we just sold the stuff to Baptiste, and then he went to the city and sold it to scrap dealers and garages for a small profit?' Stan asked, confused.

'Baptiste always gave us the same amount of money for whatever we gave him, did it ever cross your mind that $800 was a bit generous in exchange for junk and from someone living in a run-down shack in the jungle?

'What was really happening was that Satan was paying Baptiste to keep his money and drugs concealed at his shack, the money Baptiste received also covered what he paid to us for the vehicle parts enterprise, making people think that it was all he was up to, dealing in stolen property.

'The authorities are not usually interested in small illicit enterprises, they are more interested in serious cross-border drug distribution, and it was all a front to put them off and no one was suspicious enough to work out something much bigger was going on in the background.'

Lewis reached for the rum bottle, emptied it into his cup and continued.

'So, Baptiste said I must never come into the shack again as his cousin had been visiting more frequently as his business was growing.

'He feared that if Satan or his cohorts were there on a day I visited, and went into the shack, they would kill me, and they always carried guns and machetes for protection. In fact, he said they were so sadistic and violent, he would carry a gun to protect himself from them.

'I was told that whenever I entered the clearing, should another vehicle be there, I was to turn around and drive away fast, and hope to God, they didn't follow me.'

Stan slammed his cup on the desktop, rum splashing on the desk's surface.

'You piece of garbage; that is why you stopped going down there and then asked us to join the enterprise, then you sent Gareth on his own while you became the 'coordinator', you cowardly spineless miscreant.'

'Look at it like this Stan, a wise sailor always avoids the storm,' Lewis replied, drinking the last of the rum from his mug.

'More like a rat fleeing the sinking ship, you judas, you have got to be the most conceited, conniving shyster I have ever met Lewis, and all this so you can profit while putting everyone else's life in danger.

'When Gareth found Baptiste overdosed and hid the money and drugs, you knew they belonged to this maniac Satan and he would be pissed when he discovered his stuff missing, and you also knew if any of us went down there, it was possible he or his crew would be waiting for us.

'Oh, I see it now; that's why you were so reluctant to go. How fucking dare you do this to us, you spineless coward.'

Lewis sat in silence and stared at his empty cup.

Evil originates not in the absence of guilt
but in our effort to escape it.

Shannon L. Alder

The foliage around him began to cast longer shadows, and the amount of shade increased as if a curtain was being pulled slowly closed.

He shivered as the temperature abated in the shade and made his damp clothing feel even colder. Sitting motionless by the river, Jack had been distracted from his adversity by watching wildlife which had been therapeutic and calming, and had not realised that time had been passing so quickly.

Knowing that spending the night in the jungle without specialist equipment would not be a sensible option and not something anyone should risk without appropriate survival training, and in any case, couldn't remember any scenarios involving a murderous machete waving, drug-dealing maniac.

He recalled that the temperature in the jungle could drop to as low as thirteen degrees at night and how uncomfortable that would be after experiencing a constant thirty-five degrees during the day in sunlight, quickly prompting him to try to work out what he would do next.

Wearing just a tee shirt and shorts, which were already

sodden with sweat and humidity, and showing too much bare flesh made him vulnerable to hungry insects and animals which came out at night; they would smell his odour and sweat.

He already had an abundance of mosquito bites on his exposed skin, including his hands and face, but there were far worse parasitical insects in the Belizean jungle just waiting to bury themselves into soft flesh, laying their eggs; then there were the snakes, spiders, and vampire bats, he shivered and stood.

It was time to be positive again and stop thinking about what could go wrong. Convincing himself that he would escape the wilderness, he forced himself to climb up from the riverbank and began hacking his way through the thick green foliage towards the jungle edge facing the clearing.

Walking through the thickest vegetation was challenging and dropping to a crawl made progression easier. Eventually, he found a position not far from where he had earlier observed Satan.

His eyes scanned the clearing; there appeared to be no movement apart from a few hens pecking and scraping the ground, searching for food scraps.

He calculated that the distance across the clearing to the exit path was about one hundred metres, and the brown river appeared from his left, bordered the side of the clearing, and then disappeared into the jungle by the exit. Thinking of possible options to escape, it seemed possible to run across the clearing to the exit, along the track, and then onto the main road.

Another option, he thought, would be to search Gareth's body, locate the Land Rover keys, and then drive out. The issue with either option would be the element of surprise and to succeed, he would have to do so under the cover of darkness.

It was quite possible that the maniac may have a gun and Gareth had mentioned seeing a firearm on Baptiste on a previous visit, he thought it would be safer to wait until Satan was asleep.

His thoughts returned to Lewis and Stan and wondered if they had guessed, because they had not returned, that something had gone terribly wrong.

Perhaps they had decided to take a vehicle and drive to the clearing on an insane, suicidal rescue mission.

Although it would be a relief to see them, he hoped they hadn't because they would have no idea of the dangerous lunatic or his determination to increase the body count.

Rubbing his face and feeling a stressful throbbing in his temple, he thought he really must see a doctor about that when he got home, smiling as he realised the irony.

He quickly turned his head and stared into the darkening undergrowth when he heard a terrible low vibrating wail. Then another followed by short whooping noises that cut through the dense vegetation.

The sound of a howler monkey was deafening and close enough to remind him that whatever he decided to do, he had to get on with it soon. It was starting to get dark, and the night wildlife were waking and would soon be searching for fresh meat.

He smelled smoke, a fire somewhere, it was the smell of burning wood. Then suddenly, he heard the sound of a loud shattering crack across the open space of the clearing. It was so loud it reverberated around the surrounding jungle causing monkeys to shriek and a flock of annoyed birds, alarmed by the noise, to take into the sky from their hidden perches amongst the trees.

A manic rustling of foliage all around as animals decided that this no longer felt like a safe place to be.

Satan had walked a little too close to the british soldier's body and noticed the number of surging rats nibbling at the flesh had substantially increased; rather than making him feel repulsed, it only helped him to understand how hungry he was and so decided to light a fire and eat, feeling that it would be good to get the smell of roasted chicken in the air to assist the soldier determine his next move.

Having collected several broken branches, dry vines, and other chunks of wood, he set them on the ground, then stuffed paper between the wood, flicked the flint on his lighter and watched the flames flicker as it began to burn.

Then, he walked to where the hens were scratching around for food and saw a large hen which he tried to snatch, but it quickly darted away and out of his reach. He tried again, but it was useless; whenever he got near, the hen would quickly run in the opposite direction he wanted to grab it.

His patience was wearing thin; Satan removed the gun from his shirt, aimed and shot the nearest hen, feathers erupting into the air around the dead bird.

He remembered that Mikel always prepared the hen before cooking it because the head, innards and feathers had always been removed. He had never seen how his lieutenant did it, so thrust a long stick through the middle of its body and supported the dead bird over the fire with other sticks and watched the feathers singe and burn.

It was the unmistakable sound of a gun being fired on the other side of the shack, obstructed by the hen house and out of his vision.

Well, he thought, that answers the question regarding Satan having a gun, quickly eliminating running across the clearing, unless under the cover of darkness, as an option to escape; he would have a couple of bullets in his back before he reached halfway; then he tried to guess which pocket Gareth would have put the vehicle keys.

If only he could get closer to the shack, he thought, so he could see exactly what Satan was doing and would perhaps provide some other ideas on how to escape.

Crawling from his safe place in the foliage, he slowly made tracks in the direction of the rear of the shack. Darkness was beginning to creep in as the sun's light faded giving him confidence to walk slowly between the cover and open ground.

Within a short distance, he came across a large tree trunk lying on the ground and thought it would be ideal for squatting behind and surveying the area.

He looked at the side of the shack and saw an old rusting oil barrel which he thought would provide better cover and allow him to see more of the clearing. He left his position behind the tree trunk and walked quickly towards the barrel.

Two minutes later, he was crouching behind the drum and had a view of the side and rear of the shack, and saw nearby, the rear half of the old Land Rover where the drugs and money were concealed, Mikel's body now lying on the ground in front of the vehicle.

Further on and about twenty metres away, his own Land Rover, standing cold and lifeless.

It would have been the perfect escape if only the keys had still been under the sun visor, he could have sprinted to it, started it up and within seconds would be driving onto the exit track.

That was not going to happen because the ignition key was in Gareth's pocket and now he had the dilemma of finding his friend's bloodied body and searching for them.

He was distracted as the wood-burning smell had changed to the delicious smell of roasting chicken and saw smoke bellowing from around the front of the shack, guessing Satan was obviously preoccupied and cooking a hen on the fire.

He had never been to the rear of the shack before, and noticed one or two ramshackle outbuildings, realising the smallest must be a toilet. Then, surprised when he noticed a vehicle tucked between the two buildings.

It was a very early model Land Rover and one the British Army disposed of years earlier. Trying to work out why it was there, then deciding it probably belonged to Satan; how else had he and Mikel arrived at the shack? He felt exhilarated, realising he may have just stumbled across another possible escape and prayed that the ignition keys were still in the vehicle.

Looking around, he worked out that he could reach the vehicle reasonably quickly, but there was hardly any cover and decided he would just run as fast as possible and would reach it in a few seconds. He felt his heart begin to beat faster as he began thinking that if only the keys were in the vehicle, all this could be soon over.

Gently biting his tongue, knowing the sharp pain would make him focus, he stood and was about to step out from behind the barrel, then felt the cold steel of the handgun gently touch the rear of his skull.

'Hey, *amigo*, your friend called you Jack, is that your name?' Satan asked.

He froze, then raised his hands.

'Jack, my friend, there has been much death today, it is such a waste, and there should be no more. If you stay in the *selva*, you will become weak and vulnerable then the animals will eat you alive. The killing must stop, come with me now, and we'll eat together.'

Realising Satan had probably observed him in full view as he walked from the tree trunk to the barrel, he would have quickly circled the chicken shed, getting into a position to creep up unseen and surprise him.

Suddenly startled and hearing the rustling sound close to the oil barrel, Jack quickly stepped sideways while Satan aimed the gun at whatever had decided to join them. Searching in the fading light, Jack became instantly alarmed when he saw the squirming body of a scraggy, dark brown snake which must have been curled up a couple of feet from where he had been crouching.

Their voices caused detectable vibrations and unsettled the reptile, which was uncurling, seemingly unhappy and began moving towards them; the serpent's tongue frantically darted, tasting the air and collecting their odours and position.

Being very aware that almost every snake in Belize was venomous, none got any worse than this and he recognised its spear-shaped head; it was a fer-de-lance, the most dangerous and venomous snake in Belize.

Even Satan was aware of the immediate danger to them both and, taking hold of Jack's shoulder, pushed him toward the shack.

There was no hesitation, and he quickly walked towards the building, feeling his machete being removed from his waistband.

His captor spoke as they walked, 'First we shall eat; then you will show me my money and *drogas*. When that is done, you can leave here; I do not fight with you, my friend; I only want what is mine.'

Jack didn't believe the psychopath; it was lies, and he knew the monster had no intention of allowing him to leave.

They arrived at the front of the shack, a small fire burning on the ground in front of the porch and the suspended body of a charred and bloated chicken, feathers burned black and propped over the flames by three branches sticking from the ground.

The carcass swelled and blistered as internal juices spilled out, dampening the fire below. He didn't care, the smell was mouth-watering and tempting, and he couldn't remember the last time he had eaten anything.

'Sit there,' Satan demanded, pointing to the porch near the door of the shack, a half-empty bottle of rum propping the door open.

Jack sat next to his own petrol-filled jerry can that he had placed there earlier, and watched as Satan stepped onto the porch then entered the shack.

Suddenly, he thought about running across the clearing and into the darkness, then realised it would be useless and Satan would easily be able to shoot him before he could make it to any sort of cover. He thought for now, it would be better to comply with the beast and wait for a better opportunity to escape. He sat and held his hands towards the small flames, feeling the warmth and smelling the delicious odours of roasting chicken.

Satan returned holding a reefer, picked up the rum bottle and sat on the porch, about two metres from him. He watched as he sucked a long draw on the joint, then gently released the thick musty smoke from his nostrils, eyelid fluttering over his lone eye and puckering his lips, took a long drink from the bottle.

'Hey, soldier, let me say, you and your friends killed my cousin Baptiste and stole my *drogas*. Then you killed Mikel; that was not good, my friend. That is why I ended the life of your friend, perhaps I should make things more even, after you show me where you have concealed my property.'

Jack didn't answer.

Satan put the bottle on the porch boards and, walking to his captive, bent forward and placed his face close to his. Jack smelled sickly pungent marijuana odour mixed with rum, it was disgusting, he winced as Satan began to shout.

'You imperialist pig, tonight you die here in the jungle. The *animales* and *insectos* will eat your rotten corpse after I have cut you into little pieces. I give you a chance, *amigo*, answer me, you *cerdo.'*

Jack, holding his breath, grimaced as spittle flecked his cheek and maintained his silence.

Satan, incensed, returned to where he had been sitting and continued to smoke the reefer, staring at him with his grim single eye as Jack sat quietly looking at the flames of the fire, desperately thinking of running into the darkness, if it had not been for the gun.

Turning from the swirling flames to his watch, he saw it was 7 pm and dark in the clearing except for the light of the moon and the dancing orange swirls of light emanating from the fire and reflected and flickered eerily off the furthest foliage around the clearing.

Suddenly, as the fire's dry crackling wood splintered and sparked on the fire, he heard a loud thud and the porch vibrated.

Satan had fallen backwards and was lying on his back across the porch, eye closed and was beginning to breathe heavily followed by snorts, the marijuana and rum had overcome him, and he had fallen asleep.

Quietly watching, knowing it would be foolish to act too soon, Jack thanked God for presenting him with an opportunity to escape earlier than expected.

A minute passed, Satan had not moved, and his grunting snore was steady and consistent; he quietly and slowly stepped over to him and, with his foot gently kicked his leg, nothing.

Then bent over and pushed his finger into his chest, then again but firmer, still nothing. Satan was in a deep sleep, and now was his chance to escape.

Looking around, he watched in the darkness as the flames from the fire flickered, causing irregular and dancing shadows which he thought would surely be in his favour.

Should Satan wake and search for him, the creature would undoubtedly be influenced by alcohol and weed and would be at the very least confused; besides, moving around in the darkness, interspersed by the flickering light from the fire, and with only one eye, would prove difficult to see him.

The snoring became more profound and louder, enabling him to relax and providing generous time to think about his options to escape.

He again thought about the vehicle at the rear of the shack, which was the closest, and was the most straightforward and accessible, assuming the keys were there, he decided to quietly make his way to the rear.

Walking around the side of the shack, he was engulfed with darkness as the building eclipsed the light of the fire. Then stepping carefully and cautiously, trying not to trip, he reached the vehicle; a 'click' sound as he gently and slowly pulled the door open with two hands.

He felt around the ignition switch, but there was nothing. Then pulled down the sun visor, and again nothing. Lying across the driver's seat, he gently opened the glove box, it was empty.

'Dammit', he said to himself thinking about what he should do next. The thought had crossed his mind to return to Satan and search his pockets, then thought better to let sleeping dogs lie.

He looked around the seats, and then into the rear cabin, seeing a grip bag near the tailgate.

Quietly creeping to the rear and opening the gate, he removed the bag, feeling that it had a bit of weight to it, and guessing it could contain drugs, food or if he was lucky, perhaps a gun.

Unzipping the bag, he reeled from the sickening wave of stench, quickly pulling the sides open. There was just enough light from the moon, allowing him to see what was inside, a badly decomposed human arm. The flesh was black, fingers curled, bony and withered, and the stench overbearing.

Sickened, he swung the grip bag and its horrific contents into the undergrowth.

What kind of miscreation was Satan? Jack thought, then decided to locate Gareth's body and search for the vehicle keys.

Before walking, he scanned the area, and assisted by the moonlight, saw the old Land Rover bonnet. He had calculated earlier that approximately ten metres or so further would be the place his friend's body lay whom Satan had so savagely and horrendously butchered.

He looked at the shack and then his Land Rover and realised that between Gareth's body and the vehicle, he would be in full view of the front of the shack and hoped the darkness and the distance would make it difficult for Satan to see him should he wake from his sleep.

He walked towards the bonnet, turned ninety degrees, and stepped over Mikel's feet, then continued counting each pace to measure as close as possible to ten metres. It was eerie in the dark, and the moon's light assisted him, and the only sound came from the flowing river.

Eventually, he saw a lump on the ground appear and guessed it was the body of his friend; confirmed when, a couple of steps closer, he recognised Gareth lying on the ground, face down in his congealed blood.

He heard a faint squealing and then rustling, realising there were several rats on his body and around his head, at least two on his back gnawing at his shirt. Searching in the darkness, he saw an old windscreen wiper blade and picking it up, waved it over his friend's body, alarming the feeding rats which scurried into the darkness.

'I'm sorry Gareth, it was never meant to end this way,' he said quietly, then tentatively slipped a hand into his pocket. He was successful; in the first pocket, he felt the keys and removed them. The relief was almost unbearable, and he felt himself shaking with excitement.

Satan needed to urinate.

He was overly tired and a little confused, the condition he hated being in after having smoked ganja, it always made him cantankerous and grouchy. Anyway, and more importantly, he felt the need to do his business.

Rolling from the porch, he saw the fire had almost burnt out. It did not matter to him, the rum and marijuana made him tired, and he would crash on the mattress when he returned. He walked to what was left of the glowing embers, the sticks supporting the chicken had collapsed and the burnt carcass lay amongst the ashes. Pulling down his zipper he fumbled to find his penis.

Then in the haze of his befuddled head, he realised something was not right. Looking back at the shack and the porch, he remembered the soldier had been there before he fell asleep and, pushing his member back into his trousers, began searching for his gun.

The bright full moon assisted his vision, and he could see the shape of the Land Rover some fifteen metres to his front and knew that in only a minute or two, he would be in the driver's seat and driving the hell out of what had seemed an impasse.

Gripping the keys in his hand tightly, he walked towards the vehicle and hopefully, escape.

After a few paces and being aware he was now in full view of the shack, he looked over his shoulder, hoping he would see Satan still lying on the porch asleep, then suddenly began to panic, his heart thumping when he saw that Satan was no longer lying on the porch.

His demeanour became more urgent as he realised that he had to get to the Land Rover quicker than he had planned.

Fifteen metres…

That was about twenty paces, but he had to do it without making noise and tried to walk a little faster, stretching his pace. He exerted more energy, feeling sweat begin to run down his face.

Twelve metres…

Being careful not to stand or trip over anything in the moonlight, he continued walking, relief beginning to overcome him as he approached the vehicle and liberty.

Eight metres…

He stopped, fearful when he heard the noise and realised it was a small animal shuffling; then a scuffle as whatever it was headed towards the river. Annoyed at the valuable seconds wasted, he continued.

Four metres…

The tailgate was still open, jerry cans and rags still on the ground, and would remain there when he started the engine; hearing it roar into life, he would engage the gears and be out of there in no more than a few more seconds.

There…

Gently touching the open tailgate, he hurriedly walked to the driver's door, ignition keys still tightly gripped in his hand, then closed his fingers around the door handle, overwhelmed, excited and shaking with relief.

The hard metal to the bone impact of the handgun striking the base of his skull caused momentary head splitting, intense pain, and a split-second later loss of consciousness as the central amygdala in his brain switched off. He slumped to the ground, concussed.

The full moon reflecting light and casting an almost ghostly shimmer over the river and across the clearing as Satan strode across the ground, dragging his quarry by his leg, and returning him to captivity.

2 0

Sometimes life must strip us in order to save us.

Craig D. Lounsbrough

Following Lewis's disclosure, Stan left the radio store office in a furious mood and walked to the bar; two soldiers sat at a table in the bar area and were drinking and talking. He ordered a coke, paid, then carried the bottle and a glass to the same table he had sat at with his friends the previous evening, and slumped in a chair, attempting to take in, and understand what Lewis, had just told him.

He poured the coke over the ice, watching the brown froth fizz and expand to the rim and then begin to reduce and settle, ice floating.

Then he heard the familiar voice.

'They could have just broken down on the way back; there is nothing to suggest they ran into trouble. Let's face it, they might have buggered off with all the money, I wouldn't put it past Gareth, he's a dodgy fella you know.'

Lewis, who had followed him into the bar, said quietly, sitting in a chair opposite. He turned and called to the barman, requesting a bottle of rum and four cokes.

Stan ignored his assertion as Lewis continued, 'Don't be too surprised if they walk in here in a few minutes, anyway, as you suggested the radio set would have been useful.'

'Tell me what else you know about these homicidal drug dealing thugs you made us deal with,' Stan asked, breaking his silence.

'Well,' he replied, 'Baptiste said that they're depraved and would kidnap, torture and kill their own family if they felt they had to, apart from that, nothing other than I already told you.'

Lewis stopped talking when Pete approached, setting the bottles on the table, they watched him leave and then carried on with their conversation.

Stan filled his glass with rum, pouring the same into Lewis's glass, and asked, 'I guess you are just going to carry on with your life and try forgetting all about this, perhaps waking up in a sweat in the middle of the night wondering if you could have done something more, but never did?'

Lewis grabbed the glass without adding coke and drank the rum, the sourness making him wince.

Stan added, 'What I don't understand Lewis is why you can just ignore the fact that Jack helped us all get out of that prison truck in Cancún, and even volunteered to stay with the police and take responsibility, even risking going to prison to allow us to escape if he had to.

'That's what you call being honourable to your friends, being loyal and not letting them down.'

Lewis slammed the empty glass on the table; the barman, who was reading a book at the bar glanced over at them, as did the two soldiers sitting at the table nearby.

'Stan,' he said, trying not to appear angry, 'you simply don't get how bad these bastards are; Baptiste told me that these maniacs don't just kill you; they want you to feel the pain

265

first, we wouldn't stand a chance, how many times do I have to tell you.'

Stan stared into Lewis's eyes, noticing how bloodshot and glazed they were.

'Listen, Lewis, what do you think we would do if it was your sorry arse down there and you needed our help?

'Do you think for one second, we would be saying, oh poor Lewis, he could be hurt or dying, but let's leave him because we are too gutless.

'Are you prepared to live the rest of your life a scheming quitter or do something you can look back on, hold your head high and say you did the right thing and did everything possible when your friends were in need?'

Stan watched as Lewis lowered his head, staring into his empty glass; after a short time, he looked up as a tear meandered down his face, conscious, he rubbed his eyes, releasing further tears then removed a rag from his pocket and wiped his face then blew his nose noisily.

Stan refilled their glasses.

After composing himself, Lewis shuffled nervously in his chair and looked around the bar as if preparing to say something, drank from his glass, then placing it on the table said, 'All right, Stan, I get it, I've listened to you and I know I've messed up big style, but you have to remember, it could already be too late, it's pitch black out there and we would never be able to navigate the track from the road to the clearing without the risk of driving into the river.'

Stan sighed, relieved. 'I know, but we should have gone earlier.'

He stared at Lewis who was sheepishly glancing around the

bar, thinking. Then after a short silence said, 'We go before first light; can you meet me at the store at 5 am? We can load up with stuff when I meet you then, I think we will need some water and a first aid kit, a rope and spare petrol, and anything else you think may be useful if we run into trouble, oh, and machetes, we will need weapons, is that okay with you?'

Stan nodded eagerly, his relief obvious and replied, 'Thanks mate, I will be there and ready to go, but I am warning you now if something dreadful has happened to either of them, or we could have prevented it, what I will do to you will be far worse than Satan ever would.'

Lewis shook his head slowly, pursing his lips, then said, 'You really have no idea how depraved and blood-thirsty these people are Stan.'

Lewis half-filled his glass with rum, drank it in one, then stood from his chair and walked out of the bar, leaving Stan to pay for the drinks.

However much he tried, Stan couldn't sleep; lying on his bed, fully clothed, he stared into the darkness, the rhythmic sound of chirping crickets and the annoying high-pitched buzzing of mosquitos depriving him of any sleep.

After paying for the drinks, he had left the bar and walked to his room, stripped out of his sweaty and damp clothes then climbed between the cool bed sheets, tucked his mosquito net around the mattress, lay back and closed his eyes but a short time later, he was still awake, eyes open.

Looking at his watch, he saw it was just after 2 am and dark outside. He pulled the mosquito net aside and rolled out of bed, dressed, then walked to the rest room, and splashed cold water on his face before heading out and into the darkness.

Unlocking the radio storeroom, he collected the equipment Lewis had suggested and what he felt was necessary for the mission and placed two machetes on the floor close to the door, followed by two petrol jerry cans.

He filled a water bottle from the sink and collected a first aid box and tow rope from the shelves.

Then taking the keys for a Land Rover from the desk drawer, he loaded the equipment into the rear of the vehicle parked outside the door. It was still very dark, the only light came from the moon and feeling unusually cold, shivered and because he was only wearing a tee shirt, rubbed his bare arms in a vain attempt to keep himself warm.

He thought of what could possibly have happened to his friends, wondering why they hadn't come back and hoping that wherever they were now, they were safe and coping with their situation.

Anyway, Lewis had appeared to have accepted that they were possibly in danger and needed their help and had finally agreed to drive to the clearing to find them. He already knew that if Lewis didn't turn up at 5 am, he was going without him.

When he finished loading everything he needed, he climbed into the driver's seat and turned the ignition key with a single click, checking there was enough fuel in the tank for the journey; satisfied, he switched off the engine, then lay across the seats and within a short time, he slept.

The words were no more than a distant whisper but enough to startle him. He jerked and looked around, trying to understand where he was as he quickly surfaced from the light sleep.

'Wake up, Stan.'

He pulled himself upright in the seat, rubbing his eyes, it was cold, and the sun was beginning to rise, the sky a greyish blue.

'It's time to go, mate,' Lewis said, wiping condensation from the driver's side mirror.

He watched him walk to the passenger side of the vehicle and, pulling the door open, climbed into the passenger seat.

'Did you sleep here all night?'

Stan's voice was croaky when he replied. 'I couldn't sleep, so I thought I would get everything sorted. Besides, I thought there was a chance that you wouldn't turn up, and if you hadn't, I would have gone without you. I take it you are still up for this, and whatever has happened down there, we deal with it?'

'Yes mate; I've done some dreadful things in the past and admit I've been totally selfish.'

Pause.

'Are you sure you have everything, including a machete for me if I need to use it?'

Stan nodded, slightly impressed by Lewis's self-reflection and honesty, but still didn't feel that he was ready to fully trust him, then turned the ignition key and the engine roared into life.

Lewis, buckling his seatbelt said, 'All right, mate, let's go find our mates and bring them home.'

He engaged the gear stick and began steering the vehicle towards the exit gates, heart pounding in his chest in anticipation of what they may find or have to confront when they arrived at the clearing.

*Those crazy enough to think they
can change the world usually do*

Steve Jobs

He was suffering from a sharp pain in the back of his head, which turned to a dull ache across his shoulders and down his spine, so Jack lay still, trying to figure out why he hurt so badly.

He opened his eyes, but his focus was hazy and blurred, and could only make out murky fog and shadows as his vision readjusted to the light.

He realised he was lying on something soft and comfortable, providing some relief, but felt an annoying discomfort in his lower back, he tried to recollect what had happened and where he was.

Closing his eyes tightly and using his weakened neck muscles, attempted to lift his head, then experienced a sharp pain across his face as if the skin had been ripped or torn. He lowered his head back to the softness and rested, drawing breath and begging the pain to subside.

He was lying on his back, arms behind him which accounted for the discomfort between him and whatever he lay on. Lifting his hips slightly, he attempted to pull his hands from behind, then realised his wrists were bound tightly behind his back.

The rhythmic pulsating in his hands and fingers helped him understand that whatever secured his wrists was far too tight and like a tourniquet, restricting blood flow, and causing his hands to swell.

He knew they would soon become numb unless whatever was securing them was removed and wondered how long he had been bound.

Ignoring the pain in his face and shoulders, he lifted his head from the softness, opened his eyes, vision now a little clearer, and gently moved his head, searching to the left and then right. It came as no surprise that he was lying on the mattress in Baptiste's shack.

Resting his head on the softness, he tried to relax for a short while, knowing that being tied up, he wasn't going anywhere soon then closed his eyes, willing the pain in his head to subside.

He gradually felt himself beginning to drowse then remembering how vulnerable he was, opened his eyes, urging himself to stay awake and trying to stay conscious of his predicament.

Grimacing with pain, he lifted his head again, his neck weak, but just enough motion to look around and satisfy himself that he was alone in the room then ignoring the pain, leaned to his side, bent his knees and pulled his feet towards his body, attempted to twist himself into a sitting position.

It was useless; the pain, coupled with tiredness and hesitant muscles sapped his motivation and he remained half curled on his side in a foetal position.

Two minutes passed while he rested, trying to motivate himself and then tried again. Inhaling deeply, he shuffled his body across the mattress using his feet to push, enabling him to move and stretch his wrists, slightly adjusting the ties and allowing much-needed blood circulation but he still felt warning signs of a prickling and tingling sensation in his fingers.

Resting for a moment to allow the pain to subside and to gather strength for the next move, his thoughts drifted again to how he had ended up in this position.

He remembered feeling excited, and elated but was panicking, he was holding the door handle on the Land Rover, it was dark, and he could hear the river nearby, he recalled looking at the porch, Satan should have been lying there but was gone.

Then, like a small tsunami, the obscure events of the previous evening flooded into his mind.

He felt utter misery, almost dispirited, realising how close he had been to escape.

Freedom had been in his grasp and he remembered holding the ignition keys in his hand, now all that was lost but felt he had to find it in himself to be positive, there was no time to mull and reflect on what had gone wrong because now he was in an even more perilous situation and could not afford to wait around for Satan's next act of malevolence.

First, he needed to understand any new injuries and areas of pain, he guessed he must have been hit on the head with something hard and had fallen to the ground, accounting for the ache and pain in the back of his head and shoulders. The painful stinging sensation across his face was puzzling, nevertheless, very unpleasant and sore.

Above everything else, his concern focused on the tourniquet restricting his wrists which he knew had to be removed soon, otherwise he would be useless without hands.

Then an intermittent scraping sound outside the shack disturbed his thoughts. It was close, probably originating from the porch, lying still, listening carefully to the sound of a scrape, a two-second pause, then another scrape. Then, with dread, recognised it was the sound of a metal blade being slid against a flat stone.

He reclined on the mattress, feeling distressed, and then without warning, the door to the shack swung open with a loud shattering crash. The sun's bright rays prevented from entering the open doorway, obstructed by Satan's large build filling the door frame.

Jack lifted his head and saw he was holding a machete, slightly raised and at that moment understood the terror instilled in his victims and the last thing they would see before death, his scared and mutilated face and his intention to be their final horrifying living memory, as they shuffled off this mortal coil.

The fiend spoke, 'I gave you a chance to live last night, soldier, but you have disrespected me.'

As he spoke, droplets of saliva sprayed in front of him. 'I offered food in return for my *drogas* which you and your rat-infested friend stole from me. You leave me no choice now; I will make you beg for your life.'

Satan raised the machete, taking a step towards Jack, who was defenceless, bound and feeling terrified, he tensed his sore muscles and closed his eyes waiting for the sharp blade to strike.

Then nothing.

He slowly opened his eyes and saw him close, standing over him, holding the machete blade uppermost and sliding his forefinger along the length of the sharp blade. Blood dribbled as his finger continued sliding along the cutting edge.

He shuddered, not quite believing what he was witnessing; the beast was cutting deeply through his own flesh and not even wincing while doing it. Then turning the blood-soaked blade, Satan plunged the tip of the machete into the wooden floorboards next to the mattress.

Jack saw the hand coming and quickly moved his head as Satan grabbed his hair. He was too fast and strong and forcibly turned Jack's head until he stared at the yellow, smoked-stained ceiling.

His strength weakened, and with his hands trussed behind his back, he could only watch as the beast's blood-soaked finger approached his eye.

The bloodied incision on Satan's finger went deep, and blood seeped from the parted flesh, dripping to the floor. Jack thought he intended to gouge his eyeball and recoiled, squeezing both eyes tightly shut.

He felt warm blood drip on his cheek as the finger neared his eye, and then, just as he expected his eyelid to be pushed open, he felt a gentle stroke on his forehead, then another. Keeping his eyes tightly closed, he felt the warm bloodied finger slide across his skin in gentle but well-intended strokes.

Then the grip released his hair, and he opened his eyes, Satan had stepped a few paces away from him and was smiling or grimacing, Jack wasn't sure which, and stared down at his forehead as if admiring his latest piece of work.

'*Muerto*,' Satan said, laughing as spittle sprinkled on the floor before him.

Satan had written something in blood on his forehead, but that wasn't what worried him most, and more pressing was what the unstable psychopath would do next.

He did not have to wait long as Satan bent forward, pulling the machete from the floorboard, then leaned forward, and with lightning speed, gripped hold of Jack's chin, pushing the tip of the blade onto his left cheek, the light pressure splitting the skin.

The pain was unpleasant and stingingly painful, and he winced, making a squealing sound, then felt warm blood trickle down the side of his face, across his temple and dribble into his ear.

'When I return,' he said vehemently, still holding his chin, 'I will remove bits from your body until you tell me where my *drogas* are.'

Satan nodded towards Jack's crotch, and laughing, said,

'I will remove the smallest piece first, soldier, starting with your *pene*. Then I will remove your feet and hands and then feed them to the rats.'

Releasing his chin, he leaned back, rummaged in his pocket then removed the soldier's vehicle keys. 'Now I have these, *amigo*, you will not be leaving,' he said, grotesquely smiling, then walked out of the door, slamming it closed behind him.

Lying on the stinking mattress, he turned his head and attempted to wipe the blood from his face and onto the rough material. Then lay still and thought that unless he did something soon to change his situation, there was a strong likelihood that he would die today, and probably extremely painfully. The thought of being eaten alive terrified him, he detested rats.

It seemed that Satan was becoming excited, even imaginative, about how extreme he would inflict pain on him and knew he had to somehow find some inner strength to try to break the current sequence of events.

Then his mind began to drift, and he began to think of his parents, reminding him he had once learned that when extreme fear triggers in the human brain, the extremely anxious mind attempts to cloak the distress by creating soft emotions like vulnerability, empathy and affection.

His parents had always been there when he was in need, both possessing some weird parental intuition, always knowing when he was in trouble, occasionally before it happened, stepping in, preventing, and providing solutions.

They asked for little in return, just his honesty, truthfulness and deference, they instilled hope. Now they were five thousand miles away and squeezing his damp eyes closed, wondered if their intuition alarm was flashing as they were sitting in their living room in Yorkshire; he bet it was.

Well, he thought, he had no intention of letting them down today, then he felt something comforting, a presence perhaps, as though they were there with him, his mum distressed and appealing to him to climb from the mattress and release his wrists and his dad, standing behind her as always, berating him for not doing something more to escape from the savage miscreant; that was all he needed to find the conviction and determination, he opened his eyes and decided it was time to go home.

Wincing but trying to ignore the various aches and pains, he lifted his head, eyes searching the room, looking for something obvious or inspiring that might prompt him to figure out what to do.

Unable to see anything conspicuous, he relaxed his neck muscles, resting his head back on the mattress. It seemed useless, he couldn't see anything within a close enough distance that might cut the ties binding his wrists and knew that he needed to stand and search for something sharp.

Inhaling several deep breaths and counting backwards from five, and with every bit of strength, he quickly rolled to his side, pushing himself from the mattress, while at the same time twisting his hips and colliding into the nearest wall, landing awkwardly with both knees on the hard wooden floor.

The pain was almost unbearable and surged across his back and he started to feel the beginnings of a ferocious headache. His knees hurt but he had no intention of being in this position longer than necessary and knowing that getting to his feet would be a considerable challenge.

Now he needed to shuffle across the floor to a wooden chair not too far from the bottom of the mattress. The pain in his knees was excruciating as he knelt on small wood chips and chicken bones but eventually was able to lean forward, placing his chest as far over the wooden seat as possible.

Then centring his weight on the chair by using his head and chest, he was able to straighten a leg behind him while bending the other and allowing him to manoeuvre his foot until it was flat on the floor.

The movement and imbalance caused his support to tilt and threatened to fall over due to his uneven and shifting weight, but he was able to push down with his upper body to steady the chair.

He paused, rested, then sucked in several long breaths, and feeling ready, and with all the strength he could find, pushed his body up with his bent leg, allowing him to elevate his hips and crudely slide his other foot flat onto the floor.

Now in an awkward position, half standing with his chest and head lying across the chair seat. He knew that the next movement would require every bit of strength possible while trying to balance and prevent falling over.

He took more deep breaths then, when sure he was ready, tensed and using all the strength of his chest and stomach muscles, jolted his head quickly backwards and upwards.

He groaned when his legs strained, taking the weight and stomach muscles ripped, almost losing balance, then straightening his back, tottered around the room from one foot to the other until he could steady himself and finally panting, leaned against a wall, upright and relieved but experiencing strong and surging pains throughout his body.

While waiting to catch his breath and for his racing heart to slow down, he remained still, knowing that if Satan heard any noise, he would come running into the shack, and all the effort would have been for nothing.

Then, after a full minute and dripping with sweat from the exertion, he slowly and quietly walked around the room, searching for something to release his bound wrists.

Walking into the cooking area of the room he saw a mirror hanging from the wall and thought the glass could be used to cut his bonds then saw that it was a piece of smooth polished metal.

He looked at the reflection staring back at him and moaned. His face was terrible; his right cheek was streaked with deep black and purple grazes and wields, blood still oozing from the wound.

His left cheek had a half-inch open gash caused earlier by Satan's machete; fresh blood had run down his face, covering his ear, and his hair stiff and matted with drying blood.

He looked at the word written in blood on his forehead and read the backward reflection. '*Muerto*' had no meaning, and thought it had to be some sick ritual inflicted on poor mortals Satan was about to torture and kill.

Thinking of Satan reminded him that he should check where the creature was and walked to the window overlooking the clearing.

He was standing shoulder-high in a trench and using a shovel to dig fresh earth from a hole. He bent forward, head and shoulders disappearing, and a second later reappeared swinging the shovel and tipping soil to a mound of earth next to the trench. Then he bent forward and repeated the action a second or so later.

Jack curiously observed his captor, sweating and panting, wiping sweat from his forehead with the back of his hand, then stopping to rest.

He looked at the mound of fresh soil, trying to work out why Satan was digging such a deep hole, and then his eyes caught sight of Mikel's body lying in front of the old Land Rover bonnet, just beyond that, Gareth's body, then his heart rate quickened as it dawned on him; Satan was digging a grave. The beast was going to dispose of the bodies and if he didn't get his hands released soon, he would be going in the grave with them.

In a sudden panic, he began to pant and quickly stepped away from the window. He returned to the cooking area and noticed a door in the back wall which allowed access to the rear of the shack. For a second, he thought of running back into the jungle but then quickly dismissed the idea, there would be no point with his wrists firmly tied, and anyway, Satan would be on him in seconds.

He studied the door frame and the hinges, and saw, on the left side of the door, part of a wooden wall plank had rotted away, and a small piece of corrugated iron sheeting was tacked over it, filling the gap. Importantly, the sharp bottom edge of the metal was bent outwards and protruded from the wall.

Assuming he could turn his back and step backwards, feeling for the metal, he could perhaps rub the bonds securing his wrists against the sharp edge.

He turned and pushed his elbows out and then painfully moved his fingers, feeling for and then gently touching the piece of metal. The movement helping him to realise his hands were becoming almost entirely numb; ignoring his concern, he moved his fingers along the edge of the metal, pulled his wrists apart and against the ties then began to rub backwards and forwards, feeling vibrations in his wrists.

Five or six strokes and his hands fell apart as the sharp metal edge sliced through the rope binding.

He carefully lifted his painful hands to his face and saw that vasoconstriction had caused his fingers to swell and had turned a greyish colour.

Gently rubbing his fingers together and encouraging blood to circulate, he winced, feeling a sharp stinging sensation as the blood began to flow and pressure increased.

He looked around the disorganised and messy room and then began searching for anything that could be used as a weapon and saw a small wooden work surface covered with chicken bones, and a dented tin box. He removed the lid, and tipped the contents onto the work surface, amongst the chewed bones and saw old coins, a cigarette lighter, a razor blade and a lock knife.

Examining the lock knife, he pressed the lock, and unfolded the six-inch blade, which was old, rusty and blunt, then snapped it back into a closed position, placing it into his pocket. Then he picked up the cigarette lighter and flicked the flint, it worked so also pocketed it.

Then went back to the window, bent slightly, and dropped to his knees, slowly raising his eyes to the glass.

Satan was panting and struggling, dragging Mikel's rigid body towards the grave; he was beginning to clean up and bury the dead.

Mikel's body had stiffened, his arms curiously splayed from his sides in the form of a crucifix. Rigour Mortis prevented the arms from bending which caused further drag and friction as Satan grappled to pull the body across the rough ground.

He saw him slip over, then pulled himself up, taking hold of the legs and continued dragging.

As he neared the grave, Satan dropped the legs, fell to the ground, exhausted, and lay on his back, chest heaving and panting for breath. When recovered, he stood and began to pull the upper half of Mikel's body as close to the grave as possible and then attempted to swing the body into the trench.

Grotesquely, instead of Mikel's body disappearing into the abyss, the contorted body freakishly lay, face up, suspended by the stiffened arms and legs, lying bizarrely across the opening of the grave.

Satan stared at the transversally dangling corpse, the stiffness of death preventing Mikel from falling into the trench.

Then, as if in the act of lunacy, he raised his machete above his head and attempted to chop at Mikel's arms at the shoulders in a display of absolute disrespect for his dead lieutenant.

The blade was repeatedly brought down, but the drying leather-like skin and dense bone only caused the blade to rebound, doing nothing.

Frustrated, he dropped the machete and wiped his brow, then to Jack's utter astonishment, he placed a foot onto the middle of Mikel's chest and applied some of his weight, the outstretched arms and legs flexed slightly, but the stiff limbs showed reluctance and refused to give way; his lieutenant obviously not yet ready to go to his grave.

Jack continued to watch Satan, as he raised his other foot from the ground and positioned it next to the foot already on Mikel's chest, then unsurprisingly Mikel's arms snapped at the shoulders, and both disappeared into the dark hole.

It was the moment that Jack had waited for but hadn't expected, he didn't even think about what he would do; he just did it, impulsively.

Pulling the door open, he rushed out of the shack and, jumping from the porch, running with every ounce of strength he could find.

Heading towards the track on the far side of the clearing, he saw that he would have to run between the grave and the Land Rover and guessed Satan would struggle to leave the steep-sided trench, affording him time to gain much-needed distance.

Enduring more aches and pains than he had ever known, he knew that he had to harness every bit of strength and energy to put distance between himself and the lunatic and escape from this hell.

Nearing the grave, Satan's head and shoulders appeared above the hole, an expression of shock on his face which only gave Jack the motivation to run faster.

Maintaining his focus on the exit by the river, he realised he was formulating a plan as he ran and his intention would be to continue along the exit track, then through the jungle and finally to the tarmac road, then hopefully, flag down a passing vehicle, either that or just continue running for however long it takes to get away.

He heard Satan shouting as he passed the Land Rover but had no concern for the drug lord now. The shouting ceased and he guessed the lunatic was too preoccupied with attempting to climb out of the grave, anyway, he was well on his way and felt exhilarated.

His motivation increased and knew that in less than a hundred metres, he would enter the exit path and then would soon be running along the track to safety.

As the last fifty metres became a reality, his attention focussed on a large tree trunk which lay across the track just before the exit; curious, he couldn't remember it being there yesterday when Gareth had driven into the clearing.

He thought that perhaps his captor had somehow placed it there to prevent a vehicle escape. It was of no concern now because, in a few seconds, he would jump over the obstacle just before disappearing into the foliage.

Then, when he was less than ten metres from the exit and with utter despair, he saw the tree trunk slowly rise on four legs, turning its ghastly head towards him.

Satan had awkwardly collapsed into the grave, badly winding himself. Worse, he had fallen on Mikel's chest, collapsing his sternum, the impact had caused the already rotten stomach cavity to split open, spilling stinking pieces of innards and splashing foul congealing blood on him.

Gasping, he attempted to get his breath back, and sat on Mikel's body, nursing his grazed and bleeding chin, which he had scraped down the side wall of the grave during the descent.

The stench was terrible, heaviest at the bottom of the hole, and he knew he must get some fresh air, but as he stood and his head appeared above the trench, he saw the soldier running towards him.

Initially, fearing the soldier would attack, he dropped onto his backside only to cause more foul-smelling gas to belch from Mikel's open stomach. The fetor was overpowering and possibly the foulest smell he had ever experienced; he covered his nose and mouth with his hand and coughed, gasping for clean air.

Then heard the pounding of the soldier's feet running past the grave, and pulling himself up, used his feet to shimmy the rough side wall and was able to haul himself out and roll across the ground.

Standing, he collected his machete which had been lying on the ground and turned to see the back of the soldier, running and creating distance and heading for the exit track.

In an act of sheer rage, he swung the machete above his head and yelled at the escaping soldier, 'You are dead, *amigo*; I have people who will tell me where to find you.'

Then remembering his gun, he wiped the blood from his hands on his shirt, rummaged in his pocket and removed the weapon, then ran to the Land Rover and steadied himself against the side of the vehicle, aiming the weapon towards the escaping soldier.

He looked along the sights of the gun, then astonished, lowered the weapon trying to focus with his one eye, realising the soldier had stopped running and was standing motionless several metres before the track.

Perplexed, he tried to think why his quarry had stopped so close to freedom and was now stationary. Unperturbed, he raised the gun and again aligned the sight; the soldier had given him the perfect opportunity to put a bullet into the back of his head before his escape.

Applying pressure on the trigger, he aimed once again, but then, and for a second time Satan lowered the gun and watched the soldier turn around and began running back towards him.

He had to exert all his energy to stop running when he saw the tree trunk move, his feet acting like brakes to dramatically reduce forward momentum while maintaining balance to prevent falling over.

'For fuck's sake,' he wailed as he came to a dead stop. Although he felt like falling to his knees and crying with anguish at a further setback preventing yet another attempt to escape, the thought was quickly dismissed when he saw the outline of the creature's colossal head.

He stood perfectly still, staring at the crocodile and its thick, leathery skin, bony plate-shaped scales covered its long body which reached possibly more than four metres in length. The sheer size of its huge girth, eliminating any chance he would be able to jump over it. He considered running around, but the river was too close, and there was a danger he could fall in trying to circumvent the beast.

Ferociously thrashing its tail and revealing massive jaws lined with rows of cone-shaped and pointed teeth, the crocodile, began to adopt an aggressive and offensive posture. Its greyish-brown scaley body glistened with water droplets.

Jack remembered that crocodiles mostly left the water when desperate to eat, and considered what would be worse, being torn apart by this beast or the one he had left behind.

The animal opened its huge pink mouth, displaying large

bone-shattering teeth, then roared and bellowed, discharging a colossal plume of humid breath; he recoiled, feeling turbulence around him, then panicked when the monster began to shuffle towards him, quickly becoming a gentle trot.

Shocked and turning around quickly, he began to run towards his Land Rover, thinking he might find safety by getting inside or underneath as he heard the creature's feet pounding and gaining ground on him.

Then he saw Satan standing next to the Land Rover, pointing his handgun directly at him causing him to think there were not many near-death scenarios left that he could experience. He decided that being shot would be slightly more appealing than being eaten alive by the reptile now behind him.

As he ran, he watched Satan move his feet apart, seemingly adopting an aiming position and thought he was going to shoot him, leaving his fate with the crocodile.

A deafening crack rang out, and he jerked then lowered his head, hearing the bullet instantly whistle past him, followed by a puff of white smoke emerging from the gun's barrel. Still running, Jack glanced over his shoulder and saw he had extended a little distance from the monster as it continued its awkward but impressive trot.

His concentration was distracted, and his foot connected with a squawking hen; losing his balance, he held out his hands, falling forward, the momentum making him fall heavily and roll along the dusty ground. He tried to curl his body to limit injury and then stopped moving, lying face down in the dirt.

Dazed and winded, he lay for a second and was just about to push himself up when he felt a hand take hold of his shirt, supporting him and pulling him onto his knees.

Satan wrapped his forearm tightly around Jack's neck, forcing him to turn and face the approaching crocodile and uttered throatily,

'He can smell the rotten bodies; it makes him hungry.'

Jack looked on in terror as the massive beast cantered towards him, unable to move; then he caught a glimpse of the gun in his side vision and felt the weight when Satan rested a hand on his shoulder then aimed at the reptile, and said in a strained and rasping voice, 'Do not be afraid, if it bleeds, I can kill it.'

He squeezed his eyes closed and braced himself as two deafening shots rang out, the thundering blasts instantly numbing his right eardrum, causing an immediate high-pitched ringing and whistling sound.

Then the gun exploded again, but this time he felt the heat from the blast more than he heard the sound and thought his eardrum had undoubtedly burst following the trauma of the first two shots.

Then everything became quiet as he slowly opened his eyes, it was silent, a thick plume of white smoke surrounded him, like being in dense fog, the smell reminding him of fireworks, and then the smoke slowly began to drift and fade.

To his utter shock, a massive set of open jaws appeared through the smoke, inches away from where he knelt, frightened, he quickly recoiled against Satan, throwing his arms as if trying to hug him.

Just as he thought the jaws were about to clamp down on his head, the reptile stopped, the mouth snapping shut, and he saw blood spreading across the beast's head and two round bullet holes in its forehead.

In the surrealness of it all, he peered at its small brown eyes and watched the eyelid membranes blink as if winking. The beast was hurt, and he was convinced the bullets had ripped through its brain and waited for the colossal reptile to slump to the ground, dead.

He was wrong.

The monster managed to take a couple of steps backwards, opened its jaws and with a blast of breath, gave a massive and deafening roar.

Jack felt moisture on his face and his hair blow back as the humid waft of air blasted him. Then watched the beast close its jaws, and winking its eyes again, turned and awkwardly shuffled its colossal body, deftly walking towards the river.

The hand holding the gun disappeared from his shoulder and then Jack could feel the hard metal press against his temple. Satan tightened the arm around his neck, causing him to gag and unable to properly breathe.

His left ear was still deaf and ringing as he was forcibly pulled backwards, falling from his knees and pushing his legs forwards, attempting to dig his heels into the ground, creating resistance, but it was impossible.

Satan was insanely strong and maintained a vice-like grip around his neck, dragging him along the ground, gun against his temple; he began to feel lightheaded as a burning sensation filled his head, indicating blood and oxygen restriction. Then realised he was being dragged towards the grave and thought it quite possible, he could pass out before getting there.

'All right, I've had enough,' he croaked weakly. 'I'll show you where your drugs are; just stop choking me.'

Satan released his grip, allowing him to fall to the ground, coughing, gasping for air, and lying on his back. Then, conscious of the lunatic's shadow shading his face from the sun, he opened his eyes and saw him standing over him, pointing the gun at his head.

Gasping for breath, he spat on the ground, and waited until could begin to breathe normally, then turned over and attempted to stand, as Satan gripped his shirt and pulled him to his feet.

He turned and faced his captor and stared at his usual hideous grimace.

Then incredibly finding some humour amongst the horror of the situation, thought the crocodile had seemed a lot less menacing to look at.

'You show me my *drogas*, pig, and I promise I will make it very quick for you. Just one bullet in your tiny brain will be enough.'

Ironically, after what he had been through already, Jack thought that may be the best offer he had heard all day. 'Wait,' he croaked, 'just one minute, please.'

'No soldier, your time has run out; I want my things NOW!'

Jack felt warm spittle speckle his cheek.

Weakly lifting his hand, he pointed toward the old Land Rover bonnet. 'It's there,' he said.

Satan flicked the gun in the vehicle's direction, indicating that Jack should start walking.

He stumbled towards the vehicle as his captor fell in behind him, pointing the gun at his back.

He walked past the grave and glanced down seeing the crumpled corpse of Mikel, then walked past rusting vehicle parts and a pile of tyres towards the old dilapidated vehicle.

The hens, having calmed down after the trauma of the

crocodile incident, innocently clucked and scraped the ground with their claws, searching for insects amongst the old British army vehicle parts.

'If you do anything, I will shoot you dead, do not think that you can escape.' Satan announced.

Jack felt that he was almost past caring now; too weak and hurting too much; there wasn't much fight left in him. Every opportunity to escape had disastrously failed and at least the pain and anguish would be over very soon.

Arriving at the front of the rusting Land Rover, he saw Mikel's dried blood, caked on the grill and bumper. On the ground a large patch of dark blood, a line of ants busily biting tiny blood fragments, taking them back to their nest to store and be eaten later.

'I have to open it,' he said.

'Do it slowly and remember I will blow your head off if you try anything stupid,' replied Satan.

Using both hands, he carefully pushed the bonnet upwards; his arms were weak, and he faltered at least twice, then holding the metal plate, he reached inside and used the hood rod as support, knowing Satan would be reluctant to look closely after what he had done to Mikel.

Jack suddenly became troubled, realising he couldn't identify the air filter housing or ever having seen one, and all he could see was a rusting engine. He looked around, but there was nothing obvious.

'What are you waiting for pig? What is the delay,' Satan shouted angrily.

He recalled Gareth had said something about a centre screw, removing it using his fingernail, so searched again until noticing a large rust-eaten casing in the centre, a screw protruding and loose.

He reached in and, turned the screw with his finger and thumb, removed it, then using both hands, pulled the top casing which came away easily and threw the round metal disk to the side of the vehicle.

Inside the oily cavity, he was relieved when he recognised Baptiste's dirty towel which was wrapped around something bulky, and assumed it was the bundles of money and packs of narcotics. 'It's there, inside the filter, you can see it; there are your drugs and money.'

He glanced at Satan and saw the side of his mouth turn up and realised the monster was smiling at what he thought had been worth all the violence, bloodshed and death.

'You think I am stupid; you *gilipollas*; take it out and put it on the ground.'

Jack leaned forward and placed both his hands into the filter, removing the towel-draped package, then stepped away from the vehicle, and turning towards Satan, placed the package on the ground in front of him.

'Step back, *amigo*, and don't do anything stupid.'

He did as he was ordered as Satan continued to point the gun towards him, cautiously watching with his single eye, then using his foot, kicked at the towel until the sides fell open.

Jack looked at what lay inside the cloth and saw four large bags of brown powder and several large bundles of cash notes. There was a lot, an awful lot.

Satan gave a cackled laugh through the side of his mouth as if relieved, then crouched and wrapped the towel around his possessions. At no point did he take his eye off Jack, then stood upright and grimaced.

Oddly, Jack felt relieved, realising the mayhem was almost over. It had taken the lives of three men for Satan to reclaim his property, and now there was only one bit of unfinished business standing in his way, him.

He knew that the monster would have to eliminate the last issue before leaving the clearing and continue leading his cartel business.

Jack stared back at him, gazing into his single bloodshot eye, then thought he would try to establish if there was even the tiniest bit of humility in the monster's soul and asked, 'You have it now; why don't you just leave in your vehicle? I'll set fire to the whole place and burn the bodies and I will make sure nothing will ever be found. Let me have my vehicle keys and I promise you will never see me again.'

Satan stared at him for several seconds without reacting and for a second Jack thought that there could be a possibility that he may accept what he had asked, that was until he began to laugh loudly, his chest energetically heaving and shaking.

'You think I am stupid, soldier? There are already three stinking bodies here, and, in a moment, there will be four. Now walk to your vehicle, and then I will end your miserable life; now move!'

Jack turned and began the short walk to his Land Rover, followed by Satan holding the gun and carrying the drugs and money wrapped in the towel under his arm.

They stopped at the back of his Land Rover and Satan asked, 'What do you have in this vehicle, soldier?'

So much had happened in the previous twenty-four hours, the trauma had caused slight amnesia and Jack had honestly forgotten.

'I can't remember,' he replied.

'Show me,' Satan demanded.

Jack moved the tarpaulin hood to one side, revealing the ammunition box and a coiled-up rope in the vehicle's rear.

'What is that,' asked Satan.

'It's a rope,' he replied.

'No not that you fool, the box, the box; what is in it?'

Jack reached into the vehicle's rear, slid the box onto the tailgate, and snapped open the stiff fastenings. He was about to open the lid when Satan pressed the gun into his temple, saying, 'Be very careful if there is something I don't like in this box; I will kill you instantly.'

He slowly pulled the lid upwards, tilting the box towards him at the same time, Satan carefully glanced inside and nodded, confirming it was empty.

'That's good, I will put my drugs and money in the box, and each time I open it, I will remember you and what you did to Mikel,' he said, grinning.

Jack didn't care, he felt exhausted.

Satan then flicked the gun, indicating he should step away from him while he placed the package into the box, then snapped the lid shut, ensuring the clasps were fixed, grasped the handle and instructed Jack to turn around and walk to the grave.

He complied and as he turned to face the grave, heard the ammunition box sliding from the tailgate then heard Satan position himself behind him and felt the gun touch the middle of his back.

As they walked, Satan felt enthusiastic about what he intended to do. He planned to shoot Jack in the head, allowing his body to fall into the grave along with Mikel, then would drag what was left of Baptiste and the other soldier, also throwing them into the hole.

He knew the autumn rain would arrive soon and without human attention, and over the coming days and weeks, the jungle would quickly spread and repossess the area, and the bodies would be gone forever.

Then he began to embrace an overwhelming feeling of dominance and authority, having been responsible for the demise of three men and a fourth was about to join them in minutes, he felt it was an outstanding achievement in such a short time, finding difficulty to contain his exhilaration and felt himself trembling, saliva dribbling down his chin.

Jack stopped when he reached the edge of the grave and looking down into the bottom, where Mikel's body lay, frowned when the odour of decay and rot hit his nostrils.

Satan pushed his weight against him, almost causing him to fall forward into the grave, then held his shirt and pulled him back, allowing him to regain his balance.

Jack expected a nano-second of splitting pain as the bullet entered the back of his head before collapsing into the grave. Squeezing his eyes tightly closed, he tensed every muscle in his body and waited.

'Turn around, soldier,' Satan ordered.

Opening his eyes, he did as he was told and turned to face what he thought may be the last person he would ever see, staring into the single eye and festering eye socket of the most disgusting, hideous, and evil man he had experienced in his short life.

Then taking a step backwards, Satan, still holding the

ammunition box under one arm, raised the gun in his other hand and pointed the barrel to the centre of Jack's forehead, no more than a centimetre from his skull.

'I will make it quick for you, and I would like my face to be the last thing you see before death, so when we meet in hell, you will recognise me,' he said, smiling in his usual facially contorted way.

Jack thought he could hear a vehicle's engine in the distance.

'You British came here with the false pretence of protecting us but now think you own us; we never wanted you here. You brought nothing to my country except your stinking rules, domination and disease. You have made my brothers and sisters greedy; do you think paying for sex with our women makes us proud?'

Jack tried to listen to the rant but was distracted and was almost certain he could hear a vehicle in the distance, and it was getting closer.

Satan spat on the ground as Jack, staring at the gun, saw his finger begin to squeeze the trigger.

He who establishes his strength by command
shows that his reason is weak

Michel de Montaigne

'For Christ's sake Stan, slow down!'

Stan had steered the Land Rover off the main road and was manically fighting with the steering wheel as the vehicle sped along the track, parallel and close to the river.

'Slow down; otherwise, we'll end up in the bloody water,' Lewis shouted with no effect.

Stan was too preoccupied and concentrating on his mission, he hadn't spoken to Lewis during the entire journey and that wasn't going to change now. He was determined to get to the shack as fast as possible, convinced his friends were in trouble and needed his assistance and no one was going to stand in his way.

Lewis realised it was useless talking to him, he seemed to be in some type of hypnotic state and instead, concentrated on bracing himself as the Land Rover bounced and jolted on the unevenness of the track.

Eventually, the relief was overwhelming when he saw the opening to the clearing ahead of them.

The vehicle's speed launched them through the foliage and

into the sunlight, the soldiers immediately made a visual search of the area across the clearing, then astonished at what they could see unfolding in front of them.

Two men were standing and facing each other close to the river. They were perhaps two feet apart, the larger of the two was holding something small at the head of the other man.

The vehicle was travelling fast and as the distance shortened, they both recognised that the smaller of the two men was their friend, Jack.

Relief was quickly replaced by confusion, then anguish when they saw that the other man, who neither recognised, was holding a gun to their friend's head and appeared as though he was about to discharge it.

Stan's determination turned to distress and pushed the accelerator to the floor, steering the vehicle towards the men as the one holding the gun looked over his shoulder, staring at the fast-approaching vehicle.

'Christ Stan, hurry I think he is about to shoot Jack.'

'I've got it Lewis; you just make sure your seat belt is on,' he shouted above the noise of the roaring engine as the vehicle increased acceleration.

The moment he had seen Satan's finger begin to squeeze the trigger, his thoughts once again turned to his parents and the devastation which would be followed by shock and disbelief when the army notification officer visited their home to inform them of his terrible death; he only hoped they would be informed that he had tragically died and not the events leading to his demise.

He quietly said to himself, 'I love you, Mum, tell Dad to be strong and please forgive me,' then squeezed his eyes tightly closed, causing a single tear to trickle down his face while waiting for the shocking blast from the barrel of the gun.

Nothing

The ever-nearing sound of the roaring engine compelled him to open his eyes and saw that Satan had half-turned away from him and was observing the fast-approaching British Army Land Rover.

Awkwardly shuffling his feet, Satan completely turned to face away from Jack and heaved the ammunition box to his chest with one hand then raised and pointed the gun towards the vehicle, the engine roaring and accelerating towards them both.

As the distance between them and the vehicle reduced, Jack tilted his head to look around Satan and feeling relieved, recognised the unmistakable features of Stan driving and Lewis as a passenger.

'You have to slow down, Stan,' Lewis shouted above the noise of the screaming engine, 'you're going to hit them both.'

Stan, ignoring him, was busy trying to calculate the distance between the two men and the river behind them. He knew that if he didn't apply the brakes at precisely the right moment, there would not be enough ground to stop and could launch the vehicle into the river.

Lewis saw Stan lean slightly forwards, straining against his seatbelt, preparing for impact and then looked ahead in time to see that the unknown man had turned, the gun now pointing directly towards them.

He felt himself begin to nervously tremble with fear and shouted, 'You realise you are going to kill Jack, don't you Stan?'

There was no response, so placed both his hands on the dashboard, bracing himself for the inevitable impact.

The vehicle accelerated towards them at a terrifying speed, and Jack understood the impact would be devastating, then he began to panic, his mind racing and believing that this was the end for them both.

Then he heard a voice whispering from somewhere deep inside of his mind, a gentle female voice, supportive and vaguely familiar; she spoke three words, '*Use the knife.*'

He wasn't confused or alarmed and didn't need to hear it again, there was no need, and remembering he still had the lock knife he had found in the shack, removed it from his pocket, released the blade from the handle and forcibly thrust it forward, watching the rusty metal disappear into Satan's lower back.

The beast gave a gut-retching wail, and blood instantly spread across his shirt, then wasting no time, Jack withdrew the blade and quickly thrust it into his back again. This time, twisting the handle and felt warm blood gush across his hand and wrist.

Satan shuddered and faltered then suddenly began trembling and leaning forward, he lowered his hand and the gun fell to the ground.

Then, as if greed was more important than death, he tried to straighten and using both hands, heaved the ammunition box and held it to his chest as if he could somehow protect his possessions from the fast-approaching vehicle.

In the final few seconds, before the vehicle made a bone-crunching impact, Lewis saw, in detail, the terrible and contorted expression of his friend's assailant, and at that moment, knew he was looking into the face of pure terror and torment and any concern for what was about to be inflicted on him, quickly evaporated.

At the same time Stan said something which was drowned by the thundering and roaring engine. 'Do something Jack, do it, do it NOW!'

Then, in a fraction of the final second before impact, he squeezed his eyes shut and stamped, with all his weight, on the brake pedal.

The noise of flesh and bone being hit by a mark III Land Rover travelling at 60 miles per hour made a repulsive and nauseating sound, they had prepared themselves for perhaps a noticeable jolt but barely felt anything as the forward trajectory of the 2900 lb vehicle ploughed into the human bodies.

It was more of a nudge than an impact, almost like hitting something soft and squidgy with a hard rock. The two men in front of the vehicle instantly disappeared as both front wheels alarmingly jolted downwards and then lurched into the air.

Stan continued to apply his full weight, pushing down on the brake pedal, at the same time pulling the handbrake as the wheels locked into a brief skid. Then, in an instant, when the front wheels fell to the ground, the rear wheels dropped as if the earth had opened and swallowed the back end.

The vehicle abruptly and instantly stopped, jolting Stan and Lewis forward, and if it had not been for their strained and locking seatbelts; would have been thrown forward through the small windscreen.

The Mark III, which had been designed for driving across the world's most inhospitable terrain, and whose leaf suspension and telescopic dampeners were able to cope with almost anything but not prepared for driving over a broad, and deep soft-sided trench at high speed and the rear wheels were now firmly stuck in the hole it had been driven over.

The acidic smell of burning brake pads and grinding clutch filled their nostrils, steam and smoke pouring from the engine, and escaping from the sides of the bonnet and grill.

Slightly traumatised and suffering from mild whiplash and perhaps a fractured rib or two, the soldiers silently stared ahead at the calm and serene slow-moving river as disturbed birds flew into the sky and wildlife, perturbed by the commotion, created an orchestra of hooting and wailing across the clearing.

Then, together they witnessed something so unimaginable, the memory was seared into their minds, and they would never forget.

Within seconds of the vehicle stopping and while listening to the noise of the stalled engine ticking and hissing as it began to cool, they saw the body of a man in the air above the water having been struck with such force, his body catapulted upwards and over the river. They watched the body descend and splash into the muddy brown water, followed by the ammunition box splashing close by.

The box floated for a moment then slowly submerged while the limp body resurfaced and bobbed in the water face down, both the soldiers staring in astonishment.

'No way, did you see that, or did I just imagine it?' Lewis asked, aghast.

Stan quickly clambered from the vehicle and ran to the water's edge, followed by Lewis; they looked towards the body floating in the water.

'It must be the guy who was holding the ammunition box; I

think that's what splashed in the river next to him, it couldn't possibly have been Jack, he was too big.' Stan replied.

Then the water around the floating body began to swirl and froth as the air was released from under the surface, the water bubbled and gurgled as a huge crocodile surfaced alongside the floating body, opened its massive jaws and then smashed its teeth down and onto the head in a vice-like grip.

The creature remained motionless for a few seconds, then gradually sank under the surface, taking the body with it, the feet last to disappear into the brown water, as the body was dragged to the depths by the enormous reptilian beast.

Lewis felt his heart pounding against his chest and continued to watch as the disturbance on the surface of the water began to settle and then quickly return to its calmness, then he shuddered and said, 'There is no way Jack could have got out of the way, I saw him disappear under the front bumper when we hit them.'

'I know, I'm sorry but I thought he would have a plan; he normally does,' Stan replied.

Lewis walked to the water's edge and watched the ripples of water still washing to the muddy sides, wondering what had been in the ammunition box. He waited with the hope it might resurface, and at the same time, Stan, on his hands and knees, tentatively searched under the front of the Land Rover, looking for any evidence of Jack's body; inspecting the undercarriage, he saw traces of blood across the front bumper and grill.

Standing, he walked to the rear of the vehicle and sighed when he saw the rear wheels had sunk into what looked like a broad trench, then realised the hole had effectively stopped the vehicle when the rear tyres dropped down into it, the weight preventing any further traction coupled by the locked brakes.

'Lewis, I can't find him, would you look around the undergrowth by the river for any body parts, please?' he shouted.

Then to their utter astonishment, a muffled and croaky voice could be heard from deep in the hole below the Land Rover.

'I'm in here, you silly buggers; come and help me climb out!'

Lewis ran to the rear of their vehicle joining Stan and together dropped on their hands and knees, crawling around and searching between the sides of the hole, obstructed by large clumps of earth and the half-sunken rubber tyres.

Then, from the depths of the trench, Lewis thought he saw movement and crawling under the vehicle chassis, saw Jack's face, partially covered in soil, eyes staring up at them.

His hands appeared from the earth surrounding him and he started brushing loose soil from his face while spitting and coughing. Stan and Lewis used their hands like shovels to pull soil from around him and only when they got deeper into the hole, inhaled the overbearing and disgusting stench of rot causing them to retch and gag.

'Try standing and hold your hand towards me; watch your head on the tyres mate,' Stan said and leaned between the side of the hole and the undercarriage of the vehicle, reaching with both hands to his friend.

Lewis assisted, and together, they carefully hauled him, as he supported his weight by holding onto the side of the wheel arch, then he was pulled from the hole and dragged along the ground and away from the trench.

Helping him to his feet, he coughed and blew soil from his nostrils, and they helped by brushing him down with their hands, then they laughed, hugged, and cheered together; it was an emotional reunion and he felt tears welling in his eyes.

When they calmed, Jack explained that a fraction of a second before the vehicle struck, he had pushed against his already fatally wounded captor, creating a momentum for him to descend rapidly into the grave.

He had looked up seeing the front bumper passing over his head, followed by the front axle lurching upwards, his fall had been cushioned by Mikel's decaying body, and then as he lay facing upwards, saw the rear wheels crash into the trench, causing the soft earth sides to collapse and clumps of soil to fall and almost bury him.

The elation and relief of surviving the impact had overwhelmed him only to be replaced by dread realising that the falling soil could have buried him alive.

Stan apologised and explained that he had prayed seconds before, hoping Jack had worked out how to avoid the impact but then thought it must have been impossible and they had both been killed.

Jack placed his hand on Stan's shoulder, reassuring him that he had done the right thing and that there was no one else who possessed the determination or courage to do what he did, then thanked them both for deciding to launch a rescue mission, because if they hadn't, he would be dead.

Lewis cast a shrewd glance towards Stan, who stared back in disgust.

Stan looked closely at Jack's visible injuries and said, 'You look dreadful, Jack, what happened to your face? You're going to need some stitches in those cuts, I'll get the first aid kit and see what is in it.'

'Not now,' Jack said, 'there is more important stuff we need to do, but firstly, where is Satan's body? He has something in his pocket that I need.'

'Satan?' Lewis asked, 'isn't that the name of Baptiste's cousin? Bloody hell, was he the guy who was holding the gun? I can't believe it; he's got a gruesome reputation and is head of Belize's biggest drug cartel.'

Jack curiously looked at him for a few seconds then inquisitively asked, 'Exactly how do you know so much about the guy who almost killed me and his reputation, Lewis?'

Stan interrupted 'If you are talking about the ugly bloke who was pointing the gun, he was flung into the river when he got hit by the vehicle, and then a massive crocodile dragged his body under the surface, I don't think anyone is ever going to be bothered by that vile and evil beast again.'

Jack smiled and paused for a second, then asked, 'Did the crocodile have two bullet holes in its head?'

Stan and Lewis looked at each other, perplexed.

Trying to laugh at his own humour and wincing simultaneously, he raised a hand, touching his painful jaw. 'Forget it; I'll explain later. Anyway, I don't know about you two, but I need a strong drink, and there should be a bottle of rum on the porch.' Then he began to walk towards the shack, followed by the others.

As they walked, Lewis increased his speed and catching up with Jack asked, 'What has happened to Gareth? Is he okay?'

'He's dead, mate,' Jack dispassionately replied without looking at him and feeling he had been to a terrifying and dark place and witnessed too much death to express any emotion at this time. 'Let's sit on the porch, guys, and I'll tell you everything.'

The rum was still where Satan had left it the evening before, Jack removed the cork from the bottle and gulped the clear liquid, then screwed his face as the cheap alcohol stung the back of his throat.

Then he told them everything.

He began by describing the shocking events of the last twenty-four hours, calmly and succinctly, from the moment they arrived at the clearing, finding that Baptiste's body had gone and the warning etched into the wall, Mikel crushed under the bonnet and Gareth's gruesome death.

He told them of his experience being trapped in the jungle and of his frequently failed escapes, the massive crocodile blocking his escape and plunging the knife into Satan's back moments before impact.

Throughout the recount, his friends sat silently in almost disbelief; there was no need for any clarification and no questions; they just listened, quietly dumbstruck until he had finished, then watched in silence as he drank the last of the rum from the bottle.

He had intentionally withheld some of the most extreme and shocking detail for another time, conscious they had a lot of work to do and eager to get as far as possible away from the clearing.

Stan had been hoping to attract his attention when he had finished talking, feeling it was important for him to be aware of Lewis's detailed historical knowledge of Satan's involvement.

Finding the moment, he said, 'There is something you are probably unaware of Jack, if you were, this might have ended quite differently, particularly for Gareth.

'This backslider,' nodding towards Lewis, 'admitted that he

306

had been aware that Baptiste was working for Satan and knew all along that the drugs and money belonged to the cartel. The vehicle enterprise was a cover and Baptiste was used by his cousin to store the drugs and keep his head below the drug enforcement agency's radar.

'As soon as Lewis discovered that visiting the clearing and dealing with Baptiste was becoming dangerous, he stopped but was more than satisfied for the threat and risk to transfer to Gareth and then you.'

Silence

Lewis spoke quietly, 'I'm sorry Jack, and know it's too late to change anything. What happened to Gareth could have been avoided and none of this would have happened if I had been more honest, what can I say?'

'It doesn't matter now; there's no changing what has happened, just learn from it and we have to move on,' Jack said, then paused, adding, 'I had probably always known some things just don't add up with you Lewis, but now is not the time to finger-point; we need to work as a team and what happened here needs to be cleaned up and confined to this place.'

He stepped onto the porch, turned to face them then gave instructions on what needed to be done.

'Firstly, we winch your vehicle out and use the rope to tow my vehicle to the edge of the clearing. It will have to be towed all the way back to camp later because, the ignition keys, along with Satan, are in the stomach of a crocodile. Then we will have to put Gareth and Baptiste's bodies in the grave along with Mikel and cover them up.

'When that is done, we pour petrol everywhere and on

everything, and I mean everything and then only when we are satisfied that the whole place is drenched with accelerant, we set the entire clearing ablaze and then allow the jungle and wildlife to reclaim its territory.

'That's what Gareth and I came here to do and now that is how we will finish it before we leave.'

Lewis asked, 'What do we say about Gareth? He has family back in Cardiff, they will want to know.'

Jack looked at him, thinking, then said, 'Firstly, we should understand that however we handle this, I know that Gareth will forgive us; if it had been one of us in the same circumstances, he would have done the same.

'So, we say nothing, when we are back at work, they will ask where he is, and we say we don't know, we haven't seen him since, (*pause*) since leaving the Moonshine bar the day before yesterday, we say no more than that.

'He'll get reported as a missing person; he won't be the first or the last; they'll assume he got drunk in town and ended up dead in a ditch or perhaps gone absent without leave with a prostitute or some local girl; remember that bloke from the Parachute Regiment who went missing a couple of months back, well they haven't found him, and there doesn't seem much effort to do so.

'Now let's get on with it, there are some jerry cans of petrol around here, and there's one that we brought here on the porch.'

'We brought a couple of jerry cans of petrol, they are in our Land Rover,' Stan said.

'Good, the more, the better, we need to make sure everything is incinerated, and nothing can be identified or traced back to us. Anyone who sees the fire, or the smoke will think someone is burning the undergrowth. After a few weeks and good rainfall, the jungle will take it back.'

Then Lewis asked, 'Can I just ask about the money Jack? I'm not sure you explained what happened to it?'

'How did I know you would be the one to ask Lewis,' he replied. 'I didn't say where it was earlier because I knew you might want to know specific details, and I was right; after showing Satan where it was hidden, he put it in the ammunition box. The same box he was holding when your Land Rover hit him. If you saw the ammunition box end up in the river, then that's where the money and drugs are.'

Lewis queried, 'Do you think he closed the latches properly? If he did, it should be watertight.'

'Oh, give it a rest Lewis; I told you; the priority is to dispose of all the evidence, including the bodies; now help me drag Gareth's body over to the grave and bring a stick, I hate rats.'

Using the vehicle-mounted winch, they quickly hauled the Land Rover from the trench and attached the same rope to Jack's Land Rover, towing the vehicle to the edge of the clearing and facing the exit track.

What was uneaten of Gareth's remains were carried to the grave after having removed anything that could identify him from his pockets, then they rolled their friend into the grave and on top of Mikel's body.

Baptiste's body was much more manageable; his remains were carried on shovels and dropped into the grave.

Jack instructed Lewis to search around the grave area and using rags, recover the handgun and Satan's machete, advising him not to touch either of them without the rag, then he was to throw them in the grave with the bodies.

'If the bodies are ever discovered, I want Satan's fingerprints to be found on weapons, not ours,' he added.

Lewis, impressed by Jack's attention to detail, began searching.

After shovelling the earth back into the grave, it was patted down; then petrol poured everywhere, inside and outside the shack, Satan's Land Rover, the vehicle parts, tyres and the chicken shed, leaving the hens to their fate.

When they had finished, the last of the petrol was used to pour over areas where the bodies had lain and been torn and eaten by rats.

Stan and Lewis walked to the vehicles parked close to the exit track and watched Jack, standing close to the edge of the petrol-soaked area.

Turning to his friends, he called, 'Are you ready for this, guys? When this goes up, it will go big style so have your engine running and ready to leave, okay?'

They indicated that everything was set and prepared to get in the vehicle following Jack's instructions.

Flicking the lighter, he moved the small flame along the edge of the rag, then paused, as Satan's abhorrent image appeared in his subconscious, and he recalled the torture and near-death experiences he had endured.

Then from some dark and inner place, deep inside his mind, saw Satan slide the blade across Gareth's throat, the shocking grimace spreading across his friend's face in the last seconds of his life, Gareth saying his last ever words *'Run Jack, run.'*

He recalled the message on the wall, a warning they had not understood at the time they had seen it.

'The jungle will devour your screams when you die.'

Then he was abruptly brought back to reality when he felt

the heat from the flaming rag begin to burn his fingers, he quickly moved his hand away from the flame to another part of the cloth, then looked at the mound of the earth-covered grave containing the remains of the three dead men, thinking, all this because of the extreme and evil greed associated with merciless violence and illicit trafficking of narcotics.

Still looking at the grave, he quietly said, 'Forgive us.'

Then threw the burning rag onto a tarpaulin soaked with petrol, and turning, ran as fast as he could towards his vehicle.

He only managed a few yards, before hearing a deafening 'WHOOSH' sound as the petrol exploded; intense flames quickly and fiercely spreading across the whole area behind, feeling the blast as he ran, the heat severe and uncomfortably hot on his back.

Arriving at the rear vehicle, he quickly climbed into the driver's seat and pressed the horn, immediately feeling a jolt as the rope between him and the lead vehicle jerked and began to take the strain, then steered as his vehicle coasted towards the exit track.

He looked at the rear-view mirror, surprised at the enormity of the fire and how quickly it spread, the entire clearing engulfed in massive flames that danced erratically and fiercely, incinerating everything in its path.

Just before his vehicle was swallowed by the foliage surrounding the track, he saw frightened monkeys jumping in the trees and birds launching, trying to escape the flames.

Then watched as the hanging vegetation, draped over the clearing entrance begin to thicken with distance, gradually smothering the sunlight, as if a final curtain was being closed following a surreal theatrical finale.

Realising that the events he had experienced had almost been like theatre, a tragic stage play, but also knew that this had to be its closing night, sensing he would never see or return to this place again

Then became immersed in dull, shaded colour as the jungle vegetation drowned the sunlight and for the first time since he had arrived in the clearing, felt almost relaxed sitting alone and in silence while gently steering the vehicle along the track, the same track he had attempted to get to so many times in the last twenty-four hours.

Stan drove the lead vehicle as slowly as possible, conscious that Jack may have difficulty steering his vehicle due to his injuries and exhaustion, and constantly checked his rear-view mirror.

Lewis had been silent for a while, then asked, 'Do you think we will get away with all this?'

'We didn't get away with it; Gareth is dead, as are three others; that's not what I would call getting away with anything,' he replied.

'You know the ammunition box is watertight, don't you.'

Stan tutted then replied, 'I don't care, it's gone, far too many people have died in grotesque circumstances for that gear, and we could have joined them; Jack almost did, so forget the money, it's at the bottom of the river, and besides, you saw the size of the crocodile.'

Lewis ignored him and said, 'Can you remember a couple of weekends ago when we went snorkelling off Ambergris Caye? Well, I recall speaking to an American guy in the bar there, Dennis was his name, anyway, he said he was a marine biologist based at the Belizean Crocodile Sanctuary facility on the island.'

'What's your point?' Stan asked.

'Well, they're responsible for marine GPS tagging in Belize and he told me that they have this device that they use to make marine animals placid, I think he called it an electronic sonar pulse device or something like that.

'Anyway, it gets lowered into the water and emits sound waves, he told me that anything in the water nearby will go into a trance, it sort of makes them sleepy. That is how they safely enter the water and attach a GPS tag to register and track them, mainly crocodiles.

'Well, I was thinking that maybe we could have a word with him and ask if we could perhaps borrow the equipment for a short while. It would just mean getting hold of a rowing boat, and some snorkels; finding the ammunition box in the water wouldn't be difficult, we both saw where it sank in the river.'

Stan ignored Lewis, shaking his head with frustration and carefully concentrated on steering the vehicle, occasionally glimpsing from the windscreen to the mirror, checking the vehicle behind.

Eventually, the Land Rover burst out of the jungle track and into bright sunlight. Stan manoeuvred and steered the vehicle onto the tarmac road leading to the city and continued to drive in silence for a few miles.

He looked at the rear-view mirror and saw, behind the vehicle Jack was steering, a huge billowing plume of black smoke rising above the jungle treetops, and began to think what Lewis had said about electronic pulses, crocodiles, recovering the ammunition box and the wealth contained within it.

He continued to steer the Land Rover and again glanced at the inferno as it incinerated the evidence, then asked, 'Do you have the contact details for Dennis with the sonar device? I fancy snorkelling in Ambergris Caye at the weekend, and besides, I know a guy in San Pedro who owns a rowing boat.'

Lewis couldn't hold back his excitement. He smiled and clapped his hands, then said, 'Okay, I'll give Dennis a call in a couple of days when the dust has settled, but whatever you do, don't tell Jack just yet, let's wait until we think he's ready.'

If you want to keep alive in the jungle,
you must live as the jungle does

John Wyndham